A Handbook
of
American
Prayer

A Handbook
of
American
Prayer

A NOVEL

LUCIUS SHEPARD

THUNDER'S MOUTH PRESS • NEW YORK

A HANDBOOK OF AMERICAN PRAYER

Published by
Thunder's Mouth Press
An Imprint of Avalon Publishing Group Inc.
245 West 17th St., 11th Floor
New York, NY 10011

AVALON
publishing group incorporated

Library of Congress Cataloging-in-Publication Data is available.

ISBN 1-56858-281-1

9 8 7 6 5 4 3 2 1

Book design by Paul Paddock

Printed in the United States of America
Distributed by Publishers Group West

To PG

Chapter 1

When people look back at things they're ashamed of having done and say it must have been another person who did those things, and they have no idea who that person was, what they're actually saying, though they may not understand it, is that they *do* know that person and they don't know who they are now. They believe or pretend to believe that age and experience have combined to make them larger, wiser, a grander and thus less knowable soul than their former self, one incapable of such miscreance. Perhaps committing an act of extreme violence helps to clear away these confusions, for I know exactly who I was on the night twelve years ago when I killed Mario Kirschner, and while I'm more patient than once I was and have rid myself of certain delusions, I'm essentially the same man today, equally susceptible to stupidity. Prayer has made a difference in my life, yet it hasn't proved to be the glorious difference-maker that evangelists suggest. Of course my prayers are aimed lower than the prayers of priests and mullahs, intended to produce not miracles but small, calculable effects.

I came to murder as might an actor to a role. I had worked as a bartender ever since dropping out of college and had learned that an attitude of studied indifference posed a challenge to drunken women. Over the years I grew into the part of a cool, disengaged man of the world (though I had yet to travel beyond the state of Washington), letting that false color permeate my character. By the

winter of 1991, when I was employed at the Galley, a tourist restaurant on Lopez in the San Juan Islands, near the mouth of Puget
Sound, I had developed a heartfelt disaffection for the world. Even
the women I slept with bored me. Our encounters were merely
opportunities for the exercise of my cynicism. I suspect that all mur-
derers, to one degree or another, must be egoists in this same way.

There were few tourists in winter and usually the rest of the
Galley's staff would go home by nine o'clock, leaving me to close
and deal with stragglers. I did my best drinking during those times.
One night in late January, while I was working on my fourth double
vodka, sitting in a booth by the picture window, watching the hot
blond lights of anchored boats bobbing on the polished black water
of the bay, a red Porsche pulled into the lot and a good-looking thirtyish woman with long auburn hair came into the restaurant and
began flirting with me, trying to hustle a free drink. Her face, beau-
tifully made up, a painting of skin and subtle umber shadow, had
strong cheekbones and satiny lips that reminded me of the lips you
see painted on the façades of carnival strip shows. I told her I was
sorry, I couldn't help her. She leaned tipsily against the booth,
clinging to the chrome coatrack that extended from the back of the
seat. "Come on, man! I've had a really shitty night," she said. She
was wearing gray slacks and heels, a blue angora sweater. Heavy gold
bracelets, gold-and-sapphire loops in her ears.

"You can afford a drink," I said.

"I left my purse at my boyfriend's."

"Call him. Tell him to bring it."

"He's the reason I'm having a shitty night." She slumped into the
seat opposite me and buried her face in her hands, speaking through
interlaced fingers. "Just give me a drink, okay? I'll catch you
tomorrow."

"What's your name?" I asked.

She kept her fingers interlaced, lifting them as though they were
a visor, and stared at me blankly. "What's yours?"

"Wardlin Stuart."

"Wardlin?" She repeated it, imparting a comic emphasis, and grinned. "Like *warblin'*, huh?"

The grin lapsed. I assumed she was reconsidering the wisdom of teasing someone whom she had hit up for a drink.

"I'm Wanda," she said, and gave her hair a toss, signaling, I thought, that she might associate wildness and wantonness with the name. "Wanda and Wardlin. That's kinda cute!"

"Wanda," I said musingly. "I don't see it. It's not right for you. You're more of a . . . a Brooke. I think I'll call you Brooke."

She didn't like that, but kept it to herself.

"Yeah," I said. "It suits that damaged post-Vassar look you've got going. Little wear and tear, but sexy. Smart."

She perked up at the word *smart,* crossed her legs, settled back in the booth. "You're seriously an asshole, aren't you?"

"Part of the job description, Brooke."

"You want me to be Brooke? That's cool. I'm Brooke. I'm so very, very Brooke. Now are you going to fix me a drink?"

"Why don't you show me what's holding up that pretty blue sweater," I said. "Then I'll pour you something."

A measure of what was happening inside Wanda's head seeped through to her face. Anger, resentment, indecision, reluctance, and, finally, because she needed that drink, bemusement. "You want me to show you my tits?"

"If you're up for it, y'know. I'm fine either way."

"Is this like your custom?" she asked. "How you do things on a daily basis?"

"You're the first. We don't get many people in here who can't pay for their drinks."

"No wonder!"

"Even if we did, I wouldn't be asking them to take off their sweaters. If you like"—I allowed softness into my voice—"you can think of this as a provocative form of flattery."

She laughed, a single sardonic note. Her eyes went to the red Porsche. I expected her to leave, but she shot me an I-am-reading-your-soul look, concerned no doubt with issues of trust, perhaps deciding how much of a Wanda she might let herself be that evening. "All right. But not here," she said, and gestured at the window. "Somebody might drive up."

I led her back into the kitchen. Standing by the steam table, her back arched under the fluorescent lights, Wanda displayed an exhibitionist's flair, doing a half-pirouhette as she pulled the sweater free of her arms. Her breasts were large, yet not so large, I thought, as to warrant the heavy multipaneled fortress-style brassiere that packaged them. It could have been a Victorian implement of torture. Something for the recalcitrant maiden in your life. The coarse off-white fabric was ridged by thick underwires; the straps were wide as restraints. With a coy smile, she reached behind her and unhooked the thing. The straps slid down off her shoulders, the cups fell away from her flesh. The skin beneath was discolored by cloudy yellow and purple bruises. Surgical stitches crisscrossed everywhere, transecting her areolae. They were Frankenstein breasts. Shapely but monstrous. I stared at them.

"Don't squeeze 'em too hard, okay?" Wanda said. "I just had a reduction."

"So what do you want to drink?" I asked. "Scotch? I got a really good single malt."

I imagined that not telling me in advance about the surgery and then flaunting her untouchable breasts was her way of making me look like a jerk, but she seemed genuinely angry that I wasn't interested in groping her. She glared at me, hands on hips, as I started back into the bar. "Hey!" she said. "Where you going? Hey!" A minute later, fully clothed, she took a seat at the bar and ordered a Manhattan, which she drank in silence, casting the occasional furious look toward me. I began going over the night's receipts, and as I bent to pick up some coins I'd dropped, I heard hurried footsteps, then the front door opening.

After watching the litle red car swerve off along the curve of the bay, I dragged a stool behind the bar, set a fresh bottle of Ketel One at my elbow, and reflected on the workings of Wanda's mind. She had come to the Galley directly from a traumatic confrontation with the boyfriend and permitted me to harass her sexually, possibly because she believed a meaningless encounter would consummate revenge. In her drunkenness she might have neglected to think how the sight of her mutilated breasts would affect a potential lover. Then again, it was conceivable that she had played me and that her anger was pretense; but I hadn't thus far met anyone that self-possessed on Lopez Island. Whatever the scope of her manipulaton, I admired her. For a drunk Porsche-owning child of privilege, she had handled herself fairly well.

Three drinks after Wanda had driven away, a gray Mercedes pulled into the parking lot. A burly middle-aged man with a shaved head, wearing a gray tweed overcoat with velvet trim on the lapels, climbed out and, leaving the engine running, made for the door. I realized I had forgotten to lock up.

"We're closed," I said as the man entered.

He said, "Yeah, you are," and walked to the bar and stood in front of me, resting his gloved hands on the countertop. He stared at me without expression, but I felt hostility streaming from him. His skin was pallid, his cheeks mapped by a blotchy redness. A goatee sketched by a few days' stubble dirtied his chin and upper lip. By contrast to the fleshiness of his features, his brown eyes seemed feminine in their considerable size and luster. The overall effect was butt-ugly, but looked as if he had worked hard to achieve it.

"I'm Mario Kirschner. Janet's friend," he said, his voice big and, I suspected, pitched artificially deep, as if he were announcing something more overtly ominous like, "Name's Ringo. Johnny Ringo."

I had to laugh. "Janet," I said. "You mean *the* Janet?"

"You know who I'm talking about."

Although drunk, I was cannily drunk. I was pretty sure I knew who Janet was. Clever girl, I thought. "Tall? Fuzzy blue sweater, reddish-brown hair? She told me her name's Wanda."

"Twenty years ago I woulda broke your bones," Kirschner said with a wistful air. "Now I got lawyers doing it for me. Hurts more that way."

"Before you call in the lawyers, wanna let me know what I'm supposed to have done?"

"You think I'm fuckin' with you, don'tcha? You don't take me serious?"

"Let's see. Wanda . . . No! Excuse me. Janet! Janet comes in after a fight with you. Drunk as a fish. She wants another drink so bad, she flashes her tits. The sight of which, by the way, would turn off a fucking pit bull. I give her a drink, she leaves. Now here you come threatening legal action." I sipped my vodka. "I guess you're right. I don't take you serious."

Kirschner eyed me coldly. Though I remained, basically, amused by the situation, I felt the nip of paranoia. "So what did she say happened?" I asked.

"Don't gimme that shit!"

"Naw, tell me, man! I'm intrigued. See, I know I didn't do dick to her. And since she obviously fed you some garbage 'bout I did . . . Think maybe she's got an agenda here? Like she's trying to stir up trouble?"

"Maybe I should bring her on in. You think you can face her after what you did?"

I peered at the whitely smoking Mercedes, trying to divine a shape behind the fogged glass. "She out there? Bring her, man. If I can face those tits, I can face fucking anything."

Kirschner caught a fistful of my sweater and pulled me close. "Son of a bitch!" he said, spraying me with spittle.

He said something else, but I didn't register it. The warmth of his spit, his primped and powdered smell, the entire specificity of his physical presence so repelled me, like the flare of revulsion you feel when a spider crawls across your hand, I disconnected from the moment, from any individual appreciation of him. I barred a forearm under his chin, pushed him back, and as he twisted away from the pressure, I struck the crown of his head with the bottle of Ketel One. The bottle didn't break. It made a dull *bonk*, an innocent sound, like someone bumping their head on a beam. Kirschner's face emptied and he went down as if his electricity had been switched off.

Though I know now that he lay dying as the result of a skull fracture and a subdural hematoma, Kirschner's pulse was strong and there was no sign of blood. I assumed he'd wake up in a minute or two. I walked to the window. Wanda (née Janet Pietkowski) had wiped a porthole of clarity in the fogged glass of the windshield. I could see her sweater, the frame of her hair, her shiny red mouth shaped in an O. It was obvious she had witnessed everything. We looked at each other for quite some time, at least twenty, thirty seconds, I'd say, and it was during those seconds that the remainder of my life was molded, that Wanda—I never think of her as a Janet or a Brooke—consolidated the details of the story she would tell, an account of unprovoked assault that inspired the district attorney to file a charge of murder two.

I'm tempted, when I recall those seconds, to enhance memory, to persuade myself that I felt fate gathering about me, palpable as the white boil of exhaust from the Mercedes, a turbulent cloud; but the truth is, I had no great sense of moment. I wondered what lie Wanda had told Kirschner to so enrage him and I speculated as to her motivations. She'd had cause to be angry at us both. She might have sicced the boyfriend on me in hopes we'd hurt each other. She clasped her hands prayerfully, the tips of her fingers touching her chin. Her eyes were closed, her lips moved. At length she relaxed from this pose and punched up a number on her cell phone and spoke into it. I wasn't worried. Discounting my own drunkeness, I figured that with a spotless six-month record at the Galley, I had no reason to doubt my word would stand against that of a woman who would blow two percent on the Breathalyzer. I lit a cigarette, exhaled toward her, and gave her a wave, all fingers, a blithe, dismissive signal. Wanda finished her phone call. Our eyes met through the double layer of glass and she smiled. It was such a disarming smile, devoid, it seemed, of any duplicitous alloy, I was moved to respond in kind. Briefly, until the police siren drew close enough to hear, I labored under the impression that we were only slightly less than friends, accomplices in the good.

Chapter 2

I once gave an interview in which I said that prayer, the act of making prayers, had refined me, drawn out my essential substance into a simpler shape. Though this statement is true on the face of it, I perhaps failed my interviewer, Mr. Ed Bradley of *60 Minutes,* by not adding that the new shape of my soul was mostly the result of opportunism. The human spirit is malleable to a fault. We're all sociopaths to an extent, benign ones for the most part, capable of squeezing ourselves into whatever dress is required for success in a particular environment. Studied indifference and disaffection, my typical clothing, don't buy you much in prison. Passion is called for, passion in the interests of survival. I had thought I might be able to plead my charge down to involuntary manslaughter, but Wanda's story of how I had accosted her in the ladies' room while she was medicating her breasts, her sorrow at having told Kirschner about the incident, Kirschner's temperate approach and my ultraviolent reaction . . . under the circumstances I had little choice other than to plead to man one and so was afforded ten years to practice the art of passionate survival in the state prison at Walla Walla. For the first few years I devoted myself to my appeals and to the contemplation of what I might do to Wanda upon my release. It turned out that Kirschner was a brutal abuser and that Wanda had cohabited with him for a period sufficient to establish common-law rights; thus she was entitled to a significant portion of all monies deriving from his chain of grocery stores. I doubted she could either have planned or anticipated what happened at the Galley, but I now believed that the simple shape into which Kirschner's abuse had refined her soul was a vengeful one and that she had seized the opportunity I presented, engineered a confrontation, and prayed for the best possible outcome.

I wasted a good deal of time in prison visualizing improbable forms of revenge. I pictured myself as a phantom hovering in the purple air of Wanda's boudoir, merging with her dreaming body, perpetrating a metaphysical rape that seeded her flesh with infant tumors. I saw myself committing fiercer, more literal debasements, violent seductions that would leave her yearning for Kirschner's comparably unimaginative rapes, yet were so masterful that they bred gentler feelings in her, creating a perverted dependency that would enthrall her for a period of no less than eight, no greater than fifteen years. It was not until midway through that minimum term, when a car thief named Roger Dubon whom I scarcely knew, acting out a prison fantasy of his own, one in which I presented a dire menace, stabbed me and left me to die in a stairwell . . . Not until then did I pass beyond the desire for revenge and begin to understand the nature of prayer. As I recuperated in the hospital ward, my mind turned again to Wanda, recalling the moment during which she had prayed. At trial it had become apparent that she was by nature grasping and amoral, a party girl who held no significant religious convictions. Prayer for her had been the product of a powerful impulse, offered at an instant of pure opportunity when she felt inadequate to the circumstances. Whatever she had prayed for— whether asking that my blow be fatal or for the power to persuade the police her story was true—it was plain that the prayer had been answered. I recalled my own recent prayerful moment. Lying in the stairwell, tasting blood in my mouth, the shadows closing in, life slipping away. I had prayed serially for the strength to stand, to negotiate the stairs, to walk along the corridor until I met with someone who would call for help, aiming my prayers at no god, but toward a vast indefinite region over which I believed nothing ruled.

And yet a sudden strength had washed through me. I stood, I ascended, I walked. A miracle, my surgeon told me, given the seriousness of my wounds. This suggested the possibility that prayer itself was the miracle worker, that whatever name one attached to a prayer, be it Allah or Jesus or Damballa, was less important than the intensity and particularity with which one prayed, and the moment one chose to offer up one's prayer. Thus prayer, perhaps even faith, might be seen as an immoderate act of physics, a functional means of effecting small changes in reality.

This idea, initially a whimsy, came to possess me. Such obsessions are a consequence of having too much time on one's hands and explain the high incidence of cities made of toothpicks, ships in bottles, and matchstick mosaics found in prison cells. But the idea had more developmental potential than did those pastimes. It occurred to me that if intensity and opportunity were the criteria for effective prayer, the former might be fabricated to serve the latter. Prayers might be created to focus the intensity of the person praying whenever the need arose. Why else had the Psalms been written? The trouble with the Psalms, however, as with all the ancient prayers, was that their grandiloquent language didn't suit the modern age and so their power to focus the mind sufficiently to create change had been diminished. A new style of prayer was called for, one that posited no god or else summoned lesser gods to attend, transitory beings with limited powers and not the all-seeing eminence invoked by biblical authors. One that spoke more specifically to need, that engaged the sensibility in a contemporary way, as might a self-help text, a handbook teaching a basic skill or the attitudes and disciplines essential to developing said skill.

The first prayer that accessed this idea, which I wrote while still in the hospital ward, asked that I be allowed thereafter to hear "the footstep in the dark, the feathering of the murderer's breath." I can't say whether or not it effected any change other than to make me more conscious of danger, but I repeated it whenever I left my cell and endured no recurrence of my experience with Roger Dubon (now whiling away his years in a supermax facility), and no further assaults from any quarter. Indeed, all my prayers came to be answered. I asked for small benefits only and chose my moments carefully. One evening prior to putting in my application for a library job, I was working on a prayer to assist that purpose when my cellmate, Jerry Swain, a chunky, middle-aged redneck from Yakima doing a six-pack behind a trafficking charge, offered to pay me five packs of Camel Wide Lights if I would "whip out one of them prayer dealies" for him. The request startled me. Though a camaraderie of sorts had been thrust upon us, Jerry had maintained a sneering distance since being assigned to the cell and I had not attempted to close it. We were different breeds. He was slovenly, fat, long-haired, his chest, back, and arms disfigured by monochrome tattoos, all apparently the work of the same artist, mainly caricatures of voluptuous women, the centerpiece being the rendering of an octopus having many-tentacled intercourse with four such ladies. His numerous prison friends all resembled him and when together in a group they would talk madness about "niggers" and "beaners" and a secret kingdom, now in its infancy, that would one day come to dominate the world. By comparison, I was fastidious, slim, short-haired, unadorned, and kept my views on race and politics to myself. I asked Jerry what he wanted to pray for and, waxing voluble for the first time in our relationship, he related a dismal family history. Father missing for years, mother dead from alcoholism, two brothers killed in criminal enterprises gone awry. His sole surviving relative, a sister, Serena, had "turned lesbo" and they were now estranged.

"It was her girlfriend fixed Serena's mind against me," he said. "Marcy Sharp. This fat ol' pig-bitch. Her mama's a damn lesbian, too, if you can believe that."

Moved by the spirit of isolation, Jerry had written a letter to Serena, asking for a reconciliation, but was leery about mailing it, feeling he had little credit with her. "I seen things has got better for you since you started up with them prayers," he said. "So I figger, what the hell, y'know."

After inquiring further about Serena, thus enabling me to strengthen the specificity of the piece, I set to work and two days later presented Jerry with the finished product, the earliest of the prayers that I was eventually to collect between covers, beginning with the line: "The pig-nosed daughter of Genevieve Sharp hates me . . ."

Jerry read it over several times, nonplussed, and said, "Don't sound all that religious, does it?"

"You have to supply the religious feeling," I said. "You use it to focus your feelings, to generate intensity."

He read it again and then said, "It's just it ain't your typical prayer."

I sought to explain that the virtues of what I'd taken to calling "prayerstyle" lay, as was the case with all concentrative verbal devices, prayers, mantras, and so forth, in the weather of the words, their precise sonority and the resonance achieved between sound and meaning. Rather than emulating the ponderous architectures of the past, I was attempting a contemporary expression. If it didn't satisfy him, I said, I'd give him back his Camels.

"Naw, I hear ya," Jerry said. "Lemme work with it a while. I'm likin' it . . . I swear I am. Just it's kinda weird, y'know."

Three weeks later Serena Swain came to visit Jerry and soon thereafter I received my second request for a personalized prayer. The petitioner was a wiry lit-fuse of a man named Skinner Wallace, a murderer so afire with agitated energy, it seemed I heard a faint buzzing whenever he came near. His stated desire was for a prayer that would cause the death of the hooker whom he payed to visit once a month and put on a sex show in the booth where they met, talking dirty over the phone, separated from each other by thick glass. He claimed that his frustration level had become such, he couldn't abide the thought of any man having what he could not. To my surprise, because I hadn't thus far associated prayerstyle with any sort of moral code, I told him that killing someone likely exceeded the capacity of my work and, even if it did not, I wasn't inclined to try it. Skinner's expression of prim ferocity flickered when he heard this. I thought he might hit me, but apparently Jerry Swain's testimonial to my ability as a miracle worker earned me a reprieve.

"What do you really want?" I asked. "I mean you don't want her dead. You want to fuck her, right?"

"They don't allow me no conjugal visits," he said.

"You know things get done in here that aren't allowed. You might do better addressing a prayer toward influencing one of the guards."

"I'm not prayin' to no damn guard! Guards fuckin' hate my ass!"

"What I'm suggesting is, you pray for a way to get next to your hooker . . . whatever it takes."

Skinner gave the idea a turn. "Okay. Fuck! Write something up."

"It's not just me writing . . ."

"Yeah, I know! I gotta get behind what you write. Be intense with it."

"There's more than—"

"I know! Okay? You gotta ask me a buncha questions. So come on! Let's do it!"

It took nearly six weeks for Skinner to engineer—by means of prayer, threats, and negotiation—a circumstance in which he could enjoy an ongoing physical relationship with his hooker. From that point forward I was deluged with requests for prayers. I was able to satisfy those I accepted, but I rejected most of them. Either they were morally unsound or they proposed goals that lay beyond the limited scope of my creations. My high success rate could be attributed in part to a rigorous selection process, but from watching Jerry and Skinner and various other of my customers, I realized a more legitimate process was in play—the act of praying had modified their behaviors, made them calmer, more agreeable men. The fulfillment of their desires served to reinforce those traits. They returned frequently to ask for new prayers and I would catch sight of them in the yard or wandering a corridor or sequestered in their cells, head down and lips moving silently. I was certain that their prayers had been answered because prayerstyle concentrated their efforts toward that end, and I believed that the practice itself was the actual sponsor of their behavioral changes, that no traditional spiritual component had contributed. And I saw evidence of this in myself. I had been thirty-one when I entered prison, and although any period of five years during one's thirties generally encompasses a time of psychological growth, I could trace the majority of that growth from my involvement with prayerstyle. I had grown devout, contemplative, methodical, quiet, my cynical edge rubbed dull by the exertions of my craft, replaced by an eager, earnest quality. My conversational personality, formerly sardonic and quick-witted, became increasingly bland and nonconfrontational, and I would often hear myself giving forth with folksy-sounding homilies, a mode of expression I once would have ridiculed. Inherent to my reconstructed simplicity was my belief that God did not figure into any of this, yet considering my enhanced capacity for self-delusion, for vapid sermonizing, I might have been a convert to some tedious, undistinguished Christian course. Whereas I was merely under-taking a change of mental dress, adopting a personal style more suited to my environment, I began to view myself as an artisan engaged in honing and reshaping his own spirit, preparing it for great things. The man who had killed Mario Kirschner . . . I could no longer have told you who that person was. I was a grander soul now, less knowable, incapable of such a casual, thoughtless crime.

Chapter 3

Toward the end of my eighth year in prison I prayed for a woman and for success. I crafted a single prayer to encompass both possibilities, because I had the notion the two were bound together. I recall that this prayer was the first in which I addressed myself to a god. A fictive god, a cartoonish poetic gesture, a quasi-divine color added for effect, but a god nonetheless:

> *Oh, Lord of Loneliness,*
> *drowning in candleflame,*
> *sitting with your cup of raw spirits*
> *at a back table in the Cantina de Flor Negra*
> *in Nada Concepción,*
> *spittle and mezcal dribblings*
> *beaded up on your mustache . . .*
> *Listen, this night is a black border*
> *around the photograph of life,*
> *this night is a strip of blindness*
> *across the eyes of the condemned.*
> *Let me wander in it a while,*
> *let me find some softness there . . .*

As I've said, I asked for small things only, and after finishing this prayer I wondered if I had resorted, albeit humorously, to the mention of a god because I felt I was asking for too much. I decided I was not.

During the previous four years I had through the use of prayerstyle improved my life and level of accomplishment to a point at which success and the potential of a woman waiting for me on the outside were viable goals. I had created the opportunity for prayer to be effective. Bryan Sauter, a writer who taught a weekly class at the prison, had helped me to assemble my prayers and notes on prayerstyle into a manuscript that read like a cross between a collection of poetry and a pop psychology book, and was preparing to send it to his agent. As to the woman, for several years I had placed personal ads in various magazines that offered this service free to prisoners. The ads had dredged up a number of responses, some from teenage girls pretending to be sluts, some from lonely old women pretending to be young, others from neurotic wives seeking a fantasy life. I was in process of refining my ad. Since the prayer I was creating addressed the success of my written work, I thought it appropriate to let it do double duty and include the ad, and once I finished the prayer, once I committed it to memory and used it to focus my mind on the task at hand, I wrote the following:

Incarcerated, Not Dead: prisoner, SWM, 39 yrs., seeks correspondence with SWF, comparable age. Object: to learn, to engage hope, to find true correspondence.

Several weeks after the ad was published I received a reply, one among seventeen, from Therese Madden of Pershing, Arizona. It came in a crisp business envelope imprinted with the name 'Zona Madness and a street address, standing out in its white simplicity from the rest: pastel-colored high school stationery decorated with songbirds and roses and such, some with addresses scribbled in pencil and bearing the scents of trailer park desperation. In my hand, Therese Madden's letter, negligibly light, had a cool precise value. No perfume wafted out when I opened it and the letter began not, as did so many, with the word *hi* punctuated by a jaunty exclamation point, the downward slash comically fat and the period beneath it round as a berry, but with a typed:

Hello, Wardlin,

A magazine with your ad in it was left in my shop by a young housewife married to a drunk from Ohio who manages a restaurant and halfway believes he is the descendant of cowboy heroes. She had circled your ad. It occurred to me after reading the ad that my reasons for responding to it were more or less the same as hers. I'm certain that we both feel isolated, imprisoned by stupidity, and the sense of an actual intelligence out there, especially one who is also imprisoned, resonates with us. That said, I'm not clear on why I'm responding, but I obviously am. For some reason, I feel it's right to respond. The feeling seems impervious to examination.

I run a gift shop in a small town. It was left me by my mother. When she died I was out in San Francisco, working in a bank, writing plays for a theater group. I'd just been through a terrible romance—terrible in the sense that it ended terribly—and everything I was doing seemed empty, worthless. I intended to sell the shop and return to San Francisco, but when I reached Pershing . . . it was a combination of things that caused me to stay. I fell in love with the desert again, for one. For another, I thought the shop would make me comfortably independent. I'd been living in cheap apartments with roommates. My life was disorderly, cluttered, always in a state of financial emergency. I was twenty-five and the thought of being my own boss and free to travel was alluring. Operating a small business had made my mother happy. Why not me?

That was seven years ago. The shop barely makes enough to sustain me and my employee. I never can afford to travel. I'd sell the place if I could, but there are no buyers. Even if there were, where would I go? I have no connections anywhere except Pershing. Thirty-two is not twenty-five. I don't have the courage I once had and the prospect of taking flight and forsaking the known is daunting. That may be cowardly of me. I've been told I underestimate myself. Many nights I'm tempted to empty my bank account, abandon the store, and drive away. I'm lonely and there's no one here with whom I want to share my life. Yet I haven't been able to make the move. And so, too frightened to leave my prison, I'm doing something foolhardy and reaching out to you in yours.

I understand you are limited as to the number of words you can use in an ad. It seems to me that you've used your limit intelligently, you've tried to send a very precise message that's designed to attract a certain type of woman. Perhaps this is just another dumb mistake on my part. Perhaps you're not intelligent, or if you are, perhaps you're violent and unstable, as well. I guess this is my risk for the year . . . the decade. But whatever type of woman you wanted to attract, you've at least attracted my attention. I'd like you to tell me about yourself. I think I'll know if you lie. Eventually, anyway. Tell me anything you want. If you want to tell me about your crime, that's fine. But I'm less interested in the past than in the present.

Good night.

The letter was signed "Therese" and enclosed a photograph with a processing stamp dated several months before. In the photograph Therese was leaning against an adobe wall, one knee drawn up. She wore a tan suede jacket, jeans, and a white shirt. The strong sunlight brought a glare to her face, erasing detail, lending her features a dovelike simplicity, but clearly she was pretty. Her hair was strawberry blond, her body slender. She was smiling, yet she looked anxious, as if she were uncomfortable with having her picture taken. I thought I could see the woman who had written the letter. Lonely, nervous, hopeful. The quietness that solitude had bred in her. Holding the photograph between thumb and forefinger, I lay back on my bunk and let Therese's image be a small sky. The sense of presence I'd felt while reading her letter grew pronounced, as if that glossy rectangle were a portal opening onto the blazing place where she stood, allowing the picture to be snapped yet unhappy, embarrassed by something the photographer had said, annoyed by the unwanted attention, by the sun, her mind partly somewhere else, probably on business, a worry concerning bills or an overdue order, and I imagined the torpid pulse of the town around her, the griddlehot hoods of pickups parked on the slant along the main street, onestory buildings of prestressed concrete with glass fronts and heavy-duty AC, wakes of bitter yellow dust rising from every passage, gaunt white-haired men with string ties and bracelets of silver and turquoise sliding loosely on their bony, brick-colored wrists, a pretty Native American woman eating an ice-cream sandwich outside a convenience store, waiting for the dented shitbox that would carry her home to the reservation, and at night Pershing would respond to the wild stars above with its own bright signals, neon pyramids, dice, sun emblems, the names of bars, a glowing scatter of less-than-sacred signs across the blue-dark flats, and the wind would blow down from old Indian ruins in the hills and rearrange sand grains into uncanny wrinkled faces, and the faces would whisper in a counterfeit of the wind. I knew how a beer would taste in that arid heat, how the smells of gasoline and diesel would knife through the alkali perfume of the desert. It seemed I knew everything about the town just from holding Therese's picture, and though I had only that picture and a letter for proof, I was inclined to believe that my prayer had been answered, to consider myself already a part of her life. I recognized that an assumptive leap of this sort might be a prison twitch, exemplary of a convict's tendency to seize any opportunity, and not necesarily the right one, to work some angle. However, my faith in prayerstyle persuaded me that in this instance my instincts were correct, that Therese's letter had been dislodged from her heart and hand by the small power of my prayer, and when I responded I did so with what I believed to be painstaking candor, though I think now that what I took for candor was merely a facile means of denying accountability.

Dear Therese,

You say that you think you'll know if I lie to you. I suspect you will. My difficulty lies in the fact that I may not know myself. Life has always seemed to me in essence a deceit. The things we say to each other are such poor approximations of the truth in our hearts, they might as well be lies. People tend to interpret themselves when they speak and they do so clumsily for the most part, like actors with a superficial understanding of their roles. A brighter, more precise truth can sometimes be communicated when two people look toward each other with similar intensity and aim, when certain compatibilities are involved, and perhaps when you say you'll know if I lie, you're really talking about whether or not those compatibilities in fact exist. Whatever the case, I promise I'll tell you nothing that I know to be false.

Our correspondence flourished, evolved, passed through stages of flirtation, courtship, misunderstanding, repair, and lastly to a mutual acknowledgment that we were becoming more than pen pals. We talked on the phone, always briefly, but we said love things, and after hanging up from her I would feel dazed and comforted. We were walking together on some extraordinary plane, I believed. Having a soul conversation. The thoughts I had about her each night streamed up and joined the thoughts she was having about me and braided together into a single smoke. I confessed to her, I admitted everything. Each sentence of those letters had the ring of truthful revelation. They let me know myself in a way that was both painful and instructive. I embraced the hope she represented, yet I doubted her embrace of me was wholehearted. She kept saying that circumstances prevented her from visiting. It was not until thirteen months after we had begun, when I told her that my book, entitled *A Handbook of American Prayer*, had been accepted for publication, that she suggested the time for a visit had arrived:

. . . we've discussed your being paroled to me and how my
willingness to accept that responsibility would help you with
the board, since you're estranged from your family. We need
to take this step now, because it seems that what with the
book, you have an honest-to-God chance for parole. I've
come to care about you during this past year (has it really
been that long?), but I must admit I'm a little afraid of finally
coming face-to-face with someone who has become so important to me and yet remains such a mystery. What if things
aren't as we hope? What kind of pressure will that put on me?
I realize the pressures on you are immense, and I know what
I'm saying only exacerbates them, but that's how things are.
Anyway, I believe I can come to Washington in a couple of
weeks and see you at the prison on the twenty-first of May, if
that's all right.

I had acquired a dozen pictures and over a hundred letters, yet
when I looked to her upcoming visit, I felt more confused about her
than I had after receiving her first letter. Forced to examine my feelings, I was unable to separate the real from my sexual fantasies and
the elaborate speculations I'd entertained regarding our future
together. It was as if all that had been a mist designed to obscure a
literal gulf between us, and it seemed unlikely that the bridging of
this gulf could be achieved within a span of a couple of hours on a
May afternoon. Panicked, I set out to write a prayer relating to the
occasion and failed to come up with anything. I'd been nine years
and several months without a woman and my confidence with the
opposite sex had eroded. Not a bad thing, since that confidence had
been based almost entirely on contempt. What I felt now, though,
was a complete lack of confidence compounded by desperation
regarding my parole and the thought that Therese might be a last
glimmering chance. As the day of her visit approached, I passed
from anxiety into a state of calm acceptance like a condemned man
coming to terms with the inevitabilty of the needle. On the morning

of the day itself I experienced a resurgence of panic and felt wobbly in the knees as I went along the corridor that led to the visitors' yard, a rectangle of grass, apple trees, and playground equipment—swings, a seesaw—enclosed by a chain-link fence topped with razor wire. The sun was so bright, it brought a weakness to my eyes. I could smell the river that ran beyond a stand of spruce to the west of the prison. All my senses were stripped of their baffles and the world came as a shout of hot colors. The breeze wrapped around me and the cries of kids scampering near the swings were sharp like the pop and flare of sap catching in a hearth fire against the soft conversational crackling of prisoners and wives and parents sitting at picnic tables, eating take-out food and touching one another.

There must have been sixty, seventy people in the yard, but I saw Therese at once. She was sitting alone at a table in the shade of an apple tree, wearing a blue sundress with a white pattern. Her hair was loose about her shoulders. Spotting me, she gave a tentative wave. I walked toward her, one hand shoved in my pocket, trying for casual, but afraid that I resembled some idiot playing Johnny Cool in a bad fifties movie. Close up, she could have been an ad for American Purity, pretty like milk and sugar cookies. The pattern on her dress was of white soaring birds. She got to her feet as I walked up and stepped into a sisterly embrace. The scent of her shampoo made me want to go to sleep, but the feel of her breasts aroused me. My erection pushed into her thigh. Embarrassed, I made to pull away, but she held me and said, "It's okay." After a second she laughed, a little water music, and said, "I guess you're glad to see me," and I said, "Uh-huh," speaking into her hair. I couldn't tell if she was trembling or if I was. Both of us, probably. My heart was all through my body. I didn't know what to do, except stand there. Finally we sat down, holding hands across the picnic table. I was so accustomed to mistrusting everything I felt that now, confronted by an emotion too big to mistrust, all I could do was stare. She was paler than her pictures showed. A pale moonbird living out in the rough sun country. And though I'd known her eyes were green, now

I saw they were different from most green eyes—they had a cloudy mineral shade like snowmelt in a Colorado creek. She looked out of place among the wives and girlfriends of carjackers, armed robbers, and worse, and I thought that this was a woman who'd look out of place everywhere, except someplace solitary, because her beauty was that quiet and handmade, as if her features and form had been pressed into shape over a slow contemplative time by a sculptor's thumbs, all her smooth curvature worked into being.

"Well," she said, "it appears we don't have to worry about chemistry."

"That's what this is? Chemistry? Feels more like metaphysics."

I thought she might have found the response too glib. She held my hand a little longer, then reached beneath the table and hauled up a paper grocery sack with the top neatly folded over. "Sandwiches," she said.

The sandwiches were chicken breast with lettuce and tomato and some kind of dill spread. As we ate we talked about nothing much. I told her what was happening with the book, how the publisher was basically a literary press and *A Handbook of American Prayer* was something of a departure for them, but they thought it was a unique item and had plans to put some real money into promotion.

"My editor says they might want to do a new edition every coupla years. Add new prayers to it." I had a bite of sandwich and chewed. "You know, treat it like Whitman's *Leaves of Grass*. Keep enlarging it. So I told her it was a hell of a long walk from me up to Walt Whitman, and know what she said? She said, 'God, Whitman would be so marketable today. A macho Ginsberg!' And then she asked if I was gay. Like she was hoping, y'know."

Therese told me about Pershing, about her shop. "I am the only source in Pershing for stuffed Gila monsters," she said. "I move a lot of stuffed Gila monsters." She poured iced tea from a thermos. "Sometimes when I open up in the morning, I really like being there. It's such a strange conglomeration of things. Geodes and tarantulas. Postcards and Navajo artifacts. Refrigerator magnets, fake treasure maps. With nobody else around, it's like I'm the mother of this exotic dysfunctional family."

Time ran off downhill. The tension that had been in the air seemed to glide and flow between us. With about twenty minutes left of visiting hours, Therese checked her watch. She pursed her lips, gave me an all-business look, her hands clasped, and said, "What are you feeling?"

"You mean about this? Us?"

She nodded and kept her eyes steady on mine.

"Couldn't you tell?" I asked.

A blush rose on her cheeks. "It's been a long time since you've been with a woman. Not as long since I've been with a man, but still it's been a while. That might be confusing things."

"Maybe . . . or maybe it's just making things clearer." I tore off a strand of chicken meat and nibbled at it. "We been saying *I love you* for months, but before today it was like high school, kind of. I got all caught up on details. When you started signing your letters *Love, Therese,* that was huge for me. I stared at those words a long time and when your next letter came I went right to the end to see if you'd signed it the same. There was more than that going on, but it needed this, today, to be solid. When you leave now, it won't feel like a high school thing anymore. It's going to feel worse . . . and better. Isn't that more or less how you see it?"

"I think so."

"You have doubts, though."

"This prayer thing of yours . . ." She gave her head a fretful shake.

"What about it?"

At a picnic table about twenty feet away, a convict's family was putting plates and jars back into a hamper, preparing to leave, and a little Mexican girl in shorts and a purple Washington Huskies T-shirt began crying. Therese watched as the convict, a man with full-sleeve tattoos on his arms and shoulder-length black hair, consoled her.

"You're so certain about all of it," Therese said. "I've always associated that kind of certainty with crazy people."

I joined my stare to hers and watched the tattooed convict pick up his wailing daughter. "I'm not certain about that much. Not really. But I'm devoted to creating certainty. That's the whole point of the book."

"The book . . ." She firmed her mouth, as if trying to keep back a wrong word. "I enjoyed it, you know. But it's got this peculiar weight. It's so obsessive."

"Look, I'm making this up as I go along," I said. "Not just the book. Me. I'm not sure a person can change who they are, but you can change what you try to be. I've told you how I used to act. I don't want that kind of distance from people anymore." I put my hand on hers. "I don't know what I'm going to say next, okay? I know what I want next, but when I try to say it, however the words come out, it's like I'm locked into their meaning . . . and that's never exactly what I intended. So words are important to me. With the prayers, I work hard at getting them to mean what I hope they'll mean. Writing them's gotten me through some bad years. Maybe once I get out I won't care about them as much. Or maybe I will. I don't know."

Saying all this, I felt evangelical about the book, yet at the same time it felt as if I were trying to convince myself as much as Therese. I had the thought that I'd bought into prayerstyle so deeply, everything that came out of my mouth embodied a form of self-coercion. As if I'd been hooked on my own line. Recognizing this knocked me out of the moment. I focused on Therese, trying to reclaim it, and found a way back in through the green constancy of her gaze.

"I talked to your lawyer on the phone this morning," she said. "He thinks it would cinch things with the parole board if we were married."

We both waited for the other to speak. At last I said, "I can't . . ." and simultaneously, with some agitation, she said, "This is . . ." I told her to go ahead. She stared at her clasped hands with a look of sad perplexity, at one of her thumbs rubbing back and forth across the joint of the other, as if they were an odd form of life that she'd just noticed, separate from her, and she didn't know quite what to make of them. I thought she must be gearing up for a major statement, an essay regarding our situation, but all she said was, "I never wanted to get married." If there was any considerable attitude attaching to that statement, I didn't hear it. She might have been saying, "I'm not partial to mayonnaise." I told her I wasn't pushing her for anything and she nodded and went back to studying her thumbs.

Gray clouds were straggling up from the south, thinning the light and lending the air a chill. On every side, visitors were exchanging last hugs and kisses with their criminal loved ones. The yard rang with false cheer and forced laughter, but Therese and I sat without a word. Oddly enough, I wasn't anxious. I had a sense of conclusion. It seemed for all my life I'd been viewing one of those miniature volumes with line drawings on the corners of the pages that, when you flip through them, make it appear that you're seeing an animation of a man running a race or a ballerina performing an intricate passage, only what I'd seen was a woman's face, a simple stylized oval morphing into the faces of old lovers and the other significant women in my life, eventually merging into Therese. I noticed that her eyelashes were blonder than her hair and when you glanced quickly at them, they resembled the delicate claws that hold a stone in the setting of a ring. There was an old trouble in the line of her mouth, a deeper stitch extending from the corner of her right eye than from the left, as if she winked it a lot. These things made themselves known as if a haze—of self-involvement, perhaps—had dispersed and now I could dial her in.

With a purposeful sigh, she stood, then came around to my side of the table. She bent down and gave me a soft, inquiring kiss. I deepened the kiss, let my hand rest on her waist, my thumb grazing the underslope of her breast, and felt I was falling upward.

"Oh, God," she said as she sat back down. "I don't know what to do."

I halfway understood that she had liked the kiss, but insecurity got the best of me and I asked if she had.

"Except for the losing-consciousness part. I'm not used to that." Then, bemused, she said, "Jesus. This is so damn weird."

I'd never heard her swear before, and although she sounded natural doing it, it was startling and increased my measure of her. I envisioned her fending off strangers in bars with blunt efficiency. "I can't help you," I said. "I'm nine years down the road from weird. Maybe more."

"Feeling so connected with someone else from just letters and phone calls . . ." She made a flighty gesture. "That doesn't give you doubts?"

"It's how I was hoping to feel, so maybe I'm not as prone to doubt."

"You wrote a prayer about me, didn't you?" This had the ring of an accusation.

"I wrote one about wanting to find someone like you. It's what I said in the ad. True correspondence."

"But you think I came in answer to your prayer?"

"If I say yes then you'll go, 'Oh, he's crazy.' If I say no . . . Well, that'd be a lie. I'm not sure which way to go."

She fussed with the ends of her hair, angling her gaze away from me.

"I don't get what bothers you about prayerstyle," I said. "Not exactly, anyway."

"You're an intelligent man and the prayers, they're so commonplace. Don't take me wrong. They're clever. Some of them are beautiful. But when you look at what you say they're supposed to be doing, the philosophy behind them, they're like . . . like Norman Vincent Peale on Ecstasy, kinda."

"That's fair," I said. "But here's another side of it. Intelligent or not, I was a bartender before they sent my ass to prison. Not all that good a bartender. Norman Vincent Peale on Ecstasy's a major upgrade. Now I've got thoughts in my head that don't have anything to do with making myself feel good by putting other people down. I think I have gotten simple in here. Simple's where I needed to start. Maybe I'll get less simple. Like the book, I'm a work in progress. Whichever way it goes, I promise you this—things don't seem right for you, with us, I'll let you be."

Ragged groups of sweethearts and parents were dribbling back into the reception building, herding their kids ahead of them. A scrawny gray-haired trustee with a seamed face stood at the edge of the yard, puffing on a cigarette, blowing smoke through the mesh of the chain-link fence.

"Do *you* want to get married?" Therese asked.

"I want to do what you want," I said carefully. "And I want to get out of here. The truth hangs between those two poles. But if you asked me that on the outside, I'd say, yeah, you bet."

She glanced around the yard. "I don't need a woodland chapel and bridesmaids, but getting married *here* . . ."

"You oughta check out the inside. It's way more cheerful."

She laughed, but her heart wasn't in it. Another handful of seconds burned off our fuses.

"Fuck!" she said, startling me again. "I've been with you in my head for almost a year now, so I might as well." She worked up a smile. "I realize that doesn't sound too enthusiastic, but this is all kind of a shock."

"You don't have to decide anything now."

"Yes I do. That's why I came today."

A guard strolled past, said, "Better say your good-byes," and moved on to another table.

Therese started crumpling sandwich wrappings, putting them into the empty sack. Her movements were unhappily hurried, as if all she could think about was getting clear of me.

"Hey," I said, catching her wrist. "Are you all right? I want you to be all right. Not just because of you. I want to feel secure tonight. But if this isn't going the way you hoped . . ." I left it there for her to finish.

She looked at my hand on her wrist, then closed her eyes and nodded. "I was going to head back tonight, but I think I'll wait until morning. I liked being in the motel last night, feeling close to you. I might like it better tonight." She glanced up at me. "Okay?"

"Okay," I said.

As Therese and I crossed the yard, we passed close to the weathered old trustee standing at the fence. He took a break from killing himself and said sourly, exhaling a billow of unclean smoke in the process, "Well, one a'you looks happy."

"Which one?" I asked, thinking it could go either way, since I was depressed by having to watch Therese leave.

The trustee stuck his cigarette back in its withered, wrinkled hole and turned his face to the distant trees and puffed grayly. "I was just kiddin'," he said.

Chapter 4

We were married on July 9 by an old prison chaplain with a yellow smile and a surfeit of hammy compassion, and on the morning of November 12, Therese picked me up in her Suburban at the gate and we drove south toward Arizona. Freedom didn't seem strange at first because I'd been there in my head for several weeks, but as the hours went by, the knowledge that I was free to hurt myself any way I wanted, drink a gallon of cholesterol, take any sort of poison, it made me giddy. I limited my intake to two cheeseburgers, fries, and an ice-cream sundae. The food left me torpid and I dozed while Therese drove. I woke half-turned in my seat toward her and, watching her grave face, her sweatered breasts defined sharply by the pressure of the seat belt, the neatly clipped tendrils of hair clinging to green wool, the faded jeans stretched tight across the tops of her thighs, the whole overpowering soft sum of her, I was gripped by a dread sense of responsibility. Our lives were bound together now, albeit by nothing more momentous than an arid, perfunctory ceremony in a horrid little white room of the prison annex, the same room where the remedial reading classes were held, and I wondered how much of what I felt for Therese was something I'd talked myself into, how much of the whole prayerstyle trip was just me buying into my own con. Yet wasn't opportunity and self-manipulation at the heart of everything people felt? Sure it was. And wasn't the core principle underlying prayerstyle the idea that through the careful engineering of sounds, of words, one could focus the will so as to manifest small changes in reality, give reality a nudge and bring new conditions and potentials into existence? And that being the case, wasn't this a proof of faith, a fine validation of my stripped-down view of the mechanical nature of the universe? Thereafter I was inundated with more of the psychobabble that had come to fill my head since I became a professional prayer-meister, much of it designed to convince me that my insanity was a peculiar form of normalcy—everyone did more or less the same, right? A crawl of bland justifications was unwinding through my brain, as insistent and maddeningly destructive as a computer virus, erasing every contrary thought, every mental file that sought to resist it. I was helpless before my creation. I had become the symbiotic host for a pernicious philosophy. I'd been born again in the white light of my own stupidity. Praise Wardlin Stuart! Praise him with great praise. I had reduced the religious experience to a how-to book and wasn't that clever of me? Wasn't that ill and evil? Wasn't that precisely what the twenty-first century needed? The sacred freeze-dried. Holiness reduced to a brand name. The Word-made-flesh gone commercial, packed with a hundred vitamins essential to spiritual development. And wasn't that the modus operandi of all great corporate religions? I was a DIY evangelist, a cross between Pat Robertson and Bob Vila. I should have a TV show, *This Old House of Prayer,* and teach folks how to construct a home temple out of scrap lumber and shreds of truth left over from the premodern divine . . . .

"What're you thinking about?" Therese asked.

"Just zoning out," I said. "Nothing worth reporting."

The sky had gone a purplish gray, the sunset a band of rose along the horizon, the world a desert and a two-lane strip of asphalt. She switched on the headlights. "I bet you're worrying about us."

"Yeah. A little. How 'bout you?"

She cut her eyes toward me, gave my knee an affectionate rub. "I'm past the worried stage."

"What's that? What's the stage past worry?"

"Getting ready to find everything out. Being eager . . . scared. Mostly eager."

A semi passed us with a monster rush and the Suburban shimmied. "Fucker!" Therese said. She drove aggressively for a few seconds, hanging on the semi's tail, then fell back. "You know what I was thinking?"

"Not a clue."

"I was thinking how much you're going to hate Pershing. And then I thought, maybe not. Maybe what'll happen is, I'll be able to stand it with you around. That's what I've been hoping all along."

She flicked her high beams on and off, signaling an oncoming car to dim its lights. "Bastard!" she said, and, pretending to be blinded, veered us toward the car as it barreled past.

"I'm sure I'll get along fine with Pershing, should I live to see it," I said.

She slung me an angry glance. "You criticizing my driving?"

"I'd be a fool to do that." I pointed ahead, indicating that she had drifted over the yellow line, into the path of another oncoming car. "But I do believe you got God on your side."

We stopped for the night at a desert casino just across the Nevada line. Slots, a handful of blackjack and dice tables, motel attached. A neon sign on a pole announced JENNY'S PLACE and LAST CHANCE FOR CRAPS. The restaurant advertised a "24 Hour Breakfast" and all the dishes on the menu bore names that reflected a gambling theme. Golden Cartwheel Buckwheat Cakes. Full House Breakfast. Aces and Eggs. Sitting in a red leatherette booth, we could hear the *bling-bling* from the main room of the casino above the Muzak and the tinkling and clatter of glasses and plates and utensils and the rough parlance of gamblers taking a break to sop up some grease and carbohydrates, edgy hookers waiting for their pill man, lonesome hillbillies wearing black jeans and thin gold lamé belts and fancy cowboy shirts, their eyes shifting like nervous money, wasted on coffee and bourbon and uppers, and the rest of the assortment of losers that collect in such places. Therese had an upset stomach. She ordered the Big Jackpot Waffle and milk, and when our waitress brought the waffle, Therese stared at it as if it were a newspaper with an end-of-the-world banner headline. I knew what her mind was doing. After years by herself, getting chased by every clown who passed through Pershing, here she was giving it up to a mail-order ex-con—though she had already made a commitment, she couldn't help having reservations. Just to break the silence, I said, "Better eat that before it gets cold," and she laughed dismayingly and said, "Is everything a metaphor?"

I caught her meaning, but refused to acknowledge it. "You're not going to eat, why don't we take a walk?"

Behind the casino the moonstruck desert was smooth as a blue-white beach, the shadows of scrub and cactus etched clean over the sparkly sand. Big stars were laid out in asymmetrical groupings like those you might see on a Navajo blanket, written so clearly they might have been a language. It was quiet, just the occasional hum of a passing car from the highway. I imagined I could hear coyotes stepping beneath the black hang of a mesa to the east and the slither of a cold snake twisting from under a rock. We walked out to a point from which the neon sign spelling out JENNY'S PLACE appeared to be an astronomical object, an English-speaking constellation. The night air was cold. I put an arm around Therese and she tipped her face up to be kissed. She had this sharply acquisitive yet cautious look, as if she were hungering for something but wasn't sure it would be good for her. Moonlight painted her skin a cameo white. The kiss began tentatively, little delicate questions asked, then we found our way about a mile down into it. She pulled away and searched my face, appearing to find new cause for doubt, and I said, "Y'know, we need to live this thing, Therese, and not analyze it so much." She said, "Mmm-hmm," and moved my hand from her waist to her breast. I rolled the nipple hard between my fingers. She let out a rush of breath that had the word *God* in it and looped her arms around my neck. The hits of her heart were strong against my chest. I held her like that, stroking her hair, shaping an *I love you* with my lips, but not sounding it, afraid—though we'd said it before—that now on the threshold of our life together, I might give it the wrong spin and spook her, and as I gazed past the crown of her head, wondering if she wanted to cling to me a while longer or if she was waiting for me to suggest a return to the motel, I was alarmed to see a man wearing dark clothes and a slouch hat standing in the shadow of a saguaro cactus some forty feet away. A drunk, I thought. He must have taken a wrong turn in the parking lot and passed out on the sand, sleeping there until we woke him. An instant later he vanished. Either my mind had played a trick or he'd stepped behind the cactus and slipped into the next dimension over. I had the impression he'd been nodding in approval, implying that he was pleased by what he observed and everything was working out exactly as he had planned.

Back in our room, the intensity of desire, simmered and flavored for over a year, overwhelmed our anxiety, and though we had our share of awkwardness, overall things went so naturally that in the morning, thinking back on how we were together, the image I conjured of the night, of our part in it, was of a white centrality, the slow torsions of our bodies creating, along with the creep of lizards and coyotes, the predatory stalking of a spider across a stretch of star-blasted patio stone, a rhythm that had dispelled the last sinister, scorpion vibrations of the sun. When we reached Pershing the following day, the umbers and yellows and rose and purple tints of the town and the Painted Desert surrounding it had an illusory value, as if the moon-washed blue of our first night had diminished all the other colors. Each evening thereafter when we sat in the apartment at the rear of 'Zona Madness, like an extension of the desert with its adobe walls and Native American blankets and rough, bulky furniture, the windows darkened to rectangles of starred blue, my insecurities born of the day would vanish and I'd feel reinvigorated in my passion for this strange quiet woman . . . and she was, to my mind, more than passing strange. I had inside myself a furnace place that generated needs, but I could find no corresponding place in her. Like a maze with no mystery at its heart, her mystery ran all through her. Whenever I turned a new corner in my exploration of her, I would expect to discover a great secret, the source of her quietness, yet I encountered only another corridor. She seemed content, whole in her contentment. Knowing I was part of that contentment fascinated me, partly because I'd never before seen myself as a solution to anybody's puzzle, the missing piece that completed any picture other than one of chaos and trouble.

One night a couple of weeks after my arrival in Pershing, we drove out into the desert and made love on the hardpan stretching from the cliffs west of the town. Afterward, lying beneath a coarse Mexican blanket, propped on an elbow beside her, I told her how I perceived her. The air was cold and clear, and the moon showed its fossil self, an ancient globe of dirty bone like the skull of a Tibetan incarnation gone to some ritual use. The light it gave was silver, and as Therese rolled onto her back, her eyes gave back silver gleams. "It's not about contentment," she said, and then appeared to be listening to the breeze stirring whispers from the sand grains. "You're the first thing I've wanted in a while, but I want more. Maybe a child. Maybe a career . . . something more than the shop. I don't know. It'll come to me."

I said I didn't get the "it'll come to me" part.

"When I was a kid I wanted things people told me I should want. An education, a well-paying job. So I hurried out and did all that. I messed my life up pretty good and wound up back here." She ran a hand along my arm, her fingers tracing the shapes of the muscles. "I used to think I wasn't a risk-taker. And then I realized I'd always taken risks. I hadn't thought of them as risks because they were things other people assured me weren't risky. The things they told me I should want. I've learned not to be in such a hurry. To be sure I want something before I go after it."

"You didn't act that sure about us," I said.

"I was pretty sure," she said. "Just the mechanism was rusty."

I laid a hand flat on her belly. "So you're saying I shouldn't be in such a hurry myself."

"You've lost ten years. Maybe you need to be in a hurry."

She gazed up at the stars. The big ones twinkled so brightly, they appeared to be bobbling about like diamond lures. I wondered what the Navajo saw up there. Not Little Dippers and Ursa Minors, I figured. From beyond the cliffs issued the whiny buzz of an ATV, probably a drug courier on a run to the reservation. The sound gave me a discomforting nudge, breaching the bubble of warmth and security that enclosed us, reminding me of the world, and, in reflex, wanting to close that breach, I slid my hand between Therese's legs and made play with my fingers. Her eyelids drooped and her breath grew ragged. A dazed peacefulness came into her face. I loved watching her changes. The flickers of transport, the lost look that replaced them. I thrust two fingers inside her, working to bring her off. I felt at a rarefied distance from her, like a chef leaning over a saucepot, inhaling the steam, poised to add a touch of this, a pinch of that, reacting to every burst of subtle fragrance. Soon her belly spasmed, her thighs clamped my hand to prevent it from moving. She pulled me down beside her, gasping out broken words, and I experienced a childlike satisfaction at having pleased her, happy now to be sweet-talked and tightly held. "God, what you do to me!" she said, and kissed my cheek, my brow. After a minute she swung up astride me and began to fuck me with slow, exquisite precision, her face shadowed by the cowl of her hair. It disturbed me to feel such an undiluted passion. I sought consolation in doubt, trying to doubt her, to doubt my own conviction, but none of it would stick. Her breasts swayed against my palms, her hips rolled with powerful assurance. My mind kept shifting from intense awareness of her to an equally intense animal blankness, as if somebody's kid were toying with my light switch, flicking it repeatedly on and off. It seemed I could interpret the starry geometries that framed her, it seemed I remembered a secret whispered at my birth, it seemed my life went pouring up into her and hers down into mine.

Chapter 5

I liked 'Zona Madness. I liked standing in clear winter light and drinking my coffee beside a display of stuffed frogs playing mariachi guitars. I liked the bins of topaz and agates and geodes, the marshaled ranks of Navajo dolls, the display trees hung with squash blossom necklaces, the bright postcard racks, the vortex crystals with special healing powers nested in purple velvet, the fake-treasure-map place mats, the cactus-shaped Christmas tree ornaments. I liked the snowbirds, the elderly tourists, how they'd enter the shop with an air of suspicion, warning all sales personnel—myself, Therese, or her employee, Leannne, a chubby high school dropout—away with a fierce I'm-just-browsing glance, and then eventually would drift over to the counter and ask directions or inquire as to the possibility of a senior discount on some hideous gewgaw. We moved a high percentage of our merchandise to lonely old men and women who were basically paying for the privilege of a conversation, likely the only one they would have all day. I did my best to give them their money's worth, resurrecting my bartender skills and making up stories about the region, contriving fabulous legends to mythologize every piece of plastic trash.

I liked Pershing, too. I liked its uneventfulness, its placid acultural take on disorder, its unremarkable expression of the Great Insanity. It was a bit larger than I'd pictured, population slightly in excess of four thousand, but it conformed more or less to the mental image I had nourished. The storefront businesses, the dusty streets.

On the edge of town stood a roadhouse, Scotty's Cavern, an unsightly pinkish building with a covering of urethane molded into the shape of an immense boulder. A few hundred yards farther along in the direction of Phoenix, bordered by cliffs, was a development called Desert Wind—tracts laid out with surveyor's string and a double-wide trailer adorned with a necklace of pennants and manned by Robert W. Kinkade, a stocky white-haired gent with a florid complexion who favored loud plaid sport coats and red trousers and white belts. Kinkade came into the shop one evening for, I believe, the precise purpose of meeting me, to make an assessment of my worth, a process that required only a few minutes.

"Hot enough for ya?" asked Robert W. Kinkade after we'd been introduced. He stared at me with a sort of doggy eagerness as if he loved this game and could barely restrain himself from barking his next line. When I allowed that it was, indeed, hot enough, he said, "You could grill a burger on the roof of my trailer. Thank God for the ol' AC, huh?"

"Praise Jesus," I said, and gave him a wink.

Kinkade fingered the purple ceramic figure of a dragon, one of a brood ranked along the counter beside the register. He glanced between me and Therese. "Well, sir," he said. "Everybody's been wondering who Therese was going to settle down with, 'cause sure wasn't anyone around here good enough for her. Guess you're it, huh?"

He didn't appear to recognize that he was being rude. I thought his manner might help to explain why Desert Wind tracts weren't filling up with Desert Wind houses.

"Guess so," I said. " 'Course we haven't exactly settled. We're gonna be going crazy a while yet."

The sense of this must have eluded Kinkade—he gaped at me.

"Newlyweds," I said.

Kinkade arched an eyebow and chuckled on cue. He stroked the dragon's wings. "They say you're a writer."

"That's as good a description as any."

"I'm not much of a reader, but I like a book now and then. That Robert Ludlum fella, now. He can spin a tale."

I pictured a montage of bathroom scenes, Kinkade enthroned on the toilet of the double-wide, his vacuous face pinched in concentration, scribbling in the margins of a coverless paperback, emerging after thousands of such study sessions with the first fully annotated edition of *The Bourne Identity*.

His mood suddenly gone White Rabbitish, he stopped petting the dragon, harumphed, checked his watch. "Gotta run," he said. "You folks drop out to Desert Wind, I'll show you a vista . . ." He closed his eyes, a hand held up beside his ear as if enraptured by the call of memory. "You hafta see it! Seriously. Drop on out."

During that first month in Pershing I received similar visits from various of the townspeople and I got the idea that I was of not much more intrinsic interest to them than a crumpled piece of paper blown up against a screen door. They were curious about me simply because they remained curious about Therese. She had never, to use Kinkade's term, settled. She had kept herself apart from them, resisting inclusion in their social fabric, and there was some hope, I think, that I would enjoin her to participate in yard sales, bingo, and secret drunkenness, all the sketchy limbo of their mad, minimalist desert life. Her separateness seemed to have unnerved them, caused them to be apprehensive of the negative judgment they imagined she had made concerning the suitability of the town, as if her attitude, running contrary to the consensus view of Pershing as a haven for the fortunate, would put cracks in their hallucination and let in the devils of the real. They went away knowing, as did I, that I wasn't the combinant force they desired. I was just another barrier behind which Therese could hide—perhaps she had designed the relationship to have that effect. Instead of talking to her, now they would have to talk to me. This did not please them. I believe they felt a separateness vibe from me, as well—though I didn't consciously emit one—and soon they left us to our own devices.

I'd spent ten years trapped in an environment whose nights were as loud and replete with demented voices as those of a rain forest, and I found the quiet life appealing. The silence of the desert soothed me and, even at its noisiest, the intermittent racket of the town never approached the brain-damaging intensity of a prison day. Being with Therese, whether at the shop or taking a break from business, I felt I was slow-dancing through the hours, engaged in a cocooning process from which would emerge a unique bipartite entity, and I saw myself living that way happily ever after, becoming a bemused observer from behind a shop counter, accumulating memories of jangled entry bells and spooky visitors, involved in a clandestine passion with my wife. When *Handbook* was published in January, our quiet life changed, albeit not drastically to begin with—the book sold well enough for the publisher to order a second printing, but it didn't take off as my editor had hoped. I received a smattering of fan mail, most asking me to write prayers for the sick and dying. Reviewers were confused about how to classify *Handbook* and thus failed to review it in droves. Locally, the cable access channel filmed me reading in Scottsdale and the weekly newpaper did an interview. Several nights after the interview appeared, Lyle Gallant, who ran the local Allstate office, a tall sixtyish strip of jerky with thinning white-blond hair, a long, dour Scandinavian face (his original family name was one of those many-hinged, short-on-consonants Swedish names), and a laconic manner, dressed in brown twill trousers and a white shirt and an old tan Stetson, came to the shop and asked me to write a prayer for his business.

"I wouldn't quarrel with an uptick this quarter," he told me. "Seems the kinda thing's made for your prayerstyle. Don't need but an extra dribble."

I had rejected the requests for cures, but this appeared to be within my purview. "You read the book?" I asked.

"Bought a copy, but can't say I read it. Looked through it some. Don't get all the poetry stuff, but the instructional parts appear to make sense." He bent over the counter, examining a display of cheap turquoise rings. "Whaddaya figure you'll charge?"

I was accustomed to setting my price in cigarettes, which I then had traded for drugs; I had no clue as to the street value of a prayer. Lyle was plain as a button, dry as toast, but I liked that he hadn't thought *Handbook* weird, as had most Pershingites with an opinion. I told him the first one was free.

"Couldn't do that," he said. "Man with a book, his work's got value. Might not can pay what you're worth, but I need to pay you something."

"How about a percentage of the uptick?" I suggested. "If it happens."

After considerable negotiation, we settled on a sliding scale of percentages that Lyle wrote out on the back of a fake treasure map and then signed. I started on the prayer the next morning and that same night I went to Lyle's office and showed him a draft.

"You wrote this here for me to read," he said glumly, holding the paper close to the light of a lamp with a green plastic shade. "Can't do 'er."

"That's how it works," I said. "You become familiar with the words. You learn to focus behind them and you repeat the prayer whenever you feel a need."

"Can't do 'er."

"Why the hell not?"

"I'd embarrass myself."

"Nobody else has to be around when you pray. You won't have any reason to be embarrassed."

"Still can't do 'er."

"Okay. I'm not following here."

"Don't much care for the sound of my voice," Lyle said, and shook his head for emphasis. "Never did. Flusters me when I hear myself. Why don't you write it for you to read and I'll just do the focusing part?"

I said this might not do the trick.

"Don't see why not. You write 'em. Can't be much difference for you to read 'em as well."

"You need to say the prayer repeatedly," I reminded him.

This stumped him, but only briefly. "You're walking past the office, you could stop in and say it for me. Might could sweeten our deal to cover that."

"We can give it a try, but I don't know . . ."

"Got one other problem. The word *tits*. Doesn't sound like it belongs in a prayer. You hafta use it?"

"Yeah," I said, tired of hassling with him. "Probably."

Prayer for Lyle Gallant's Allstate Insurance

Silver tubes and plastic wires for our final bedsides.
The technology of comfort guaranteed.
Premiums dwindle to a platinum trickle in our veins.
God's specter rises in the needles and the drips,
and the perfect nurse with plum-tipped tits
and a smile like Satan's high school hooker
comes to bless us with her medicine lips.
Give us these splendid isolations,
these painless promises and miracle cures.
Grant us dreams of TV Movie of the Week endings.
Deliver us the kiss-shaped candy of the afterlife.
Insure that the musical limits of our financial independence
will never be exceeded by the threnody of pain.

Amid the secrets of contracts,
in the efficacy of his full-term life
and the glorious oxymoron of death benefits,
we see Lyle, pushing sixty, a castaway Viking
with eyes the color of glaciers at twilight,
marooned upon a hot oceanless beach.
What does he know when he stands
in his little cube of boxed-in coldness
with the immense red hands of his company above?

What does he think when we walk past?
Pray for the sentience of his hopes,
the sanctity of his nonexemption clauses,
the lustrous complicities of his neighborhood policies.

In the orange and gold evening
of our winter in the desert,
a long tongue of silence flicks out
to touch the roof of Lyle Gallant's Allstate,
and the peaceful treaties he has made
with death, with accident, with disaster,
their letters come alive like liquid snakes,
arrange themselves in cabalistic orchestrations
that speak the names of the Great Beneficiaries.
In the midst of this chaos of delirious spell,
Lyle strides between his office and Scotty's Cavern,
making his ordinary way, his supple mental rounds,
prowling the difficult moral peninsula that lies
along West Eldorado Street, out to the state road,
contriving a demarcation, a strip of thorny principle
separating the actuarial from the infinite,
while a wind troubles the brim of his hat
beneath which breeds a Swedenborgian magic,
some rickety law of devils and divinity
that requires only faith and business to sustain it,
and the sun opens, round and coral red
like a lizard's mouth, head lifted on the horizon,
trying to drink the air.

Fifteen days after I read this prayer aloud in the doorway of Lyle's office, with him standing at my shoulder, devoutly focused, Gallant's Allstate experienced the beginning of an uptick. More than an uptick, actually. A surge of new policies and additional-coverage clauses that made his year. Before long, thanks mainly to Lyle's relation of his success over beers at Scotty's Cavern, other businesses came to me with their prayer requirements, and by the beginning of spring I had written nearly thirty new prayers to satisfy them. One of the prayers, intended to bless the opening of a new business in town, became controversial after my client, Walt Rozier, had it imprinted on a thirty-by-forty-two-inch sign which he then chose to display in his stockroom window. It opened with lines that spoke to Walt's employment of several Arizona Cardinal cheerleaders to help him celebrate the occasion:

> *You pose, ladies,*
> *cowboy hats tilted perkily,*
> *leaning forward to expose*
> *the slopes of your doeskin breasts,*
> *skirts thigh-high, fishnetted flesh strapped*
> *with commemorative garters*
> *courtesy of Rozier's All Terrain Vehicles . . .*

The pastor of the Follow Jesus to the Crossroads Church in nearby Solarsburg, a village by comparison to Pershing, preached a sermon against me on the cable access channel, citing the prayer's "lewd content" and characterizing me as "a murderer who derides God and erects false idols," this last referring to the fact that quite a few of the prayers contained a mention of the Lord of Loneliness, whom I'd come to use as a structural component and—in some instances—a fictive addressee. But the businesses for which I had written prayers thrived and the winds of commerce served to deflect this little storm of religious outrage. I sent the new prayers to my editor, Sue Billick, and one Friday morning in April as Therese and I were getting ready to open, Sue called to tell me the new prayers were "exciting" and would be included in *Handbook*'s second edition.

"Can you get testimonials from these people?" she asked. "You know, with concrete numbers? How much their business improved after you wrote their prayer?"

"Probably. Some haven't paid yet, but they seem satisfied."

"I wasn't aware they paid you."

"Yeah, sure. Not in money always. Marshall's Tires gave us a new set of radials for the Suburban. And I got a deal with the Mesa Bar and Grille. Nancy Belliveau, the owner, lets us drink free and I'm supposed to supply a new prayer every six months."

"That building you mentioned, the bar . . . shaped like a big pink rock? Did you write one for them?"

"We talked about it, but Scotty's an asshole. I couldn't get in the mood."

"If your mood changes, it'd be a nice bit of color to add to my presentation."

"Tell her about the golf place," Therese suggested as she broke open a roll of quarters for the cash register.

"Is that Therese? Hi, Therese!" said Sue.

I relayed Sue's greeting and said, "A miniature golf course in Scottsdale traded us lifetime passes for a prayer."

"Have any other out-of-town businesses signed on?"

"This guy owns a waterslide park in Tucson. Couple others."

"And they came to you?"

"Right."

"This is wonderful!" Sue paused and I could hear sirens in her background, as if her thoughts had declared an emergency. "I need you to write something like you did for the first edition. Notes to insert between the new prayers. Can you do that?"

"No problem."

"Get everything to me as soon as possible, okay? We've got you scheduled for fall, but I'm going to push to include the new material and make it a Christmas book."

"Think they'll go for it?"

"There are some real hooks I can use this time. I want to set up some interviews for you. In New York. And a tour. Can you and Therese get away from the shop?"

"I could . . . but winter's our big season. I doubt Therese would leave Leanne in charge. She can't handle the books."

"How about for two weeks in early November? I'd like her here for the interviews."

I looked to Therese, busy now restocking the pop machine. "I'll run it by her," I said.

"Wardlin?" Sue used a girlish tone I hadn't heard before.

"Uh-huh?"

"Could I commission a prayer?"

"For the company?"

"For me."

"I've never written a prayer for someone I haven't met."

"Is that important?"

"I'm not sure. It feels like I should know more about you than I do."

"You know me from the phone?"

"Yeah, but that's your business side, right? I don't even know what you look like."

"I can send a picture? You can ask me questions?"

Therese sent me an inquiring look—I signaled that I wouldn't be much longer.

"What do you want to pray for?" I asked Sue.

There followed a longer pause; the sirens had gone elsewhere. "This guy I've got a crush on, I'd like him to respond to me. The situation isn't right just now, but I think that's going to change." I heard her lighting a cigarette, then she said, "This is silly."

"Maybe," I said. "But it's what I do, I guess."

"Oh, I didn't mean your work, Wardlin. I meant my thing. It's unrealistic."

"Me going off on a book tour . . . that's unrealistic. You landing a boyfriend's not unrealistic at all."

A disaffected sniff. "I'm not interested in a relationship. Just a hookup."

I told her I'd give the prayer a shot and she asked, "What about compensation? I want to pay you."

"I gotta go help Therese open," I said. "We'll figure something out later."

"She asked you for a prayer to get a boyfriend?" Therese asked after I hung up.

"Not even that. Just to get laid."

Therese said, "Hmm," and went into the corridor that led to our apartment. She still had on her pajama top and she stood in front of the hall closet, choosing a shirt.

"Sue invited us both to come to New York in November. Do some interviews."

"She plans to sell you like a candy bar." Therese shucked off her top. "Is that what you want?"

I stepped behind her and cupped her breasts. "We can use the money, can't we?"

"The money's fine, but . . ." She slipped away from me and pulled an embroidered denim shirt off its hanger. "You didn't expect prayerstyle to be a business opportunity. Now it's starting to get over commercially, you might consider how you'd like things to go."

"I like writing the prayers. That's the whole thing for me. The rest of it's incidental."

"That may be true now, but if *Handbook* takes off, everything will change."

"The book's probably going to fall flat, Sue'll get her ass fired, and I'll wind up pouring beers at the Mesa."

Therese began buttoning her shirt.

"Be kinda nice, an all-expenses-paid trip to New York. You been to New York?" I asked. "I never have."

"No, but I suppose I'll have to go." She flashed a sly smile. "I don't want anybody else taking a bite of my candy bar."

I eased behind her again, held her waist and nuzzled her neck. "Yeah, that's gonna happen," I said.

Chapter 6

It was a good summer for prayerstyle, but not for 'Zona Madness. Our business was way down and we might have been in trouble, if it hadn't been for the money I made from writing prayers for car washes, bars (Scotty's included), diners, body shops, Sue Billick (who sent a picture that showed her to be an attractive yet rather stern-looking redhead), beauty salons, electronics outlets, liquor stores, pizza joints, pet shops, and so on. I was churning out five and six prayers a week and it got to where I was rejecting dozens of reasonable requests. In June I was approached by Jeffrey Mungro, the eccentric CEO of a Southwestern drugstore chain, who offered a yearly stipend for prayers-on-demand to be used in their advertising as well as, I assumed, in whatever secret corporate rituals Mungro might intend. My agent worked out a twenty-five-prayer-per-annum deal for a decent advance. The attendant publicity supplied a healthy boost to *Handbook*'s sales and created a buzz around the second edition, which Sue planned to cram with as many of the business prayers as possible. So it was that when the book hit the shelves in November, it included more than sixty testimonials from businesspeople. However, the man whose support enabled the book to cross over into the literary arena from the motivational pop-psych niche it occupied was Michael Chouinard, a Princeton professor of comparative literature and semiotics.

Chouinard had published a highly praised novel in his late twenties and, due to his flamboyant and media-friendly personal style, had since been designated one of those people whose opinions are sought on matters cultural whenever a cultural matter rises to the level of public notice. He appeared frequently on CNN and the network news shows as a pundit, an *éminence grise*, and had a regular spot on NPR. It was on his radio spot that he declared *A Handbook of American Prayer* to be "a landmark achievement, a revitalization of populist literature that signals the movement of contemporary letters beyond the postmodern, an amalgam of the pragmatic and the fanciful that may well induce consequential cultural change." As the line on my sales chart glided higher, he grew increasingly evangelical and rhapsodic, trumpeting *Handbook*'s worth first on PBS with Charlie Rose, then in any venue that offered him a stage, and as a result small bookstores began sending in orders and featuring the book in their promotional newsletters. It was my sense that while he may have seen some value in *Handbook,* his zeal was mainly due to the fact that he'd found a horse that would take him for a ride into the upper reaches of the limelight. When I met him at a book party in New York, this view was borne out, I thought, by his deferential treatment of me: a limp handshake followed by a two-minute conversation during which his eyes drifted about the room, concluded by his running off, claiming that he had to "get somewhere," somewhere proving to be thirty feet away at the elbow of a telejournalist. Whether cynically motivated or not, the man might have been on my payroll. His widely publicized denunciation of a *New York Times* critic who described my prayers as "consummately plebeian . . . everymannish poetry dressed up like a man posing as a construction worker in a Greenwich Village bar" led directly to interest from *60 Minutes* and ultimately to *Handbook*'s being designated an Oprah book. Chouinard called the *Times* critic "a debased intellect shrouded in the mummy wrappings of twentieth-century literary elitism," and championed my work by saying it demanded "a revision of critical standards and, obviously, new critics."

The best thing that happened during the summer was that I lost all doubt concerning my relationship with Therese. I came to understand that love, like fire, existed on its own terms, unmindful of the reasons for which it might have been kindled. Though I gained a measure of acceptance, even of prominence, in the town, I preferred being alone with her, two strange birds off by themselves in a corner of the aviary of Pershing, escaping at night to the desert or the towns along the Mexican border, living large for those hours and then returning to their quiet perch. It was as if we'd spent all our lives practicing to be together. Days, we labored for the same cause, we listened to each other, and each night we attended a party to which no one else was invited. If we were not perfect in our union, then we were secure in our imperfection. We had our disagreements, but only once did we fight, this in early September, around midnight at the El Norte Cafe in Nogales.

The cafe was a tourist spot just over the U.S. side of the border, the slightly less polluted side, being free of maquiladoras. It was distinguished by a red, white, and blue fiberglass volcano atop the roof and its interior design appeared to be the work of a fetishist patriot. Hung from the walls—dark blue plaster with painted rows of large white stars—were *nichos,* little shrines made of tin enclosing tiny American flags and toy figures grouped about them. Elvises, football players, GIs, cowboys, movie stars, monsters. Laminated onto the tabletops were military service ribbons, religious medals, fiery images of the Virgin of Guadalupe, political buttons, baseball trading cards, chromed pennies, dog tags, an infinity of flattish objects. The lighting was dim and purplish red, and the secondhand smoke so old, it seemed the same clouds persisted from visit to visit. Contending with the babble of a hundred drunks, accordion-heavy *norteño* music pounded from a grand old-fashioned jukebox that resembled a neon cathedral. A mixed crowd of hookers and lowrollers were wallowing on the dance floor. The margarita glasses were big enough to drown a kitten in—Therese and I each put away several before we began to argue over the reason why business had picked up recently at 'Zona Madness. I claimed the upturn related directly to the prayer I'd written two weeks previously. Therese, hunched over her half-full glass, gave a dry laugh. "You think that's funny?" I said. "It's clear I'm doing something that works. I haven't had any complaints."

"Never mind," she said.

"Naw, you been on my case about prayerstyle ever since we met. Why don't you spit it out!"

"Fine." Therese gave me a disgusted look. "It's not the prayer you wrote for the shop that's doing it. It's the notoriety you've been getting. People are curious, so they come in to have a look at you. Sometimes they buy things."

"Notoriety. That's the word you'd choose? I'm not getting famous, I'm getting notorious?"

Therese started to respond, but I cut her off. "What you're telling me," I said, "the business is doing better not because of the one prayer I wrote, but 'cause of all of them. Like that somehow invalidates the system. Don't you understand? This *is* a system. The idea that one prayer works partially because it's standing on the shoulders of a hundred other prayers, that's a proof. A validation."

"Jesus," she said. "You're getting to sound like the asshole from Princeton."

"I'm just—"

"You don't sound exactly the same . . . like you're poking a finger up your butt when you talk. But you make the same basic noises. The same points. You're swallowing your own bullshit."

"Why's it have to be bullshit? Because you say so?" I slapped the table hard enough to slosh tequila out of my glass. "You don't believe what I'm saying about prayerstyle is true?"

"Something's true, that doesn't mean it can't be bullshit, too. You're taking it to the level of bullshit, Wardlin. You're starting to believe prayerstyle's a bona fide majestic article. Like it's literature and not just the artsy-fartsy version of the pet rock."

A drunk staggered against our table. I yelled at him, shoved him away, and stared meanly at Therese. "That's how you see what I do? For real?"

"It's worse than that."

"Don't hold back!"

Therese had a taste of her margarita, wiped salt from her lips. "I don't think you understand the potential here."

"Gee, why don'tcha clue me in?"

"I doubt you'll want to hear it."

"I'm all fucking ears."

"All right." She clasped her hands around the stem of her glass, peering down into it as if reading an oracle from the bits of pulp floating on the surface. "What you've done with these prayers, it hooks people in like a religion does. Except prayerstyle's better than religion. There's no god, no moral code. You just wish for things and if it doesn't work out . . . the notes in *Handbook* set conditions. How you have to focus, how the person praying has to choose the words carefully. And when the prayer isn't answered, it's easy for people to believe they didn't do it correctly. That leaves you as the source of these prayers, the ones that actually work. They have to come to you if they want them. Maybe your prayers do work. Or maybe it's that you limit what can be prayed for so much, you're bound to have a high success rate. It's extraordinarily clever. You've taken the basic principles of religion, tossed away the trappings, and turned them into an easy-access discount item. Like the Cliff's Notes to the religious experience. You could wind up being Jim Baker and Tony Roberts combined."

"That's it?" I said tightly.

"No. I'm worried, Wardlin. What's going to happen to your head if Sue Billick gets her way? Are you ready for all the hoopla, the craziness that comes with it? Is that what you want? You were in prison for ten years and I don't think you've dealt with that yet. There may be a lot of things you haven't dealt with."

"Why don't I embark on a course of therapy and suck down a few thousand lithium? That make you happy? That way I'd be sure to avoid success?" I knocked back the dregs of my margarita. "Is this a jealousy thing?"

She looked stunned for a beat, then her eyes teared. "Fuck you!"

"Only if you say please." I scraped back my chair and stood.

"Fuck *you*!" she shouted. "Fuck you, fuck you, fuck you!"

"Hell with this shit!" I said, and stalked off in the direction of the exit. I heard her call to me, but I pushed through the crowd on the dance floor and didn't turn back. By the time I'd gone halfway to the door, I was feeling ashamed, prepared to admit that her points were well taken. I'd had the same thoughts myself—I just hadn't liked hearing them come back at me. But the momentum of my anger carried me out into the sweltering, neon-lit, diesel-scented night. A single-file column of lowriders came lurching along the street, rap shuddering from their oversized speakers. Across from El Norte, half-silhouetted by light streaming from the windows of an arcade, some young Mexican guys wearing straw hats and cowboy shirts and creased jeans were negotiating with a whore with immense breasts and wide hips and a miniskirted waist cinched so small, it appeared she'd been squeezed through a napkin holder. The sidewalk in front of El Norte was clear except for a diminutive, mustachioed man in a slouch hat, a black sport coat, black shirt, black jeans, who was leaning against the wall and smoking. His clothes and his nonchalance lent him kind of a veteran rock-and-roll look. Still agitated, my head hot and buzzing, recognizing that I had yelled at Therese, something I hated having done, I bummed a cigarette from him, thinking a smoke would calm me. He lit me with a lacquered black Zippo and asked what was happening. His complexion was swarthy, but his features gave no definite clue to his racial heritage. His voice was unaccented, his eyes were very dark—I could detect no difference in color between the pupils and the irises. Border meat, I figured. Little of this, little of that. Shake it, bake it, and out pops an unprepossessing brown-skinned man with a slightly pudgy American face, someone who by century's end would be more or less typical of the population. I told him nothing much was happening, except I'd had a fight with my wife.

"Women," said the man musingly. "They solve so many of a

man's problems by wrapping them up into one big problem." His voice was lightly graveled, a sandy, stoned voice.

Feeling guilty about Therese, I wasn't prepared to fit her into this box, and I said, "Yeah . . . or not."

"Or not." The man nodded agreeably. "There are no fixed certainties. It's not even certain that there are none."

This struck me as a more convoluted expression than one was likely to hear on the streets of Nogales. The man's blasé manner, his retro cool—this, too, seemed out of place. But I didn't give it much thought, I was so concerned about my status with Therese. I'd never seen her so angry.

"Ideas, perhaps," said the man.

"What?"

"I suggested that ideas may become fixed . . . or not."

"Fuck're you talking about?"

"Nothing much," he said, and exhaled a couple of smoke rings. Across the street the whore peeled up her tube top, displaying her breasts for the Mexican farmboys. The horn of a passing lowrider sounded a wolf whistle.

"There's little else to talk about," said the man.

I suspected he might be setting me up for a hustle, trying to present himself as a figure of intrigue and then offering to sell me a midget burro and a boy child. "This how you come on to everyone?" I asked. "Or is it just for the tourist trade?"

"I spend a lot of time by myself. I rarely speak to anyone."

"That explains it, then," I said.

"Mostly I observe. I imagine someday I'll have to take a hand."

Drug-induced, I thought. The Ecstatic philosopher. Perhaps the godlike distance of the pre-tweaker.

"And you?" the man asked.

"And me what?"

"How would you describe yourself?"

A number of sarcastic answers occurred, but all I said was, "Drunk and stupid."

The street seemed to grow louder, to sharpen from a general discord into separate voices and musics and rumbles and the whirring rustle of sewing machines in the tailor's shop next to El Norte. I noticed a store across the way, its window stocked with bullfighting capes on which scenes from the Plaza de Toros had been airbrushed. A pride of gangbangers sidled past, their dark faces offering challenge, sinewy bodies encased in denim and white T-shirts and vests, shitkicker boots etched with Mexican eagles. Standing with her legs spread in front of the arcade, the whore shrieked at the farmboys who hurried away giggling. The man beside me asked if I wanted to hear a joke. "Not a typical joke," he said. "One that's unique to the moment."

I knew I should go back inside and repair the damage with Therese, but I wasn't ready. I liked being out in the black air smelling of gas and carbonized meat, the dusky orange murk of the inversion layer reflecting the polluted light of Nogales. I needed a moment. "Go for it," I said.

"Okay." The man flipped sparks from the tip of his cigarette and proceeded to deliver on his promise.

A Mexican, a black man, and a gringo policeman met on a corner on the outskirts of Nogales one Friday night when no one else was around. The policeman couldn't afford to turn his head either to the left or the right, so his eyes roamed ceaselessly like the eyes of a toy, like two beads rollling inside two plastic buttons. This caused the Mexican and the black man to move to opposite sides of the policeman, so he would have difficulty seeing them both at once.

"Listen," the policeman said. "I have to arrest one of you guys, but I can't recall whether I'm supposed to arrest a nigger or a spic on Fridays."

"It ain't me," said the Mexican. "I was your fucking Thursday, homes!"

"Hey, I was Thursday, cool breeze!" said the black man. "You cuffed me to a post in the station and everybody come in took a shot at me with their nightstick."

He threw a fake punch at the Mexican, who paid him no mind, lit a cigarette and blew smoke up toward the stars where his woman lived, at least that's what she told him, but everybody knew you couldn't trust the bitch.

"How come you don't remember?" the black man asked of the policeman, and the policeman said, "Something seems to be wrong with me. I have trouble—"

"Wrong with you?" The Mexican laughed. "Dude like you, his eyes rolling around in his head like seeds? Fuck could be wrong with you, man? You fine!"

"Thank you," said the policeman. "I have difficulty being fluid in certain situations and you saying that helps."

"Might wanta get yourself checked out," said the black man. "Be on the safe side, y'know."

In an apologetic tone, because he found the two men very sympathetic, the policeman said, "I still have to arrest one of you."

"Yeah, I mean, what's that about?" the black man asked.

"Immutable Law of the Universe," said the policeman. "You could kill me, of course. But shortly thereafter you'd be arrested and killed."

"Well, that fucking sucks," said the black man.

The Mexican exhaled vastly, his smoke coalescing into a ball that greatly resembled the planet Saturn, and the policeman said, "Nice!"

"What happens we just beat the crap outa you?" the Mexican asked.

"Same deal," said the policeman. "Sorry."

"This is lame, man. We ain't getting nowhere!" The black man scuffed a deep furrow in the dirt that soon began to glow red from the fires of hell beneath, where his homies were hanging out with the ultimate homeboy, the man with a million chains, Mister Scream Scream Scream himself, the one, the only, DJ Scratch.

"Man!" said the Mexican. "How's this shit get to be a law of the universe? All we fucking do is fucking rag on each other. You fuck with me, you fuck with him, we fuck with you. What's the plan, *ese?* What's all that doing?"

"It's the order of things," said the policeman, and the Mexican said, "Fuck a buncha order, man!"

"Where would we be without order?" the policeman asked, and appeared ready to supply a rehearsed answer, but the black man interrupted by saying, "Right here on this goddamn corner! Where you think we'd be? Think the fucking street dissolve there ain't no order? Think we be falling through chaos, the three of us? Symbols of the great categories into which humanity has been divided. The Instrument of Order, the poor, and the wretched of the earth."

"Better watch who you calling 'wretched,' homes!" said the Mexican.

"Hey," I said, growing antsy, but the man waved at me to be patient and continued with his joke.

"Wait just a damn minute!" said the black man. "Something's missing here. Where's the rich guy?"

At this juncture a rich person wandered in from another narrative. He or she . . . It was impossible to determine whether it was a man or a woman, because the figure wore a mask, a yin-yang symbol, and a billowing shroudlike garment. He or she was appalled by the stench, the poverty, and the sense of imminent danger. In a gender-nonspecific voice, the rich person asked the policeman for protection . . .

I started to worry about having left Therese alone. "Is there a punch line here?" I asked.

"I'm getting to the good part," said the man with a hint of mild offense taken. "Do you want to hear or not?"

"Yeah, okay. But hurry it up."

"Doing the best I can." The man tipped back his hat with a flick of his little finger, the nail of which, I noticed, was painted black.

"Where the hell was I?"

"The rich person just came in," I said.

"Right, right . . ."

"Protect you from what, muthafucka?" asked the black man. "I don't see nobody threatening your ass. I ain't saying it's not gonna happen, ya dig, but—"

"Chickenshit gringo pussy!" said the Mexican.

"The word *gringo,* that doesn't sit well with me," said the policeman. "Racial stereoptyping, y'know."

"I'm not comfortable with it, either," said the rich person.

"Screw you! Take off that mask!" said the black man.

"I'd rather not."

"Then we gonna make you take it off!"

"I wouldn't try that if I were you," said the rich person.

"Oh, yeah?" said the Mexican. "Why not?"

"In the first place," said the rich person, "I might be a beautiful woman, in which case you'd all want to fuck me. And no doubt you would, given the abusive primitivism of the male pysche. Two things might then occur. Either you'd fuck me to death or I would fuck you to death. On the one hand I would be dead and you'd be in prison awaiting execution. If I were to fuck *you* to death, however, though it might be fun at first, there would be a metaphorical humiliation involved that would suborn your spirit in the afterlife and cause you pain throughout eternity."

"Okay. That's one possibility," said the black man.

"Actually, that's two," said the policeman. "If you want to be literal."

"Which I'm sure you do," said the Mexican; then, to the rich person: "Give us another option."

"Well," said the rich person. "I, um . . . I might be a dis-embodied voice."

The black man said, "You wouldn't need protection, you was just a voice."

"Okay, I guess we can rule that out," said the voice.

"I gotta tell you, gringo," said the Mexican. "Right now I'm leaning toward fucking you to death."

"I thought this was a joke," I said to the man. "The way you started it, I thought it was gonna be like, you know . . . A doctor, a lawyer, and a priest were standing on a corner. Like that."

"I don't believe I know that one," said the man. "You'll have to tell it sometime." He flicked the lid of his Zippo open and shut, making a ticktock rhythmn. "The one I'm telling now's kind of a more intricate, more interactive knock-knock joke. Except there's no knock-knock. It's as much a social experiment as a joke."

I dropped my cigarette, ground it underfoot. "Yeah, well. It's 'bout as funny as a social experiment."

"The experiment being to see how long it would take you to realize you shouldn't leave your wife alone in a place like El Norte. It took you a pretty long time. Of course, you have to factor in the effectiveness of the joke."

I decided it wasn't worth the trouble to try and figure out his hal-lucination and headed for the door.

"It's been an experience," said the man.

Chapter 7

I drove off a two-legged fly who was hovering around Therese, and ignoring the infernal light and noise of El Norte, I talked earnestly with her for nearly an hour, apologizing, admitting that I probably did have stuff to deal with and I needed to think about how I wanted things to develop with *Handbook* and prayer-style. I meant everything I said sincerely, because I believed she was right, I knew she had a better angle on my life than I had, and maybe she even cared about it more. And when we had done talking and drinking, we went to our motel, Motel Radar 99, ten white stucco cabins on a state highway outside Nogales, a nondescript, barely functional place set amid desert brush, but which had the greatest name of any motel either of us had ever stayed at, and doubtless a great story underlying the name, although the old alcoholic mestizo who managed it wouldn't tell us what it was, and there we lay on the cool sheets in cabin 8, the starry blue glow of the desert lighting our bed, and fucked and talked and fucked until a peach-colored smear of dawn wedged up from behind the raggedy hills to the northeast. Therese was half-asleep when I told her about the man in black outside El Norte. He didn't come off as strange to her as he did to me in the telling. She summed him up as "just some stoner," but the farther he receded in my rear view, the weirder he looked and, at the same time, the more familiar he seemed. Familiar in that I felt I understood, in retrospect, something of his disengaged manner. The interlude stayed sharp in my mind as if it had existed entirely separate from the blurred night of drunkenness and argument and forgiveness. I was too foggy to do other than wonder about the man and soon I curled up spoonstyle behind Therese, comforted by the moist warmth of her inner thighs, the firm custardy heft of her breast, the smoky perfume of her hair. We drifted off to the sounds of clucking chickens, an air horn braying in the distance, the frail loopy whistle of a desert bird, and the old drunk in the manager's office cursing at a laughing child.

I think we lived that way for a while. Spoonstyle. Drunk with one another. In soft constant arousal. And when we flew to New York in mid-November, slightly less than a year to the day after my release from prison, our real anniversary, it felt like a honeymoon with prizes, though neither of us enjoyed the publicity mill into which Sue Billick thrust us. Thanks to Chouinard, the Oprah Book Club, and the airing of my interview with Ed Bradley, the sales of *Handbook* had built rapidly over the summer, and preorders for the second edition were, in Sue Billick's words, "off the charts." People were talking about me, she said during another phone call, the way they talked about politicians, arguing pro and con, angrily, vehemently.

"Is that desirable?" I asked, and then, with a laugh to show I was joking: "I was hoping for pop star, not politician."

"Pop star's not going to happen, sweetie," she said. "But we've got controversy. We can ride that a long way."

I'd been anticipating success and all that attached to it, and there came a time while I was in New York when fame felt like a good fit, when I basked in the attention; but that time lasted no more than a few days. I was being presented as a cult object, a violent felon who had miracle-cured his own soul and now offered cheap redemption, and the audiences reflected this lurid depiction. At my lectures they eyed me greedily, peppering me with requests for prayers. Each day they grew increasingly zealous and demanding. A sizable minority dressed all in black, mimicking my new personal style (Sue Billick had taken me shopping and outfitted me with an entire wardrobe of black garments). They carried my book the way preachers carry Bibles, tucked against their chests, and called themselves Wardlinites. Women occasionally slipped me phone numbers. Men clasped my hand with both their hands and searched my eyes for meaning. More dates had been added to the tour, venues changed from bookstores to auditoriums. I found myself looking ahead at almost five weeks away from home, not returning until just before Christmas. Therese and I defused the awfulness of the situation to some degree by discussing the subject whenever we were alone and on the night before she flew back to Pershing, we went to a dark, expensive little restaurant in the East Village, a place Sue had recommended whose white tables with their crystal and silver and ferny floral displays had the look of enchantments, and there I told her I was thinking of quitting the tour, that we were going to make enough money without it. She insisted I fulfill my obligations, saying that I might want to keep writing and I shouldn't alienate people who could help me.

"Finish the tour with me," I said over coffee. "Forget the shop."

"The shop's where I want to be now."

"Me, too."

"It'll be okay. I'll meet you at the lecture in Phoenix and drive you home." She stirred cream into her coffee and tasted it. "You know what I was thinking about earlier? How clean some of these people smell. The rich people. They have this . . . it's almost like that new-car smell. Ed Bradley, especially." She added another dollop of cream. "Maybe they do smell different. They eat better, take better care of themselves. Maybe that translates into a new-car smell."

"Ed Bradley didn't hug me," I said. "So I didn't notice how he smelled."

"He would've hugged you, I bet." She grinned. "You hadn't been so frowny, he might even a kissed you on the cheek."

"I could blow off the last two weeks. Quit right after Chicago. We could drive up and do Phoenix."

"Don't worry so much. Do what you have to, and when the time comes to do it again, you can decide in advance how much you want to give it."

"I'm not worried," I said. "I'm just having trouble with all this noise, this . . . everything."

"What part bothers you the most?"

"After the lectures. The need that's steaming off people. I'm getting high on it . . . like bad speed. Like the shit we made in Walla Walla. We used starter fluid, Styrofoam cores from nasal inhalers. All kindsa shit. This horrible alchemical brew. We'd cook it down and get a greasy yellow powder. That's the high I'm getting. Ragged and twitchy." I picked up our check, read it, set it down. "What's so freaky is, I am who I am because of prayerstyle, but after the lectures, even during the lectures sometimes . . . Mostly they're okay, you know. I'm having fun up there. But sometimes when I get in front of an audience and say the same things I once said to myself, it's like I'm chumping them. And—"

"It's not—"

"—I think, Am I chumping myself? Is everything that's in my head the result of a trick I played on myself? Is that how fucking feeble people are? Are we that flimsy? Is that what miracles are? Is it all that simple and stupid? And then I realize, of course it is! That's what *Handbook*'s about. Then I look at you and I say, No! You and me together, that's substantial. That feels different from everything else. And then I wonder if I didn't con myself into feeling that way. It's like I can't fucking find a place to stand."

Therese lowered her eyes to the table, fiddled with her spoon.

"Jesus, Wardlin," she said. "Lighten up, will ya?"

I burst out laughing and after a second she joined in. "Fuck!" I said. "You gotta come with me and keep me straight."

"I can't . . . you know I can't."

"Yeah, I know. You're a homegirl."

"I guess I am now."

I reached across the table, touched the tip of her forefinger ET-style with the tip of mine.

A chiffon voice said, "Excuse me, Mr. Stuart?" The hostess, an elegant brunette in a brown silk sheath dress was standing by our table, her right hand held behind her back. "I didn't want to disturb you while you were eating, but . . ." She showed me a copy of my book. "Would you mind signing this?"

"Sure." I took the book and opened it to the title page. "Who should I make it out to?"

"Elaine," said the hostess. "Thank you so much for the book. It's made such a difference in my life."

As I scribbled an inscription I imagined the difference it had made, picturing Elaine to have been an elderly bag lady until, finding a Dumpstered copy of *Handbook,* she embraced the philosophy of creative prayer. While she huddled drunkenly in her cardboard box that night, a spiritual light descended around her and, once it faded, this long-legged butterfly emerged from its rotten cocoon to begin a triumphant career in the food service industry.

On reading what I had written, Elaine said, "That's so lovely! Thank you." She bent down as if intending to bestow a kiss, paused and glanced to Therese for permission. When Therese signaled her indifference, Elaine brushed my cheek with her lips, then performed a high-heel runway walk back to the hostess station, where she stood cradling my book to her chest and gazing raptly into the night like a high school girl dreaming about the star quarterback while hugging her biology notes.

"What did you write?" Therese asked.

"Some bullshit."

"No, seriously."

"The kind of garbage I write in every book. 'Thanks for those nights of forbidden pleasure.' I think that was it."

She looked at me with schoolteacherish firmness. "Do I have to see for myself?"

"I don't care. If you want. Okay. 'Look into the darkness, bring back a new song.' That was it."

Therese repeated it. "What's it mean?"

"Nothing! Just stuff. I sign every book that way, but different. Little bullshit sayings. It's like I'm writing fortune-cookie fortunes. Sue said people want their books personalized and that's how I do it."

Therese gestured at Elaine. "What's she doing now?"

"Standing there."

"You notice she's looking into the darkness? Perhaps on the verge of bringing back a new song?"

"Yeah . . . maybe. So?"

Therese removed her napkin from her lap and dropped it on the table. "You may not enjoy the marketing process, Wardlin. But you're really, really good at it."

The traveling portion of the tour commenced in Boston and from there made stops in Philadephia, Baltimore, D.C., Charlotte, Atlanta, Jacksonville, Miami, and New Orleans, Houston, St. Louis, and Detroit. I did A.M. television shows in each of those cities and on several occasions I was ambushed on these shows by religious pundits. In Charlotte a fundamentalist preacher declared me to be "a tool of Satan," and in Atlanta, an author of Christian-themed children's books (*Yo, Jesus, Yo!* and *Paradise Groove* among his titles) advised me to "chill with the Man, and dig on the Master's Plan." I did a *Scarborough Country* remote from Jacksonville during which a ditsy middle-aged woman who ran a Mel Gibson Web site begged me to see *The Passion of the Christ*—I told her I'd seen it already, thought the movie sucked, but afterward I had confessed to stealing a box of Goobers from a concession stand when I was twelve. A Cuban Roman Catholic bishop in Miami accused me of "spiritual insensitivity," and in New Orleans I was accosted by a trio of sectarians led by a strident black woman dressed in a gypsy-style blouse and skirt and turban who clutched with a pathological level of agitation at a necklace of yellow teeth and laid curses upon my mission in a Creole patois. I dismissed the fundamentalist as a fool and mentioned certain Roman Catholic spiritual insensitivities to the bishop, but by the time I reached New Orleans, with the help of Sue Billick's coaching,

I'd learned to bend beneath rather than resist these attacks, to say that prayerstyle was properly used as an adjunct to organized religion, that its craft ran contrary to no sacred principle. The idea, Sue said, was to be controversial, but not to act controversial. By the time I reached Detroit, I was in full self-parody mode, sounding—as Therese had once noted—like a lowbrow version of Michael Chouinard.

Sitting in an easy chair on the mock living room set of Detroit's local version of *Good Morning America*, flanked by the hosts—Forrest, a shirt-model type with a fruity baritone, and Sherry, a thin anxious blonde, with a surreally wide mouth—I answered the usual questions and was then confronted by Professor Duval Rowan, a tall black man with a receding hairline and a salt-and-pepper goatee who taught comparative religion in the anthropology department at the University of Michigan. The graciousness and incisiveness of his questions forced me to rely on ignorance as a defense, to say repeatedly that prayerstyle was a method of focusing the will, not a magic spell, a statement that Rowan eventually countered by asking, "What is a magic spell if not a focusing of the will?" When Sherry, beaming her stupefyingly daffy, capped white Cadillac smile, suggested that we sum up our positions, I said merely that prayerstyle seemed to work for some people and that was sufficient to my hopes. Weak. Rowan, as poised and assured as a diplomat, said, "I think we have to view Mr. Stuart as a not altogether unwelcome addition to the cult of personality. What his prayerstyle does, its effectiveness—this is in the end a consumer judgment. I very much doubt, however—"

"Excuse me, Duval." With groupie-like intensity, Sherry leaned toward him. "When you say Wardlin's not an unwelcome addition to the cult of personality, in what sense do you mean that?"

"In the sense that prayerstyle isn't the usual passive panacea to fear offered by televangelists," Rowan said. "Traditional religion promises reward in return for the rigorous practice of faith. Prayer, regular attendance at services, adherence to a moral code. But faith is a nebulous quality and the practitioner can never be sure if he's being faithful enough. Prayerstyle challenges the believer to create his own path to salvation through the practice of a craft, the almost forsaken act of literacy. It offers not rules to govern behavior, but techniques to help achieve goals. *A Handbook of American Prayer* might be seen as an instructional book that teaches people how to write bad poetry in the service of their self-interests."

Forrest nodded solemnly; Sherry tittered as if she understood what was going on.

"Thanks a lot," I said.

"I'm not disparaging *your* poetry," Rowan said. "But I doubt many of your devotees will be so fluent. The point is, your book appears to be stimulating people to literacy. That in itself is welcome. Ultimately, however"—he turned toward Sherry—"Mr. Stuart's success will depend upon the shelf life of his personal style and the extent to which he engages in self-promotion."

To my surprise, Rowan invited me for coffee after the show at a downtown diner, and as we sat looking out onto the dreary winter aspect of Woodward Avenue, crusts of gray snow on the curbs, cars hissing through slush, bedraggled working-class pedestrians hustling along with their collars turned up beneath a concrete sky, I told him he'd really done a number on me.

He looked startled and said, "You think so? I imagine the switchboard at Channel Seven is being overwhelmed by calls from your devotees howling for my blood." He forked up a bite of his Danish, left it suspended above the plate. "Television journalism has gone to hell since the Gulf War. Issues are no longer analyzed, they're placed in a sort of WWF format. They bring in a hero and a villain to hash the matter out. It's more entertaining, I suppose." He chewed and swallowed. "I'm an academic. That, in the eyes of most television viewers, makes me the villain."

"You still kicked my ass."

"I made my points. I don't see it as an ass-kicking." He slurped his coffee, grimaced. "The thing is, Wardlin . . . That's quite an unusual name, by the way. I've never heard it before."

"My daddy was named Ward, my mama was Lynn. Rednecks do shit like that."

He laughed and said, "You're from a blue-collar family, then?"

"White trash . . . blue collar. Whatever."

"The thing is," Rowan went on, "you're not the typical hustler I encounter on these shows. You believe in your product. You may even be an honest man."

"Funny you should mention that. I been wondering lately if this whole thing isn't a shuck. Little self-doubt creeping in."

"They say only an honest man will admit he's a liar."

"That sounds fancy true, but I don't know."

Rowan smiled, had another bite. "This figure in your prayers, the Lord of Loneliness . . . where did he come from?"

"He's a cartoon character. I was lonely in prison. I started personifying loneliness. The reason I keep using him, it feels right sometimes. Maybe because most of the people who ask me for prayers are lonely."

"That's a huge demographic you've tapped into. The lonely. Cuts right across the spectrum." Rowan gave his plate a disgruntled nudge, as if the Danish weren't to his taste. "Do you realize how remarkable all of this is? Your success?"

"My editor says I'm a publishing phenomenon." I chuckled. "Like the *Men Are from Mars* guy."

"That scarcely covers it. Whether you're aware of it or not, and after talking to you, I don't believe you are, you've started a religion. That idiot Michael Chouinard served as your John the Baptist. Preparing the way for your advent. Now you—"

"I'm sorry," I said. "That's just not happening."

"No? Then why has organized religion been so aggressive in their rejection of your book? They feel threatened. The practicality of your approach is appealing. You're addressing the spiritual needs of nonchurchgoers and you're also beginning to drain off their converts. You've been out on the road a few weeks and the cult has already formed. The Wardlinites. I've found hundreds of Web sites devoted to your work. *Time* and *Newsweek* are doing cover stories, I believe?"

"Yeah. They're not about me as much as they're using the book to talk about how it's all going to shit with the culture. I love that. They soft-pedal war and dope, poverty and crummy education, and with me they get hard-hitting."

"It doesn't matter. Your picture's on the cover. That's the significant thing. You're a charismatic fellow, Mr. Stuart. You have a compelling story. In terms of the religious tradition, your antecedent was Saul of Tarsus, a violent man struck by the white light of salvation on the road to Damascus."

"It wasn't a white light with me. It was someone sticking a shank in my back got me going."

"Perhaps it was something similar for Saul. The Bible's hardly a literal rendering. The fact remains, you're in a tradition of men who've fallen from grace and claimed to find a sustaining principle. From Saul to Bill Clinton."

Our waitress stopped by to ask if everything was all right and Rowan told her his Danish was stale, he'd like a fresh one. I was disturbed by what he'd said about me, yet I took a perverse pleasure in thinking I might have pulled one over the eyes of America, even if that hadn't been my intent. Rowan handed me a business card and said he hoped we'd stay in touch.

"That's flattering," I said. "But seeing you don't think much of my book, I don't understand what benefit you'll get from it."

"It's my job, tracking this kind of thing." He said this defensively; then, after a pause, he went on. "When I read your book I wasn't impressed, but I kept thinking about it. The more I thought, the more intrigued I was by the practical aspects of prayerstyle. A week later I sat down and wrote a prayer. I spent several hours at it. The act of writing reminded me of when I was a student and would write painstakingly thorough cheat sheets. By the time I finished, I'd know the material so well I wouldn't need to cheat. I was focused on the process . . . as I was while writing my prayer." He gazed out the window, following the windblown progress of a young black couple, the girl wearing a Wayne State University jacket several sizes too large. "I watch televangelists all the time. I'm doing a book on the subject. Over the years I've been importuned by extremely polished pitchmen to drop to my knees, to lay hands on the television set, to perform a variety of devotions. I always resisted, even though being exposed to such a variety of Christian seduction tends to make one credulous. I was objective, I thought. I had no desire to be saved or transformed. But I didn't resist you, Mr. Stuart. You promised nothing. No golden road would open. I would feel no sanctifying touch. You placed the task of salvation in my hands. That was irresistible."

"What I'm doing's got nothing to do with salvation."

"Oh, no? You present the possibility that one can successfully pray for something small. Should the prayer be answered, one can pray for something more substantial from that platform. And so on and so on. Anyone looking for a path to salvation will see this for such a path. A ladder to climb rung by rung toward some murky form of transcendence."

"You give that an ominous ring," I said.

"The idea of god has never struck me as being other than ominous. Even at his most paternal, Jehovah's not someone I'd want for a dad. And the god you've put forward, the Lord of Loneliness, this oddly gothic figure who dresses in black, with a mustache and a black fingernail . . . he may be a whimsical creation, but he seems far from benign."

Thinking of the man I'd met outside El Norte, I felt a twinge of alarm. "I never said he had a black fingernail."

"Yes you did." Rowan took his copy of *Handbook*, which had been resting on the seat beside him, and leafed through it. The margins of the pages were illuminated with pencil-written notes. He pushed the book toward me, open to a prayer I'd written in July, two months before my conversation with the man at El Norte, and pointed out the pertinent passage:

Look up through the foliage of your days
to no god, not even he who keeps lovers apart
by crooking his little finger,
the one with its nail painted black.
Pray to know the things you know
as if they were written in lightnings.

"I don't come right out and say it's the Lord of Loneliness," I said.

"Isn't that who you were thinking about when you wrote those lines? It seems in character."

"Maybe . . . Yeah. Probably. I can't believe I forgot I wrote it."

I wished I could frame a question for Rowan, because he was good with answers and might have had one that would help me shake the ridiculous notion that I possibly had had a conversation in Nogales with a creature of my invention. But I didn't want to sound like an idiot and I changed the subject. I asked him what he had prayed for.

"Channel Seven booked Arlie MacMichaels, the minister of the largest Protestant church in Detroit, to debate you," Rowan said. "I was hoping to meet you and sometimes they'll use me in a pinch. So I decided to try prayerstyle and pray for the opportunity. Two days after I wrote my prayer, Arlie fell out of the booking. An emergency of some sort. They gave me a call. It was a coincidence, I'm sure. It would go against logic to believe otherwise, to believe prayer can be made into a craft." He took back his copy of *Handbook* and let the pages waterfall. "But I'm tempted to belief, Mr. Stuart. *You* tempt me to belief."

Chapter 8

That night in my suite at the Renaissance Hilton I looked through *Handbook* and found over forty direct references to the Lord of Loneliness and numerous other nonspecific references, including the prayer Rowan had showed me, which had been written to help a young Pershing housewife—the one who had left the magazine with my ad in it on the counter of Therese's shop—summon up the strength to break free from what was essentially a marriage of convenience. I read the prayer, hoping to recall what I'd been thinking at the time I wrote it:

Prayer for Elizabeth Elko's Divorce Action

The hour of midnight is the hour of strange guidance.
The stars are diamond pockmarks on a tight black skin,
and serpents burrow like corkscrews into the earth
seeking secret meats packaged in tiny pockets far below,
animals with no names no eyes no souls,
treasures of pure protein.
Wolf spirits howl in the high places
when the wind brings them the scent
of petroleum products, not game.
The Devil is killing Africa.

These things are known to you
who pray for less deliberate a fate,

for release from an old promise
made in a moment of pain,
from a marriage gone sour and yellow
as milk curdled in its carton,
from a life into which you're fitted
like a clipper ship into a bottle,
plying no current and sailing no sea,
a perfect model of your kind.

The tigers that come at the end
to carry you off, to weave you in and out
like a fiery thread through all the universe,
they care nothing for your heart,
for your sacrifice, your forsaken dreams.
Their compassion is a knife in winter.
Look up through the foliage of your days
to no god, not even he who keeps lovers apart
by crooking his little finger,
the one with its nail painted black.
Pray to know the things you know
as if they were written in lightnings.
Pray to go forward through the world,
to abandon the stalled suburban utility vehicle
and the soul-killing ancient mortgage.
Pray for this at the hour of strange guidance
when old men in the air-conditioned heaven of their bars
are mesmerized by baseball, presidents, and wars,
and headlights stab out from the void to touch
a young beast emerging from moonshadow,
freezing her to stone, into another twisted figure
carved by wind and magic, forever tormented
by the stillness of her lapsed blood.
Pray for a single drop of undiluted joy
to be slipped into the strong drink of your life.

I tried to convince myself that my memory was flawed, that I'd written Elizabeth Elko's prayer after talking with the man in Nogales, but I remembered meeting with her, walking with her in the July heat, beneath the bunting left over from Independence Day. I tried then, like Rowan, to pass the matter off as coincidence. How many men in America, I asked myself, went about with a single fingernail painted black. Hundreds, surely. Thousands, maybe. It might have signified a gang affiliation, an affinity for a certain sexual practice, a random conceit. But the man's diffidence, the allusive quality of his conversation . . . though the Lord of Loneliness hadn't spoken a word in any of the prayers, after glancing back at them, recognizing the lineaments of the character I had drawn, I imagined that if he were to speak he would sound very much like the man in Nogales. This led me to consider the improbability that if prayer were, as I had countenanced it, an act of physics, if it could work on a quantum level to produce small changes in reality, might it not be possible that I had summoned up a minor deity, or perhaps created one, provided a template into which some portion of the divine reservoir could flow? The idiomatic mechanisms of religion and fairy tales, wish, will, prayer, spell—given what was known about the mind's control over one's own physical well-being, was it so ludicrous to conceive that my nearly decade-long concentration on prayerstyle, on the Lord of Loneliness, had generated a miraculous occasion, a moment during which the tightly focused beam I'd directed toward the uncreate had caused the form of a sardonic dark little man with a mustache to bubble up in response? Implausible though they were, I couldn't exorcise these thoughts, and when I called Therese later that night, I paced about the room and told her about Rowan, the black fingernail, everything, and said, "Know what I think? I think I'm losing my fucking mind. It's not just the Lord of Loneliness shit, it's the audiences, the TV, the Wardlinites. There's times in the middle of it, it's like I've left the planet, I'm inhabiting someone else's body."

"Are you going to be okay?" she asked.

"I'm fine, I guess. But I get this screw-loose feeling. Nothing's quite real. Maybe you were right, maybe I wasn't ready for this."

"It's only a couple weeks more."

"Sixteen days. I'm marking 'em off like on a jail calendar."

"It's getting crazy here, too. I'm so busy I'm going to have to hire someone to help Leanne. This afternoon a busload of Japanese tourists came. They all had copies of *Handbook* they hoped you'd sign. When I opened this morning, people were waiting outside the door."

"Jesus! That's a first."

"They buy things, but they're here for you. Lots of them leave prayer requests. And the mail . . . I have sacks of letters addressed to you."

The line hiccupped, signaling that Therese had another call.

"You gonna get that?" I asked.

"No. Chances are it's someone asking for an interview. That's usually what it is at this hour."

"I'm sorry."

"It's no big deal."

"Yeah, but they shouldn't be calling so late."

"It won't be like this forever." Therese's voice brightened—an artificial brightness, I thought. "Anyway, everybody in town's delighted."

"With all the new business, huh?"

"Uh-huh. People have been asking, 'When's Wardlin coming back?' They figure once you're home, business'll pick up more. Things keep on the way they have, they'll be putting up a statue."

I opened the drapes, looked down at the Detroit River. All I could see of the water were reflected shines from the lights of the gantries and ships and warehouses that picked out the darkness— like a junkyard galaxy. "I miss you," I said.

"Me, too." After a second she said, "We're going to the desert the minute you get back."

"What if I'm jet-lagged?"

She laughed. "Don't be."

I pictured a thin curving tube arching across the masonry of the Midwestern states, a wormhole uniting the eleventh floor of the Hilton with the apartment behind 'Zona Madness, and felt the stuff of our intimate connection flowing along it. Therese told me more news of the town and I listened happily, paying little attention to the specifics, letting her voice make blurs of desert color in my head. After hanging up I considered hitting the bar adjoining the lobby, but there had been a handful of Wardlinites lurking about earlier and I didn't want to run into them. I ordered a bottle of Ketel One from room service and sat by the window and drank. Three drinks and I was able to detect constellate shapes among the lights along the river, a zodiac of inimical forms: knives, hatchets, crowbars. The phone rang, but I didn't answer, suspecting that it would be a Wardlinite who had bribed a bellhop for my room number or Sue Billick calling to remind me that she'd be rejoining the tour in Chicago or someone else I didn't want to talk to. As I sat there in my four-hundred-dollar-a-night suite, drinking a bottle of expensive vodka, it occurred to me that I owed everything to Wanda's manipulation and Mario Kirschner's unwitting sacrifice. I no longer saw Kirschner's spirit dressed in gore coming through the walls as I occasionally had in prison, but thinking of him, how his spilled vigor had fueled the engine of my success, made me uneasy. I had a fit of existential instability, an apprehension of supernatural forces gathering, and envisioned the Hilton tower growing flexible and tilting, tipping me out the window, and I would fall through the blackness to meet some uncompromisingly grotesque fate. The phone rang again and again I refused to answer. I kept drinking until I felt distant from the past, the present, isolate even from my own emotions, my consciousness limited to an observance of the night and its hotly lit machines, so immune to human concern, I might have been the Lord of Loneliness himself.

My first evening in Chicago I ducked out on Sue Billick and my publicist and went for a walk downtown. The sidewalks were icy, the windchill must have been below zero. Few pedestrians were about and those who were kept their eyes on the pavement. This pleased me because I was sick of being recognized. My image on the *Time* and *Newsweek* covers, prominently displayed at every kiosk, luridly mounted above banners that said respectively "The New Amorality" and "Cult Hero or Con Man?" (as if the two were mutually exclusive), had temporarily given me celebrity-level visibility and turned my day into a wearisome succession of handshakes and wet stares. I was at home in the cold white lights under the El, plumes of warm rotting breath erupting from sewer gratings, the bright frozen streets. It felt comfortably fictive, like a dystopian future, a world with a metal sky whose living buildings spoke in agonized windy gusts. After an hour on my own I was restored, certain that I could hang in for the last two weeks of the tour without a hitch.

As I came around the corner nearest the lobby entrance of the Westin—my lecture was to be held in the banquet room—I spotted a man leaning against the building some forty feet ahead and smoking a cigarette. Despite the harsh weather, he was dressed in a slouch hat, black jeans, a black sport coat and black shirt. He pushed up the brim of his hat with a flick of his little finger—I was too far away to determine if the nail was black—and butted his cigarette and headed toward the hotel. The sight stopped me for a second, then I ran after him, thinking he might validate my speculations of a few nights before; but I'd gone no more than five or six steps when I hit a patch of ice and went on my ass. On entering the hotel, still breathless from my fall, I found the lobby bristling with men and women dressed in black. Slouch hats, jeans, shirts, and jackets. Many wore mustaches (a few of the women had glued-on facial hair) and all sported a single black fingernail. Dozens of them. They closed in, gabbling my name—"Wardlin . . . Wardlin . . . Wardlin . . ."—sounding like a chorus of agitated turkeys, thrusting out envelopes and pieces of paper. A bungling subspecies with a herd mentality, more or less identical faces, and an utter unanimity of expression, a sort of drugged yearning. Surrounded, unable to regain my poise, I pushed through the crowd and bolted down the corridor that led to the banquet room. They pursued me, calling my name and snatching at my coat. Sue Billick poked her head out from a half-open door farther along and beckoned. I slipped through the door, which she then locked.

"Wow!" she said. "I guess the heat's been turned up a notch."

We were in a small conference room with a podium fronted by ten or twelve rows of chairs, the walls hidden by dull red drapes. I took a seat and said, "What the fuck was that?"

"The voice of the New Amorality." Sue sat beside me and began stuffing things—notepad, tape recorder, manuscrpt, pencil—into her bag. "I was doing some work and heard the hue and cry. Good thing, too. They were closing fast." She extracted a pack of cigarettes from the bag. "I don't suppose they let you smoke in here, but what the hell." She offered the pack, lit my cigarette and hers, then went pacing about, emitting little gray puffs. Engine Girl. I could hear the crowd outside, murmurous, bumping against the door.

Sue stopped her pacing and stood facing me behind the podium. She had on a gray-green tweed jacket, gray slacks, and a loose white blouse, clothing that caused her slender figure to seem genderless. Her pale red hair was pulled back from her face into a long pony-tail, and her makeup was so artful, I could never tell if she was a pretty woman who had for business purposes designed a mask of powder and paint so as to appear cold and off-putting, or if she had managed by dint of careful application to create an illusion of beauty that disguised a witchy plainness. "How are you holding up?" she asked, resting her elbows on the lectern.

I pointed at the door with my cigarette. "I'm not too fond of that shit."

"Soon you'll be back in Pershing. This'll seem like . . ." She smiled winsomely. "Like a distant apocalypse."

"Therese says it's out of control back home, too."

"Well, from what you've told me, Pershing's a pond that could use a ripple or two." She tapped the side of her head, as if in self-punishment. "I forgot to tell you. We're going to host a thing in the suite after the lecture. Just a few important people."

"Important," I said dully. "How important?"

"Some print and TV media. One of the Chicago Bears. I can't remember which. He's a sweetie, though. He claims *Handbook*'s done wonders for his game. Roger Ebert's coming, too."

"Roger Ebert? Jesus, I hate that guy! He likes every piece-of-crap movie comes along." I flicked ashes onto the floor. "If I was a movie, he'd like me."

"For God's sake, Wardlin! Don't go morbid on me just when you're about to make a zillion dollars."

"I'm not *going* morbid, I been there a while.""Then cheer up!" She cast about for a place to put her cigarette, finally stubbing it out against the side of the podium. "I wish Jean would get here," she said, referring to my publicist, Jean Singer. "We've got a thousand things to go over before the party."

"Fucking bloated, pompous elf!"

"Are you still on about Roger Ebert? What's your problem with him?"

"It's not rational, okay? I understand that."

She waited for me to go on.

"See, I used to watch him religiously when I was in the joint," I said. "I thought he was supposed to be this great critic, so I made a list of movies he recommended I wanted to see after I got out. Every one of 'em sucked! Every single one, man!"

"There's no accounting for tastes."

"I shoulda known he was a joke," I said. "There was this one movie he loved . . . the girl who plays Buffy was in it? It had a magic crab in it, too. Only way you could love that movie, you're getting paid to love it . . . or you got a hamster on a treadmill instead of a brain."

"People say he's a very nice man."

"If a convict bullshitted me like that, I woulda gone at him. I fucking was counting on Roger, man. He was part of my freedom dream, all those cool movies. I started watching those movies, I wanted to kick his fat ass. Fact is, I still want to."

Sue put hands on hips. "Are you going to behave tonight?"

"When have I not behaved?"

"Never. But I'm sensing a potential for misbehavior. We've got *Larry King* tomorrow. It would be nice if you could refrain from violence until afterward."

A firm knock at the door. Nervous as a fox, I twitched my head toward the sound.

"I'll take care of it." Sue strode to the door and opened it a crack. The murmur rose to a babble once again. I heard her tell someone to see about getting some security in the corridor, then she said, "Wait a second," and closed the door. She came toward me, wearing a perplexed expression. "Jean has a man with her who claims to be your father."

My relationship with my family was such ancient history, the idea that my father had materialized in the immediate vicinity provoked not genuine surprise, but a thinner emotion, the sort of feeling you get on learning that something trivial you'd lost, a button or a bowling ball, has turned up in an unexpected place.

"Do you want to see him?" Sue asked.

"It'll make my day complete," I said.

"Is that a *yes*?"

"It's a heads-or-tails thing."

She looked uncertain.

"Bring him," I said. "But don't go away. This reunion promises to be a model of economy."

She opened the door and there he was. My dad. Wearing a stained car coat with a leatherette collar and holding a beat-up Seahawks cap. Twenty-some years had exacted a toll. His comb-over had gone gray and his skin, too, was gray, that industrial tint you see in the complexions of old factory workers. The chest was sunken, the beer belly accentuated. Scrawny legs. But that long-jawed, hangdog face, no amount of wrinkles and liver spots could hide its depressive soul-stamp. He shuffled forward, muttered, "Wardlin," like it was something he was embarrassed to say, gave me a halfhearted handshake, and stepped back. The feeling I had was of déjà vu, not true familiarity.

"What're you doing in Chicago?" I asked. "Last I heard you were still in Spokane."

"We moved to Cicero so your mom could be near her sister," he said. "You remember your Aunt Paula."

"I remember the name. Don't believe I ever had the pleasure."

I thought he might argue the point, but after a pause he said, "Maybe not."

He seemed to be having trouble thinking of a follow-up, so I said, "Long time, huh?"

He nodded. "Yeah. Been a while." He glanced at Sue and said, "I'm Ward."

Sue introduced herself as my editor and Dad said, "Guess my boy's getting to be a big deal."

"Bigger'n Texas!" she said with an excess of cheerfulness.

He nodded again, then turned to me. "Your mama wanted to come. She's having health problems, though. Your brother's down in Dallas, working for Mobil now. Sister's fixing to give us another grandchild. Be her fourth."

"Give 'em my best when you talk to 'em," I said.

"I'll do 'er. You bet."

There ensued a pressurized silence. The hubbub from the corridor had the rumbly sonority of a distant rockslide. Sue was staring at us, fascinated and, I thought, appalled. I grew angry. Not at my father or Sue, but a generalized anger at the circumstance.

"So," I said. "I know you wouldn't a come . . . I mean, if you need something, that's fine."

Another nod. He'd always done a lot of nodding. Nods for him were a language with one root word and a thousand variations. "I feel bad for asking. Things weren't ever right 'tween you and the rest of the family."

"Wasn't anybody's fault."

"Musta been somebody's, but damn if I could ever figure out

whose it was." He stuck a hand in his trouser pocket and nudged his balls. "We got us some serious medical expenses. Your mom's had surgeries. Goddamn insurance didn't cover shit." He glanced at Sue and said, "S'cuse my French."

She pardoned him with a wave.

"I probably can help you some," I said. "But most of my money's coming six months, a year down the road. The publishing business, they're slow to pay."

He shrugged and tried a laugh. "Hope it's not slow like the insurance business."

"I could see about an advance," Sue said. "I'm not sure how much. By rights I should be able to get six figures, but you know the bean counters. I could probably get fifty."

"Am I really gonna make a zillion dollars?" I asked her.

"At least half a zillion."

"How soon can we get the money?"

"I'll put in a voucher Monday. Maybe three weeks."

My father stood with lowered eyes, holding his Seahawks cap down by his waist. I thought about serfs awaiting the justice of nobility, hired hands begging before a manor lord. I wanted to act in some way, to make him feel easier, but was unable to move, to speak, constrained by regulations that had been established long ago.

"We appreciate it," he said. "Really do appreciate it."

"I owe you," I said.

"You don't owe nothing."

"You raised me up. I owe you for that."

Something seemed to stiffen inside him. "We never gave a shit for each other, you'n me. Now here I am with my hand out. Hell, I . . ." He jammed the cap onto his head. "Makes me feel bad."

I couldn't think of a thing to add. The thin emotion that had posssessed me earlier changed colors from suprise to sadness, but it was still thin, like how you might feel while watching one of those commercials for charitable organizations that work with Third World children, an emotion that if you're a couple of drinks into your evening may bring a tear and momentarily inspire you to act, but then is erased when *Monday Night Football* comes back on.

"All right, I'm going." He hitched up his pants and started to button his coat.

"I need your address." I fumbled in my pockets for a pen and, finding none, asked Sue to take down my father's particulars. He leaned in over her shoulder and spelled out the street name—Corinthian Way—with laborious slowness. He spelled it wrong.

"Don't you worry," he said to me. "I won't be troubling you any more after this."

"It's okay. If I got it, y'know?"

He opened the door and shot me a last gray neutral glance. The babble in the corridor had subsided. Security doing its work.

"I'm married," I said. "Woman named Therese. We live in Arizona."

"I'll tell your mama," my father said. "I expect it'll make her happy."

When the door closed behind him I was startled to find myself standing—I'd lost track of my body while he was there. The silence of the room had acquired a faint ringing. I sat down in a chair at the end of one row. My head was fogged with his gray residue and I was close to crying, but I knew that close was as near as I'd get to actual tears. The space occupied by my family in my thoughts was large but attenuated, a persistent mist that foreshadowed no stronger weather.

Sue took a stand in front of me, her arms folded. "Are you still with us?"

"It's okay," I said, having only halfheard her.

"Hello? Wardlin?"

I looked up at her.

"You're not being responsive," she said. "This is a sign you need . . . what? A ride on a pony? An injection?"

"How about a coupla drinks?"

"Hang on."

Sue went to the door, talked through a crack to Jean Singer. The folds of the dull red drapes, I noticed, appeared to be rippling.

"Vodka is on your horizon," she said, returning.

"I guess that all looked pretty weird."

"Well, it's none of my business, but . . . Yes. *Weird* is a word that might apply."

"I swear to God, they adopted me. They always denied it, but it's the only fucking explanation."

Sue sat beside me.

"Bet you're thinking I was abused. Uh-uh. It's like I was a changeling. A boy raised by wolves. They're not bad people. Maybe they're good people. They probably are. But they're all the same. My brother and sister, my parents. They're not real smart. Actually that's being kind. They're stupid. My brother and sister flunked out of high school. I was skipped a grade. Even when I was a kid they'd stare at me like, What the fuck are you? There was no connection. I'm pretty sure they were afraid of me. When I left home they were relieved." I leaned back, kicked out my legs. "Me, too."

"It looked as if there were a connection."

"It shook me up, seeing him. But what really shakes me up is there's so little going on."

Sue put an arm around my shoulders, gave me a squeeze, and I was aware of her breast flattening against my arm.

"Anyway," I said. "Fuck."

She withdrew her arm and sighed. "I can cancel the party if you'd like."

"Naw, I need ol' Roger Ebert in my life tonight."

She pretended to be annoyed, giving me a pert, disapproving stare.

"I promise he'll live," I said. "But it'll feel good to have him in my sights."

The alcohol arrived. Two doubles for me and a glass of chardonnay for Sue. I gulped down one of the doubles and pressed the icy glass against my forehead. Sue peered at me through the pink lens of her wine glass. "You're an unusual fellow, Wardlin," she said. "I don't think I've ever met anyone quite like you."

I picked up the second double and sipped, let a chip of ice melt against my gums as the heat of the first drink stole through my gut and into my bones. It seemed to be reconstituting me, clarifying some fundamental position.

"Aw, I bet you have," I said, "and you just didn't know it."

Chapter 9

I enjoyed giving lectures because the crowd seemed to become a single person and it was easy, no pressure, like when I was in Walla Walla, explaining prayerstyle to a convict holding five packs of Marlboro Reds and wanting to land a kitchen job or receive a letter from his girlfriend. I would lose myself in my original enthusiasm for the creation of individualized prayer and pay scant notice to the creepy fixity of the Wardlinites, black cadres mixed in among those of brighter cloth, a crafty desire agleam in their ranked faces. That night, however, as I mounted the podium, the applause, the things I intended to say . . . it was all like a dream in which I discovered that none of my clothes would fit. Rather than connecting with the audience, I was aware of my voice booming out across the room and I saw my words strike into them, saw their flesh shudder and their pupils enlarge, as if they had swallowed poison. I grew to like the effect. I wanted to maximize it, to watch it happen again and again. I later understood that this disassociative feeling might well have been a last divestiture of my prison-bred desire to be kind, to give of myself, a frail garment that had, in the interests of survival, muffled the self-destructive elements of my character, most notably, a spiritual nonchalance that sometimes manifested as a willingness to do violence. Now that I could act incautiously with relative impunity, that garment was no longer necessary. Though I could not have articulated this at the time, I had an oblique understanding of the game that I was running.

Seeing the audience from an aloof perspective gave me to recognize that these people wanted me to control them. That's why they were here. Sitting in their rows like eggs in a carton, each one insecure in the belief that their shells contained a little golden prize. It was my job, my duty, to firm up their self-deception. Knowing that made me hate them a little. More than a little, if truth be told.

"Prayers are empowerments, not pleas," I told the audience that night. "You're empowering creation to resonate with your will, not begging for a crumb. Anybody here know what fractals are? Let me see hands."

A scattering of hands were raised.

I plucked the microphone from its stand and went pacing across the stage. "If you don't know, look it up. F-R-A-C-T-A-L. You look it up, you'll come across the notion that when a butterfly stirs its wings in a Cambodian jungle, a storm might just blow up out of nowhere down in the Caribbean. That's how connected we are to everything else in the universe. Why am I telling you this? Because a prayer is more powerful than a butterfly's wings." I took another stroll across the stage and then repeated it in sections. "A prayer. Is more powerful. Than a butterfly's wings. If it's precise! If it precisely announces the thing you desire! If you infuse it with your individuality, a prayer can become a real power in the world." I lightened my tone. "I remember giving this same spiel to an acquaintance of mine in prison. Man name of Jody Wirgman. My mistake was, Jody had been behind walls so long, he could barely recall what a butterfly looked like. The only example he had to go by was this big ol' butterfly tattooed on his chest, with pictures of naked girls on its wings." A titter rippled across the room. "Jody emerged from our discussion with the wrong idea, but we got it straightened out." I flipped through the pages of *Handbook*. "I'm gonna read a prayer I cooked up for a man back home. Robert W. Kinkade. He owned some land west of town. Been trying to get a development off the ground for years. Hadn't sold a parcel. He asked if I could help him out. Now I'm not here to write prayers for you like I did for Robert W. Kinkade. I can show you how I helped a few people, but mostly what I want is to encourage you to help yourselves, to find words that feel right for you. Like I keep saying, that's all prayerstyle is. Finding words that feel right. Devoting yourself to that practice until you isolate the voice that's in you."

I located the prayer, flattened out the book.

> *Between the white smack of sun*
> *against the prefab plastic walls*
> *of Donald Cardwell's Boron station*
> *to the mesa west of Pershing*
> *where Bobby Kinkade's Airstream trailer sits*
> *flat to the rock, decorated with flags,*
> *there lies the phantom town that he envisions . . .*

"I'm going to try something," I said after reading for about fifteen minutes. "How many of you got prayers you're working on . . . got 'em with you? Show me hands."

Perhaps a quarter of the audience lifted their hands. I let my eyes wander across their faces, skipping over the Wardlinites (too eager), and settled on a brunette in the fourth row. Late twenties; jeans and a Northwestern sweatshirt; slightly chunky, jowls in her future, and too much makeup, but not unattractive. She appeared to be of two minds about being called on, her hand barely raised, like a kid who wasn't sure she knew the answer but wanted to look smart. I asked her to join me on the podium and she came forward. Officeworker, I thought. Someone on a career track. Overlying her hesitancy was an air of defiance that marked her as an underling with some power. Her name was Diana Moss and the objective of her prayer, written in a green spiral-ring notebook, was to get a date with a coworker by the name of Barry Stelling.

"Will it embarrass you to talk about this?" I asked.

"Yeah, but . . ." She shrugged. "Women know how it is, trying to get a guy to notice you. I'm not alone."

Her voice carried over the mike. She received a rustle of friendly laughter and one shout of "You go, girl!" that triggered more effusive laughter.

"Sure this guy Barry's what you want?" I asked Diana. "Excuse me for saying so, but a man who doesn't respond to a pretty lady like you, maybe he's not worth praying for."

There was slight applause, whether in support of my assessment of Diana's looks or my low opinion of Barry Stelling, I couldn't determine.

"He's a good guy," Diana said stiffly. "He's going through some stuff, but he's a good guy."

I would have bet all my doughnuts that the relationship was based on a water-cooler flirtation and consisted mainly of her longing stares, but it was plain she had invested heavy emotion in it.

"Okay. Let's see what you've got here." I rested her notebook on the podium and read:

> *I want Barry Stelling to ask me out,*
> *something simple like dinner and a movie,*
> *a night with no pressure and no promises,*
> *like friends who're just taking a look,*
> *and if nothing's there, then that's all right.*

I broke off reading and said to Diana, "Remember what you said when I asked if you'd be embarrassed?"

"Yes . . . I think."

"What was it?"

A fretful line cut her brow. "I guess I'm flustered. I can't . . ."

"You said women knew how it was, trying to get a guy to notice them." I tapped the notebook. "That's what you're praying for, but you're not saying it here. You're putting the cart before the horse. What you want is this guy to look at you and then all else follows. Isn't that so?"

Diana studied her prayer. "Yeah, that's . . . Yeah."

"Why don't you rewrite that first line?"

Her eyebrows inched together and she pursed her lips. "Now?"

"Just the first line." I handed her a pen and stepped back to give her room at the podium. She stood with the pen poised for a second or two, then scribbled a few words and glanced at me.

"Read it for us," I said.

Diana leaned close to the mike and, with a quaver in her voice, she said, " 'I want Barry Stelling to look my way.' "

The audience offered up a murmurous noise that, I thought, implied critical approval.

"How did that feel?" I asked Diana.

"I think it's . . . better."

"You felt more connected with the words, didn't you? They pulled something out of you. Energy . . . emotion."

She nodded and then dabbed with a knuckle at the corner of one eye. I lifted a hand, palms up—a gesture to the audience that said something midway between, See, what'd I tell ya? And, Behold, a miracle. Some whispered, some shifted in their chairs, but most were still, as if waiting for my next trick, sensing it might be even bigger.

"Once he notices you," I said to Diana, "once he takes a close look and goes in past the clinical, past how men normally look at a woman . . . what do you want him to do? What do you want him to see?"

She started to speak, but I said, "Write it for me, Diana."

Her eyes went to the prayer, scanning the lines.

"Honesty," I said. "Find what you truly want and write it. You want him to look up from his desk and notice . . . What?"

She gazed at the notebook for such a long time, I thought I might have to give her a nudge. At last she bent to the paper and wrote a few lines. Then, her voice shakier than before, she read the new opening verse:

> *I want Barry Stelling to look my way.*
> *I want him to pray like I have prayed,*
> *for a sign, a glimmer, a sideways glance.*

I want him to see what I have seen,
something more than I show the world,
the evidence of genuineness and passion.

"There you go!" I said.

The audience burst into applause. Many of the Wardlinites stared with palpable envy at Diana.

"There you go!" I repeated. "That said it for you, didn't it?"

Her eyes glistening, Donna yielded up a peep of affirmation.

"Can you finish it on your own? I know you can!"

"I think . . . Yes."

"You don't have to dig deep!" I said to the audience. "You don't have to go through analysis. All you have to do is scrape off the generalities that neuter your speech, that muddy your thoughts, and say what you mean!"

Diana started to drift toward the edge of the stage, apparently feeling that her role had ended. Not wanting to lose my prize pupil, I gathered her in with one arm, keeping her close.

"What this lady here just did," I said, "you can do. Precision! Specificity! Prayerstyle's a deep, dark secret anybody can learn."

The applause, which had begun to decline, grew stronger. "Don't ask for food! Ask for exactly what you want to eat! And before you ask for what you want, ask for what it takes to get you there! That's prayerstyle! You don't hafta hear voices and see visions to strike a bargain with the universe! You don't require the assistance of a spritual professional!"

Laughter mingled with the applause, and all throughout the room, people were beginning to stand.

"All you need are the right words. The right words for you. For the moment you're living in. All you need to find those words are a pencil, and paper, and some quiet moments!"

Everyone was standing now—with all the hallelujah energy in the room, it would have been anti-American for anyone to remain seated. Old ladies struggled to their feet; the lame and the halt were rising; children were dragged from their chairs by spiritually uplifted moms who perhaps saw in prayerstyle a little something on the side that didn't qualify as adultery but felt almost as good.

"Focus!" I shouted, and released Diana back into the human stream. I grabbed the mike and strolled off into my own space. "You need focus, too. But that's all you're gonna need. You don't need somebody to sprinkle dust on your forehead! You don't need somebody to say magic words! You bring your own magic to the words."

What was strange wasn't the extent of my control, like that of a clown entertaining at a kid's birthday party or a conductor leading an orchestra, understanding how to wring just the right tones out of the musicians—the strange part was it felt like something I had been doing for a long time. I could waggle my baton any old way, sketch a giant rabbit in the air, pretend to be popping balloons, whatever, and they would respond with the appropriate noises. I wanted to see how far off the charts I could take them.

"Know what else you don't need?" I asked them. "You don't need Jesus."

The needle on the applause meter took a severe downswing, but I had a remedy. "Oh, you may need Him in some larger enterprise, but you don't need Jesus to get you that raise you deserve! You don't need Jesus to make things go easier at home. You don't need Jesus to get that new business started or keep the supervisor off your back. You don't need Jesus for the small stuff. That you can take care of yourself."

I worked them up into a call-and-response, suggesting things they might want and then saying, "What don't you need?" and they would shout, "You don't need Jesus!" It was hilarious. I was so on top of it all, I could hate them and love them in the same instant. I had that these-are-my-people glow a sports hero must feel after a record-setting performance. But then a chant of "Wardin, Wardlin, Wardlin . . ." came to underscore the litany, offered up by a group of black-clad men and women to the left of the stage, and I waved the audience to silence. The Wardlinites' chant outlasted the general silence by a few beats. I glared at them, shook my head sadly, and without a word, strode down the center aisle, ignoring outthrust hands and questioning looks. I flung open the double doors at the rear of the room and stood facing them. They peered at me with confusion, unsure whether or not I wanted them to move. I kept them guessing for a while so they could feel what I pretended to feel, my dismay over their idolatry, like, Oh, my children, why do you prostrate yourselves even as you hear me say, Stand tall! Some of those closest to the door—women, mainly—offered anxious, doting, apologetic smiles, but I suspected they had nary a clue as to what they were supposed to be apologizing for; they only knew that they had wronged me somehow.

"You don't need *anyone* to be your Jesus!" I said at long last, using a loving yet admonitory voice I had learned to mimic during countless hours of watching Christian television in the joint. "This is all about you! Not me!"

Then I stepped back into the corridor, closed the doors, and walked briskly toward the elevators, knowing I would be followed.

Chapter 10

I truly had not known how I would react upon seeing Roger Ebert. My anger toward him was petty but monumental, funded by a convict's notion of disrespect, nourished over the span of a decade. Moreover, I was in an agitated mood, juiced from the lecture and unsettled by my reaction to the crowd. But when he shook my hand, smiled, chuckled at things I said, all globular and pampered in his blue blazer and open-collared dress shirt, he seemed to have the substantiality of a human parfait one moment, of a cartoon elf the next, and I could not sustain hostility. He handed me his card and said when Hollywood came calling ("They've already called!" Sue chimed in) to buy rights to my life story, well, he understood I had an agent, but he might be able to do me some good. Later I caught him holding forth on a David Cronenberg film, the intricacy of its mise-en-scène, talking to a woman wearing a low-cut cocktail dress who was a couple of deep breaths away from becoming his lap dancer, and it occurred to me that we might be in the same business.

The party peaked, fizzled, and died. While Sue escorted a handful of stragglers down to the lobby, I poured a drink and fell out on a beige sofa the size of a speedboat at the center of a conversational grouping. My eyes drifted across the lemony walls, the grasscloth behind the bar, the fancy skylight, all the pastel magnificence and bland modernity that served to enclose me in an expensive silence. I understood in terms of continuity how I had arrived at this point in my life, yet I also felt a certain existential perplexity, as if an appreciation of continuity were insufficient to explain things and another sort of passage had been involved, one of which I was not cognizant. Sue returned and vanished into her bedroom. My train of thought disrupted, I sat and stewed in vague dissatisfactions. I wanted to talk to someone and it was too late to call Therese, so I stared at Sue's door and said a prayer. Five minutes later she rejoined me, her face freshly washed, wearing red sweatpants and a *Handbook of American Prayer* T-shirt, no bra. With a show of exhaustion, she flopped onto the opposite end of the sofa and stretched her legs, her arms. As she reached high behind her, arching her back, her nipples put in a brief but noteworthy appearance.

"God!" she said, relaxing, and shook out her hair.

"Want a drink?"

"I'm afraid if I started, I wouldn't stop."

She gossiped about the party for a few, laid out our schedule for the next day. Then she kicked back on the sofa, rested her head against the arm, tucked her chin onto her chest and gazed at me through her lashes. "That thing with the girl . . . Diana. Did you plan it?"

"Uh-uh."

"Well, it was brilliant. Your entire presentation tonight was—"

"Brilliant?" I suggested.

"I was going to say a little scary."

I had a sip of vodka and, my nose still buried in the glass, I said in a hick accent, "I's just funnin'."

"You made them see something that wasn't there . . . or if it was there, they really never saw it." She gave me a penetrating look, the same she'd worn in the photograph she had sent months before. "Don't get too slick, Wardlin. People like your rough edges. Your honesty."

"That's what they like? Not the bullshit I'm slinging?"

"Have you been to your Web site lately?" she asked after a pause. "I was online this morning. I read a post from a woman with a sick daughter—"

"Stop it."

"She bought *Handbook* a couple of months after her little girl was diagnosed," Sue went on. "She started writing prayers for better test results, a day without pain . . . like that. I'll skim over all the interim stages—"

"Yeah, please!"

"The short form is, step by step, she prayed her daughter into remission."

"You think I want to hear this shit? 'Cause I don't. Seriously. I'm not in the mood."

Sue held up her hands in surrender. "That's all!"

"Thank you."

"The point is—"

"Fuck! There's a point?"

She sat up, scooted toward me a bit, tucked one leg beneath her. "Yes. Listen. Prayerstyle may be nothing but snake oil. Or maybe it's real. Maybe your work embodies an effective principle. But screw it! You don't need to worry about that now. What you need to worry about is keeping your feet on the ground."

She had my attention. I was on Dr. Billick's couch, waiting for healing words.

"I've seen writers go through this before," she said. "None of them had fame hit overnight like with you. But it's more or less the same. Everything in their heads was blown out of proportion. They got all twisted up behind it. You, you're already twisted up, so for you it's a tremendous disruption."

She seemed earnest, ardent, caring, and again, as if it were an out-growth of those emotions, she scooted toward me. We were almost facing each other, both with an arm on the backrest of the sofa, our fingertips no more than eight inches apart.

"What you have to keep sight of," she said, "the tour's going to end soon. Then you'll be home. Things'll settle down and you can figure it all out. For now, just try and take what comes."

"Go with the flow's what you're saying?"

"Something like that," she said.

One more scoot and we'd be breaking a commandment. I knew it was coming. Sue had been scooting toward me since the outset. I saw that now. The phrase "take what comes," the soft emphasis she'd placed on the words, had twitched me out of the moment, thrown me to an angle from which I could see that her cheerful flirtiness, behavior I'd assumed to be her professional style, had a compulsive gloss and was actually part of a design leading to this counseling session on the sofa, this instant of vulnerability. I wondered if that was how she got off. Designs. I had the impression then that she was a kind of sexual serialist. Not that she tacked up hundreds of photographs of me or the other authors she had bagged on her bedroom wall. But there seemed something ritual and unemotional about how she'd manuvered us to this pass and that made me think she was getting back at someone, compensating for an irredeemable slight, a brutal rejection. It would explain the absence of a boyfriend, and maybe it explained a good deal else.

"That prayer I wrote for you," I said. "How'd that work out?"

She didn't flinch, but I could tell her soul had flinched, and I knew for a fact then what I had briefly supposed when she asked me for the prayer, that I was the object of that very prayer, and this was an oh-so-clever flourish of her design, particular to Project Wardlin, one she might have been planning to announce after bagging me. My asking about the prayer might have put a hitch in things, but— if so—she covered her true reactions and tried to turn what I'd said to her advantage.

"Well, no," she said with just a dab of coyness. "I've been so busy, I probably haven't been praying as hard as I should."

Her eyes lingered on my hand, inches away from hers, then cut sideways to meet mine, and I wanted to seize the opening, grab her and shuck off her sweats, thrust aside the crotch of her (doubtless) nicest lace panties, slip two fingers inside her and start nuzzling her neck, because though I was aware of her design, it was nonetheless sorely tempting. I was horny with success, with the faux coitus I'd had with the audience, my normal emotions—such as they were—disabled by the weirdness of fame, the spectacular weirdness of that particular day, and without her cosmetic mask, Sue looked like a sweet young strawberry, all nudge-soft and nipply, and I could tell how juicy she would be. But I didn't want her to win. Among all my thoughts—Therese, I shouldn't do this, would she find out? would it matter?—that was the only one that had any power, that stood against lust and its attendant perversities. *I* wanted to win.

"Thing about prayerstyle," I said, "it's not so different from generic prayer. Sometimes you can hardly tell when your prayer's been answered and sometimes the answer's not what you expect."

She plucked at the fabric of the sofa down by her knee, an evidence of frustration, but she wasn't giving up yet. She started to say something, probably something that would encourage me to get back on point, but I beat her to the line and said, "Hell, sometimes the answer's no. You're trying to influence a universe of influences, and there's bound to be times when too much is working against you to get even the smallest of prayer rewards."

Defiance came into her face. I was worried she might rip away the tissue-paper disguise from the real dialogue we were having and then things would get ugly, so I said, "When your answer's a no, don't give up on what you want. Just go at it different. Conditions change and you can always write a new prayer. There's space on every wall for a hundred ladders."

I was certain Sue realized that I was offering her a dignified out, but would pride allow her to accept it? Her half-smile went brittle. Frustration steamed off her. I expected her to yell at me. At last she swung around and crossed her legs and folded her arms beneath her breasts and looked straight ahead. "Gosh, Wardlin," she said in a breathy, affected voice. "If it wasn't for your wisdom, my life would be a shambles!" She smoothed down her hair with a quick gesture. "Next you'll be telling me there's more than one way to skin a cat."

"A dozen beginnings to every box of doughnuts," I said, trying to jolly her.

She gave a muted laugh. "A thousand roads with but a single destination."

"Hundred ways to slap sauce on your chicken."

"I wouldn't count on that one," she said coolly. She flounced up from the sofa, crossed to the bar, poured a couple of fingers of vodka. She had a sip, studying me over the rim of her glass, and said, "What're you praying for these days, Wardlin?"

"I'm like you, I've been too busy."

"If you weren't too busy . . . what?"

"I suppose I'd have to think on it. My life is full."

"That's funny," she said and came back to the couch, perched on the edge of a cushion. "Because I don't get that from you. I get there's a lot that you want."

Her manner was borderline aggressive and I knew she wanted to slug it out. Cards on the table. She'd work the conversation around to where we were almost speaking plainly and then maybe run some sort of editorial power game or do something seriously aggressive, like whip off her T-shirt. A tactic which, given the sorry state of my moral apparatus, would likely do the trick. I had to admire her relentlessness. The only way I was going to win was by wimping out.

"Maybe there are some things I want, but I guess I don't want 'em enough to pray for." I put on a bewildered face and, as if I were clueless, said in an aggravated tone, "Christ, Sue. What the fuck are we talking about here, anyway?"

Her expression flowed between shades of dismay, eventually hardening into one of amused contempt. "Among other things," she said, "the efficacy of prayerstyle." She tossed back her vodka and made tracks for her bedroom, moving with the exaggerated sway of a woman who believed she was being marked by a regretful eye. She paused, a hand on the doorknob, her professional veneer restored. "Big day tomorrow. I'll ring you up early."

Once her lock turned, I grabbed the vodka bottle and went into my bedroom and sat down to write Therese a letter. Having remained faithful for none of the right reasons, I wanted to prove the metal of my fidelity. I told Therese the distance between us was making me crazy, I felt lost without her, I needed her to help steer a course along this river of crap called a tour, all things that were on the face of them true, but had nothing to do with my urge to write. I crumpled up the letter, returned to the sofa and stretched out. It was so quiet I could hear the electric crickets in my head. I pictured the strip of bare tummy between the waist of Sue's sweats and the hem of her T-shirt, and considered knocking on her door. I stared not at the skylight, but at the stippled off-white ceiling in which it was set, until the surface came to resemble a lace tapestry from which hollow-eyed medieval figures emerged, some carrying skulls, some riding skeletal horses, others with signs hung about their necks and wearing doggie masks. Loneliness increased my natural paranoia. I imagined that the suite was full of invisible clockwork, a fragile Victorian mechanism that induced numbing silence and chilly light, and I could have sworn I detected the ticking sounds of glass bending inward under a terrible pressure, preparing to collapse into shards that would plunge down and neatly section me, and I recalled a day in prison, sitting in a room filled with men mesmerized by a televangelist, listening as he called everyone within hearing to lay their hands on the TV, watching a number of the men, grim and unabashed as zombies, step forward to obey, and afterward how they smiled and embraced like brothers, and I wondered if maybe I didn't need Jesus after all.

Chapter 11

Larry King was doing his show from Chicago that week and it was supposed to be the Reverend Jerry Falwell's turn to call me an ungodly blasphemer; but while Sue and I waited in the greenroom, a production assistant informed us that Falwell had dropped out of the gig. Digestive problems. His place was to be taken by the equally Reverend Monroe Treat, an up-and-comer among Christian pundits who hailed from my part of the country.

"Arizona somewhere," the PA said, twirling his pencil as if the words *Arizona somewhere* were elements of a spell he was casting. "He's got this immense church made of, y'know, those glass bricks. Are you familiar with him?"

"Yeah, I heard of him, but it doesn't matter," I said. "Treat, Falwell . . . These dorks are fucking all the same person."

The PA, a thirtyish man in college-boy clothes, wearing a microphone headset, took offense at my language. "Well, I wouldn't know, of course," he said huffily. "But this one seems a tad more intense than our usual Christian guest." After that he stopped being chatty.

"Don't," I said to Sue, who was looking reprovingly at me. "Don't fucking tell me not to fucking curse when Larry and me go fucking live. Okay?"

"Settle down, Wardlin." She said this without energy, the gassed delivery that tired moms are wont to use with unruly children.

I got up and refilled my coffee. I might have grabbed a bagel but the actress to whom the first half hour of the show was devoted had picked over them, complaining shrilly about the decline in greenroom cuisine. I smelled her perfume wafting up from the tray. For no reason I could nail down, I felt jumpy, cranked up, on the lookout for something, as if instead of waiting to appear on national television, I was casing the entrance of a convenience store I intended to rob in order to support my crystal habit. My thoughts raced. I envisioned myself jamming a gun under Larry's throat and driving cross-country, having him do his show from the back seat, wrapped in duct tape. Other criminal fantasies, absurdist noir, played out in my brain. By the time the PA led me into the studio, I had nearly persuaded myself that at heart I was a reckless boy born to kill and wander, the patron saint of petty crime, a legend to be sung by redneck poets, appearing in visions to Appalachian mystics. Sitting across from Larry chilled me out some, but also enhanced my absurdist view of things. With his suspenders and candy-striped shirt and talcum powder scent, he seemed like the Easter Bunny emeritus. I half expected the Mad Hatter to pop in with his teacup and giant hat. My adversary, Monroe Treat, was visible on a big-screen TV, sitting in a thronelike chair of ornately carved wood, being fussed over by a makeup person, and when Larry introduced us, he gave me one of those James Dean hand-glide waves, a cool 1950s salute, and said nothing. Deeply tanned; in his forties; black pompadour and sideburns. Handsome in a disreputable way, like a studly used-car dealer. He wore a dark suit and a string tie with a silver concha in the shape of a cross. I hated him instantly. It was like a panther and a wolf come face-to-face on opposite sides of a stream, recognizing that they both ate rabbits, yet had little else in common.

The interview began well enough. I talked about prayerstyle, using oft-repeated phrases to describe the method and how I had arrived at it. Then Larry asked, "Are you religious? Do you consider yourself a religious person?"

"I'm not a churchgoer," I said. "When I was a kid we traveled around a lot. I never picked up the habit. Last church I attended regularly was this old drive-in theater outside of Beaumont, Texas, where they had Sunday morning services. I liked that. Families sitting around out in the sun, eating sandwiches and listening to the preacher over the speakers. It seemed like a good, reasonable way to approach God. Regulation churches . . . I don't feel right in 'em. Sitting in ranks like you're at an insurance seminar. All that piety. Piety's always struck me as being too close to pride to be a virtue." Sue, standing back of the cameras, shook her head vigorously, signaling that I was pushing the envelope.

"Do you believe in God?" Larry asked.

"I think it was Dylan Thomas said he'd be a damned fool if he didn't. That goes for me, as well. But what I believe, that's not at issue. Not as regards prayerstyle. God and religion, the dispensing of the Word . . . I leave all that to Reverend Treat and his colleagues. If we were in the automobile industry, the reverend and I, he'd be the manufacturer and I'd be a mechanic. My job would be to make the car run efficiently. Prayerstyle, basically, is a secular appliance designed to make faith more efficient."

"It just enhances whatcha got?"

"That's right."

Larry shifted some papers lying in front of him. "You served ten years in prison for manslaughter."

"Yes. I killed a man in a bar fight."

Under Larry's prodding, I described my redemptive process, and when I had finished he said, "So you might say prison turned your life around."

"I don't want to give anyone the idea that prison's about rehabilitation," I said. "That's just not the case. Essentially what prison does is create criminals who're more violent and more committed to crime. If I'd been tough enough to deal with prison straight-on, that's what it would've done for me. But I wasn't tough. I needed an angle to help me slide through. In the beginning, prayerstyle was simply an article of faith. That's all it's ever been, really. But writing prayers for cons . . . I provided a service. It helped me survive."

We went to break, Larry schmoozed me up and Treat's digital

image stared at me like a killer who had sighted his mark. When we went live again, Larry asked Treat for his views on prayerstyle.

"Satan has a nimble tongue," Treat said, coming out of the blocks fulltilt righteous and wroth. "And Wardlin Stuart is proof positive of that. He claims to assist people of faith, but what he does is turn them from God. He claims to be a sinner redeemed by prayer, and yet he nourishes a cult of personality. He claims to stand apart from the question of religion, yet I am told that last night he exhorted his audience to reject Jesus Christ Our Lord."

"Is that true?" Larry asked me.

"Not at all," I said. "I told them they shouldn't rely on Jesus to solve their small problems. Those they can solve by themselves."

Larry nodded and said, "The Lord helps he who helps himself, right?"

"Exactly."

"Who gave you the authority to advise people whether or not they need Jesus Christ in their lives?" Treat shook a finger at me. "A felon! A murderer! You have no authority! You come before—"

"I thought this was going to be a debate," I said to Larry. "Not a name-calling session."

Treat thundered on: "You come as a lamb before us. Meek and humble. But your words are knives! You persuade people to believe faith is a trick, salvation a contest that can be won with the right slogan! You're an apostate! Nothing more." He produced a copy of *Handbook* and held it up for the camera. "This is Satan's Bible. See how it burns."

He flicked a cigarette lighter and the book caught fire. He must have hit the cover with an accelerant, because flames went whooshing up. Treat tossed the burning book off camera where, no doubt, some toadying parishioner was waiting with an appropriate receptacle, and sat back, wearing a self-satisfied smirk.

"Man, that's perfect," I said.

Larry asked the reverend if he wouldn't mind calming down, and Treat said, "Larry, I can't be calm in the face of apostasy. It's my Christian duty to shout down evil wherever it rears its head."

"That may be," Larry said. "But this is my show and I'm asking both of you to behave in gentlemanly fashion."

Appearing mollified, Treat agreed to tone it down and I said, "No problem." Larry then asked Treat what he found objectionable about people writing their own prayers.

"Not a thing. People pray in their own words every day," Treat said. "What I object to is this man telling them that the words are all-important."

"That's not what I'm telling them," I said.

"And," Treat went on, "that he's causing them to neglect the beautiful tried-and-true prayers of Christian tradition. The Psalms of David, for example."

"As far as I know," I said, "David didn't have to deal with mortgage payments, with freeway traffic, with turning up a bag of dope in his kid's dresser drawer. In my opinion, Christian tradition is strong enough, it can handle a little updating every couple of thousand years."

"Let's say this so-called prayerstyle works. Whose ear do you think such prayers will reach? Not God's! The man is teaching witchcraft. He's teaching people to approach prayer the way you'd approach casting a spell."

Though my basic impression of Treat was that stigmata could appear on his palms and he would still seem insincere, he glared at me with such perfect loathing, it gave me cause to think he might not be faking it.

"Aw, come on!" I said. "From Cotton Mather on down, anytime you people perceive a threat to your hegemony, this is how you react. You try and scare people away from it. You label it Satanism or witchcraft. If my prayers are spells, then all prayers are spells. All acts of devotion, every invocation. They're all seeking influence with God, with Creation."

Sue ducked her head and put a hand to her brow—I was straying from her guidelines. Treat didn't much care for what I had said, either. Thereafter, each time I made to speak he would interrupt, slinging wads of homily and Bible verse, going off on diatribes. Despite his bombast, he grew increasingly uncomfortable. His hands fidgeted on the arms of his throne and his eyes kept darting toward something off camera. When Larry tried to muzzle him once again, a whiny note slipped into Treat's voice and he importuned our host, saying that Larry, as a man of faith, needed to abandon his customary neutrality and get on the right side of this debate. The God-fearing side. Souls were at stake. Larry didn't like being told his business and it had become clear he didn't like Treat. "That may be," he said. "But saving souls is your job. Mine is to run this show in an appropriate manner."

Following yet another outburst from Treat, I said, "Larry, I'm getting slammed here. He's taking all of my time and he's attacked me personally. How about letting me have a minute for rebuttal . . . without interruption?"

Larry considered the request, then gave a signal to cut Treat's mike and said, "You've got your minute."

"Monroe Treat," I said to the camera. "Take a good look at the man. He turned up on your step holding a vacuum cleaner and smiling, you'd slam the door in his face, because you'd know that vacuum wasn't going to work for more than a couple of weeks. But he's not selling vacuum cleaners, he's selling God. An irresistible item. So you give him a listen. Big mistake. I mean, look at him! Look at that two-thousand-dollar suit, that rock-and-roll hair. Why's he all gussied up like that? Because he's a show! He's the Preacher Man! Got his backup singers, his hot band, a big ol' glass brick arena he calls a church. If you wanta see the show, he'll charge you all the traffic will bear. You'll pay top dollar just to watch him booty-walk across the stage doing That-Ol'-Time-Religion-With-a-Brand-New-Twist! Rose petals will drop from the ceiling. Doves will be released. But God . . . He's nowhere to be found. Because it's all just a show. Just this lame-o who couldn't make it in the music business, so he took his stale act somewhere it couldn't fail. Into the swampy bottom of organized religion."

Despairing, Sue threw her hands in the air and stalked off out of sight.

"God doesn't need a show," I said, damping down my volume. "Fact is, God abhors a show. He wants to be celebrated in your hearts, not in a glass circus tent. He wants you to use your money for your families, not hand it over to some clown needs it to put a Jacuzzi in his private jet and a year from now'll be doing a public atonement for knocking up a chorus girl in Reno. Reason this guy's mad at me, it's got nothing to do with God or evil. He's mad 'cause he thinks I'm taking *your* money out of *his* pocket. And I hope it's true. My book's a better deal than what he's selling. You give me twenty bucks, you'll get back change and a book that might help you some. Give him twenty—and it'll be a lot more'n twenty by the time he's done squeezing—and all you're gonna get is a G-rated lounge act featuring an Elvis impersonator."

"On that note"—Larry arched an eyebrow as if to suggest he'd heard it all now—"we'll take a break and then go to your calls."

Once we were in commercial, Treat started hammering on Larry, saying he'd been sandbagged and threatening to walk.

"Nobody's holding you prisoner," Larry told him.

Treat was choleric and I thought he would walk, but a blond woman leaned in from off camera and whispered into his ear. Treat nodded and the woman pulled back out of view.

"Before you take calls, I'd like to respond briefly," Treat said.

Larry looked to me for a reaction.

"What's he gonna do?" I said. "Call me more names?"

The break ended and Larry opened the floor to Treat.

"My brothers and sisters in Jesus," he said in a commanding tone. "This man, Wardlin Stuart, is the embodiment of our Great Enemy. Heed his voice and you will lose your soul. I beg you to recognize the shadow who speaks with his voice and join with me in a war against him. Arm yourself with the truth of the Lord Jesus Christ, shield yourself with the power of legitimate prayer, and contend against him until he is as dust in the wind and his—"

"Now he's referencing old Kansas songs," I said.

"—and his words are not even a rumor. Do not rest until his voice has fallen silent!!"

"You know, I bet Kansas serves as scripture in the Church of the Zircon Elvis."

"It's the duty of every Christian to become a soldier for Christ! To speak out against Wardlin Stuart!"

"Yeah, I'm a threat," I said. "Wardlin Stuart's a-comin' and he's packing a book! Hide all the women!"

Treat fumbled with his earpiece and trumpeted, "War to the finish! Let no quarter be given the messenger of Lucifer!"

"Wow!" said Larry, unruffled, after Treat had stormed off. "So now it's you and Salman Rushdie, huh?"

"I doubt it," I said. "I hope not, anyway. I hope people will consider the source and judge my book on the basis of whether or not it works for them. And I hope reading the book will encourage them to take charge of their own spiritual lives. I have great respect for the vast majority of the men and women who devote themselves to Christian service, but you put your faith in the hands of a hustler like Monroe Treat, you might as well be asking Santa Claus for world peace."

"The book is"—Larry displayed a copy for the camera—"*A Handbook of American Prayer*. Wardlin Stuart." He laid the book down and said, "Let's go to some calls." He punched open a line. "Trumansburg, New York. You're on the air."

"Larry?" A querulous female voice.

"Go ahead, Trumansburg."

"Larry, I just want to say how much I love the show, especially the ones where you have Nancy Grace on. She's so wonderful with the victims' rights and all."

"Do you have a question?"

"I have a comment, Larry. That man who was so rude to Wardlin, he needs to read his book. Because there's not one word of it's evil. Larry, I've been having health problems and nothing was doing me the least good until I bought *A Handbook of American Prayer*. Wardlin, I just want to say, bless you! I can't thank you enough for all your wonderful book's done for me."

"Thank you," I said.

Larry punched up another line. "Gallatin, Tennessee. You're live with Wardlin Stuart."

"Mr. Stuart?" The voice of a middle-aged man, brisk and businesslike.

"Yes."

"My name is Staunton Nichols. I'm pastor here at the First Congregationalist Church in Gallatin."

"Pleased to meetcha," I said, expecting to be excoriated.

"I think your book is exactly as advertised—an effective secular aid. I've asked my entire congregation to buy it and those who have already done so are delighted with the results."

"That's good to hear."

Pastor Nichols invited me to lecture at his church and Larry asked him to leave his number, then fielded a call from Florida, a teenage girl asking for advice on writing prayers The next call originated from Beverly Hills. A woman who put a sultry spin on her "Hi, Larry."

Larry beamed and tapped his temple. "I know that voice! Sharon Stone! How're things in California?"

"We're doing fine," said Sharon Stone. "And I can't tell you how much we're all looking forward to seeing Wardlin in Los Angeles next . . . Is it next week?"

"End of the week, yeah," I said.

"How're you doing, Wardlin?" Sharon Stone asked. "You look tired. Is the tour wearing you down?"

"Some, I suppose."

"Well, when you get to California, I hope I can convince you to take an evening off. I'd love to host a little party for you. People are dying to meet you."

Larry said, "Wardlin has fans in Hollywood, does he?"

"Everybody's talking about *Handbook*! Arnold ordered a copy for everyone in his administration. Tom is evangelical about it!"

"Tom Cruise?" Larry asked.

"Uh-huh. And the book's absolutely taken over Dreamworks. Johnny Depp was reading it while he was doing a project there. He gave a copy to Steven . . . and you know Steven. Now it's everywhere."

"The question naturally arises," Larry said, "what does Sharon Stone pray for? I mean, you have looks, money, fame. What's left?"

Sharon Stone laughed. "Well, of course, we're all praying for better scripts!"

It had nothing to do with Sharon Stone, or maybe it did, maybe her phone call amped up my realization that I was circling higher and higher through the tiers of the culture, borne on the wings of a jailhouse con, and that made me aware of some sour, bug-crawling corner of my head, the seat of an essential perfidy, or maybe it was simply that I recognized the heights to be no less horrifying than the depths, but whatever the reason, everything that had happened during the past twenty-four hours, the lecture, my father, Sue's attempted seduction, Monroe Treat's declaration of war, each of these events seemed to be transmitting a lurid alarm, like strip club neon winking on and off, and I understood how this flash flood of fame had washed me to a place wherein all I could see of other people were their flaws, the flaws that drove them to want to be with me, to partake of me, to be me, and that bred a cynicism far more sickly and disastrous than the petulant, juvenile cynicism that had landed me in prison, and suddenly, decisively, I did not want to go hang out in Celebrityville with Sharon and Tom and Arnold and Brad, not even for the kick, for the fizz and giggle, the deviant animal splendor of that glamorama dreamworld that only existed because we celebrated its existence, that spiritless fucking heaven of high-profile cunts and cocks and balls . . . I did not want to discover how gruesome the world looked from that vantage. I wanted to go home, I wanted to be back in Arizona somewhere.

This little brain trip ended when Larry asked me, possibly—if his concerned expression were a true measure—for the second time, whether or not I'd be able to make room in my schedule for Sharon Stone's party.

"Sounds like fun. But I'm going to break off the tour here in Chicago." I felt an odd disconnect while saying this—it seemed the words were both something I was speaking from the heart and something done for effect.

"This is a decision you just made?" Larry asked. "A minute ago you were talking about next week, being in L.A."

"Y'know, man," I said. "I'm sitting here with you and Sharon Stone calls in, and last night Roger Ebert was drinking scotch on my sofa, and . . ."

"Yes?" said Larry when I failed to finish my sentence.

Sue, I noticed, had come back into the studio and was standing behind a cameraman, doing a fine Monroe Treat killer-stare impression. The force of her anger made me feel reckless. "I don't want to be famous," I said.

Larry gave what sounded like an anxious laugh. "You haven't been doing such a terrific job of remaining anonymous."

"I bet not many people get to say that," I said. "To say they don't wanta be famous. Usually they're pulled past the point where they're still able to say it before they can get it outa their mouths . . . or before they fully realize it's not what they wanted after all."

"That's so true!" said Sharon Stone.

Looking grateful for the opportunity to shift focus away from me, Larry said, "Something like that happened with you, Sharon?"

"Absolutely. It may not have been so . . . such a moment as it appears to be for Wardlin. But there was confusion. There was a time when everything started happening at once, when I wasn't sure what I wanted. I promise it gets better, Wardlin."

"You two are talking about a problem most people would give an arm and a leg for the privilege of having," Larry said.

"That doesn't mean it's trivial, Larry. Or that it's easy to deal with."

"It's stupefying," I said.

A touch more unease crept into Larry's face. "Does this—your decision—have anything to do with the Reverend Treat's attack on you?""You kidding?" I said. "That guy's a sitcom character! The Reverend Jerry Lee Gasbag. Naw, what I mean is everything you say . . . I mean, everything *I* say, it's—"

Wardlin!" said Sharon Stone with heartfelt sympathy. "I know, I know!"

"Just now I was going to say all I wanted to do was to go home and be with my wife, but I knew the minute I said it, it wouldn't be as true as when I had the thought."

"Wardlin?" said Sharon, but I kept going.

"It probably sounds like I'm spacing out or something . . . and I am kinda. But that's just this stuff, this celebrity thing. Once you get a degree of fame, everything you say develops an ugly echo. People obsess on it. They discuss it, they distort it. They make judgments about you based on the distortions. Soon even you become unclear about what you mean. When you say something, you immediately begin to doubt it. You begin to doubt the very thing that made you a celebrity in the first place."

"Wardlin," said Sharon Stone. "I know someone here in L.A.—"

"I like writing prayers, I like going out in the desert with my wife. That's enough for me."

"I know someone who can help you through this," Sharon Stone said.

"Therapy? You talking about therapy?" I laughed. "Yeah, I guess therapy's an option."

"It seems, Sharon, you have a lot of compassion for Wardlin," Larry said. "For what he's feeling."

"I do. I really do."

"What brings that out in you?"

"To some extent, it's my own experience, but mostly it's his book . . . his beautiful, important book," Sharon Stone said. "And his honesty. It's that wonderful honesty that makes him so vulnerable."

Chapter 12

My first night back in Pershing, after spending several hours out in the desert with Therese, I wrote the following:

Prayer for the Sufficiency of Things

The Painted Desert needs no prayer
its silence is holiness enough
its ventings of wind, its tiny cries,
are sufficient in their complaint.

The Painted Desert needs no prayer,
no orison for the lizard-basting sun,
for that great pink and orange burnt umber
stretch of agate spur and shadow stripe
with scorpions for archangels—
and for the night no prayer enlightens,
only a chrome motorcycle skeleton
burnished under red evening glare will do,
long abandoned to this useless sentry post,
signaling sacred fire from a faceted eye,
while rats study the scriptures of sand grains
until their blood breaks a fever
forever in some serpent's bowel.

Therese. I have bedded down in her now,
made a home in her bones, strung a hammock
between the juts of her pelvis, settled in, and,
like the blue smoke ghosts rising from the mesa,
two oblivions twisting together, become familiar.
I know her needs, her greeds, her secret lesions,
and where she keeps her fear, an enameled box
she opens once a year, its contents supernatural
and ordinary both, a lion's tooth, a phantom heart,
an old man's face carved on an avocado seed by God
that sometimes speaks an unknown language.
I've traveled to her source, drawn maps of nations there
shaped like Egypt if Egypt were a kingdom of the air,
and drunk from the principle that purifies her face
to a moon-colored cameo of the kind a dying soldier holds
like heaven in his hand, all focused as he dutifully fades
beyond the last erratic strains of his heartbeat march.

The wind tells everywhere a lie, its old soft story.
The stars are mute, the virus raves, the sand awaits.
Tracked by a slit-pupiled eye, jackrabbits skitter,
and in our hateful American splendor we pray
with a derision of coins, a mangle of car horns,
with a mammoth music of drunkenness,
to be safe from everything we cannot see,
to end as lovers though every journey ends
in the company of strangers . . . Let this be enough.
Let this night with only thirteen stars,
pasted like spangles onto a black wallboard sky,
attended by a rumor of Tejano accordions and guitars,
be both desolation's flag and the banner of all life.
Let each breath be a promise kept not made,
each sinful minute but a part of an hourly absolution,

each word a resonance and rhyme with constancy.
Let this be enough.

The Painted Desert needs no prayer, its womanly darkness
is complete, its masculine silence contemplates
a conquerable landscape wide and beautiful as a grave
furnished with the illusion of two chairs, a table,
tequila sours, a vase displaying flowers of another world,
the effect achieved with mesas, cacti, human souls,
produced out of nowhere from nothing and a kiss
by the Lord of Loneliness, He who almost never dies
in this place where spirits vanish when we look away
they return to this place where spirits vanish
when we look away, they return, they always return,
to this place, where spirits vanish, when we look away . . .

The prayer embodied a negativity, an anxiety, I had not felt while making love to Therese, but after I withdrew from her, gazing at the sky, uncommonly dark due to a mist, I was possessed by a cynical self-consciousness that forced me to view the experience in context of my merely technical fidelity; and when Therese flung an arm across my chest and kissed my shoulder, I said, "I really fucked up."

"The tour? You said you were okay with that."

"I don't know."

She turned onto her stomach, lying half atop me, her chin resting on her folded arms. "What's wrong?"

"Nothing."

A thinning of the mist and the light brightened. Wind lifted her hair and drifted strands of it across her face. I brushed them away. Her eyes were hidden in pockets of shadow. "Did you and Sue have a thing?"

"No. She was up for it, but . . . No."

"She hit on you?"

"Yeah. I kinda knew she was gonna . . . in the back of my head. But I guess I discounted the idea."

Therese rolled onto her back and we lay touching shoulder and hip. Her lack of immediate response seemed to breed a faint vibration from the silence. Finally she said, "Then what's wrong?"

I was hesitant to tell her what I thought was wrong, worried that saying it would give it more life, more reality—this flaw, this black space inside me, an absence where I assumed normal people had a presence. It was strange to be frightened of something that was both tangible and mysterious. That's how it always struck me, this thing that enabled me to commit evil acts—like coming upon a hole in the middle of a vegetable garden from which guttural voices were emerging—and I thought perhaps it wasn't evil, perhaps "evil" was the best translation my senses could make of what it truly was, the way an ant might perceive a garbage disposal to be the Abyss, and what I had construed as evil was a less romantic phenomenon that afflicted everyone in some fashion.

"It's just I'm having trouble reconnecting with people," I said.

"You mean with me?"

"I keep getting thrown out of the moment. This river of crap flowing through my brain, it's . . . Fuck! I don't know what I'm talking about."

"Crap about Sue?"

"I told you nothing happened there."

"You must have had thoughts about it."

"It's not her, it's not any one thing."

She turned onto her side, looking pensive, and fiddled with the fringe of our blanket—it had worked down off my chest to my hips. "Yeah?" I said. "What?"

"I have a theory."

"Say."

"My feelings, my thoughts," she said, "they're all scattered, especially when I'm alone. Like dust stirred up from the floor. I think everybody's more or less the same. Like we're none of us quite real, but we become real for other people. We acquire a shape that conforms to whoever we're with . . . their shape."

She let that hang, continuing to fiddle with the blanket fringe, and I said, "It's a theory."

"You don't believe it?"

"It doesn't seem like something that demands belief."

"When you're sitting alone somewhere," she said, "and you're not focused on something, don't all these half-thoughts and wishes and memory fragments, all this mind junk . . . doesn't it start floating around in your head?"

"Yeah, sure."

"It does with me," she said. "I think it does with everybody. But sometimes we meet people who make us feel solid. Like you and me." She slid a hand beneath the blanket and let her fingers rest on my hip. "You lived in your head for ten years and then I came along. Then a minute goes by and suddenly you're out in the world with thousands of people trying to grab a piece of your soul. It shredded you. Just relax. That's all the medicine you need. It won't be long before you settle back in."

I nudged her breast with the side of her hand. "Take two and call you in the morning, huh?"

"Two, three . . . Whatever flies your flag. I can always write a new prescription."

"So you're gonna be my Dr. Feelgood?"

"Who else?" she said.

The way she looked in the half-dark consoled me: the faint lines on her face no longer visible, pale and perfected like a sexy ghost, a solemn visitation that seemed the proof of all she said. I pulled her down beside me and we lay quietly, touching, talking about nothing much. An oblate moon slipped up from behind the nearest mesa, sharpening the shapes of boulders and shedding sufficient light so I could see the ranks of blue stars on our Navajo blanket.

"You should keep out of the shop for a while," Therese said. "Too many people are coming in wanting to talk to you. You've got enough to do just answering phone messages. Must be a hundred of 'em."

"Christ," I said.

"About half a dozen are from Sue."

"She say what she wanted? She probably wants to tell me I'll never work in this town again or some shit."

"How'd you leave things with her?"

"She was pissed. She started going off on my self-destructive tendencies, but I didn't stick around for the whole lecture."

"Well, she sounded excited. Maybe it's good news. You should call her."

A coyote yipped from somewhere. The mist was thickening again and the moon had a halo. Therese shivered.

"You cold?" I asked.

"A little."

"We can go back home."

"I want to sleep out tonight. Okay? I need to be away from the shop a while."

I drew her close, told her I was sorry for having been so self-absorbed and that I knew things had been weird for her, too.

"I'm fine," she said. "We're fine."

"You think?"

"Mmm-hmm."

My cock had fattened against her thigh. She pressed herself against it. "God, I love that . . . how you grow," she said. She wedged her hand between us and gripped my erection, saying she wanted me to fuck her again. The ardency of her expression fisted me as eagerly and tightly as her hand, enclosing me in a warm pressure, and my thoughts degraded into urges. As we made love it seemed that the moon was paving my back with a cool slide of light, pushing me down into her with cool moon strength. Afterward, she fell asleep quickly and I lay with a hand resting on her most inner thigh, fingertips grazing her pubic hair. For so long as I maintained that contact, I felt grounded in her, calm and secure; yet when she shifted away, I felt isolated, insubstantial. Perhaps what she had said about people becoming real for one another influenced me, because I had the idea that were I to lift the blanket and look down, instead of hips, legs, penis, I would see stars and darkness, as if at night, separated from her, I disappeared beneath the covers, gradually vanishing from the feet upward, until all that remained sleeping in my bed, wherever I chose to make it, was a loose agglomeration of fire and stone and ice and pride and violence and love such as might occur soon after the creation of a universe.

I spent the next two mornings going through my messages and mail, ignoring the bulk of them, and put off responding to Sue Billick until early afternoon of the second day. When she picked up she said, "There you are! The man with the Midas touch."

Startled by her cheerful tone, I said, "What?"

"I should never have tried to coach you. Your instincts have been dead-on every time."

"You're not coming through here."

"*Larry King*. The 'I don't want to be famous' speech. The media's all over it. Quitting the tour struck exactly the right note. Apparently what people have been yearning for is a celebrity who declines celebrity. A real man of the people. *Handbook*'s flying off the shelves. I mean it was flying off the shelves already. Now it's out of control. We've tripled our order on the reprinting. I think you're going to have a million copies out there, Wardlin. Just this edition. I swear to God, I've never seen anything close to it! Like I said, you struck the right note. Everything you've done has been inspired. The secular religious angle, the way you look, the rough edges, the anticelebrity thing. Everything."

"I'm not going back on tour," I said.

"No, no! That would be absolutely wrong. Later, it'll be okay. But we need to retool our strategy. Maybe bring you out for a week. Spread your appearances over the year. Make them like a rock star coming out of seclusion. That fits with what the book needs. And it'll work better for you, too, since you're not good with long tours."

"Thanks for considering my well-being."

Sue didn't appear to have registered this. "We'll time the appearances to coincide with edition launches, the movie, events . . . There are going to be Wardlin Stuart events. You know that, don't you? Conventions and God knows what else." I heard the click of a cigarette lighter. "We are *so* lucky we wound up with that asshole Treat. He came off like some kind of Jesus gangster. It was perfect for you. Much better than Falwell."

"What's up with that?"

"Treat? You haven't been watching TV?"

"You think I came home so I could spend my first night back watching TV?"

That gave her pause. When she resumed speaking, her tone was subdued. "Every talk show on cable has been doing features on what happened between you and Treat. Your disappearing act. . . . Fox, CNN, MSNBC. They're having trouble finding enough people who'll say something bad about you. Even the Christian right's running from Treat and rushing to give you a hug. That thing you did about God not needing a show . . . I guess that moved some numbers in their demographics. Falwell's going to come on King Friday and talk about prayerstyle. He probably won't be a hundred percent on your side. But I doubt he's going to hammer you the way he would have if he'd showed up on Sunday."

The thought that Treat had suffered damage as a result of our debate pleased me and I asked what Sue knew about it.

"Just that the e-mails to King, to everyone, are going some absurd percentage in your favor. I don't have the figures right here. But the rats are fleeing Treat's ship. Who's that guy . . . the skinny young guy who ran some Christian right-wing political group? Ralph Something. He was on *Hannity & Colmes* saying that Treat was the kind of man Christians have to live down. He came close to calling him a fraud. They're all playing the same tune. Maybe Treat had enemies. Maybe that's how he got maneuvered into doing *Larry King*. They may have known he wasn't ready for prime time." She exhaled, then coughed. "This is about you, Wardlin. Not Treat. I used to think you were going to be a Flavor of the Month, but you can take this anywhere you want now. Except for some crazies out on the fringe, everybody's loving you."

"They'll forget me sooner or later."

"Later," said Sue. "Much later. Even if you sit there in Pershing the rest of your days, if you never do another update on *Handbook,* this edition alone is going to sell for years and years."

"You can tell all this from the last couple of days?"

"All the last two days did was demonstrate that you've crossed into the mainstream. I've been thinking you were headed that way for a while. But you did it in record time, and . . . Hang on a second." I heard her talking to someone, then she was back.

"What do you want to do, Wardlin?" she asked. "Are you going to keep writing? You're a wonderful writer. If you decide to write other kinds of books—novels, whatever—people will buy them. Or you could be Tony Roberts. It's your choice. Endless possibilities are opening up. You should think twice before passing on them."

Therese came along the corridor from the shop and gave me an inquiring look. I signaled that I'd be off the phone soon.

"Damn!" said Sue. "I've got a call. Let me get rid of it."

Therese eased past me into the kitchen. Through the doorway I watched her pour a glass of orange juice. Her hair was tied back with a blue and gold scrunchie and she had on faded jeans and a loose-fitting dark blue shirt. The sun sluiced through a window onto her face, reminding me of the photograph she'd sent me in prison, her features blurred with golden-white radiance. Looking at her made me aware of the apprehension that Sue's news had roused in me, but also acted to soothe it.

"You still there?" Sue asked.

"Yeah."

I heard the cigarette lighter again, then she said, "Saturday night . . .

what happened, what didn't happen. Did that play into you leaving? Because if it did, don't worry about it happening again. That was a wrong move on my part."

"It wasn't wrong, it just wasn't right."

She laughed. "Now I'm going to be analyzing that all day."

"I'm just saying wrong or right isn't a judgment I'm qualified to make."

"Okay." A ticking sound, as if she were tapping a pencil against her desk or the phone. "But please don't let Saturday night influence your decision. We can talk about it if you like."

"That would be fine, but I'm in the middle of stuff."

"You're not alone?"

"You got it."

"Well, sometime it might be good to clear the air. I want to be certain last Saturday's not going to affect your decision."

"I'm concentrating on the present. I don't plan to do much thinking about the future for a while."

"No rush. Nothing's going to go away." Sue dropped into her cheerful corporate I'm-signing-off mode. "We're all confident your future's here to stay."

After I hung up Therese said, "That was Sue?"

"Uh-huh."

"Was it good news?"

I gave her a digest version of the call and she made a pleased noise and said, "She's right. You shouldn't close any doors if you don't have to." She drained the last of her juice. "Would you help me out front a minute? We got a shipment in. I need you to unpack it, if you could."

I came to my feet. "What is it?"

"Baby iguana key rings. Dried baby iguanas with key rings attached." She wrinkled her nose in distaste. "They're gross, but I bet they're going to sell."

Chapter 13

Baby iguana key chains; Arizona-shaped oatmeal cookies with raisins marking the principal towns; New Age vortex pendants made in Sedona; teddy bears dressed as cheerleaders, wearing Arizona State University turtlenecks; stuffed Gila monsters; plastic coyotes; dried rattlesnake rattles; chunks of petrified wood; Painted Desert scenes painted on handsaws, printed on T-shirts, embossed on coffee cups; scorpions mounted in glass paperweights: myself an eccentric product, I felt at home amid this trivial mutant spawn of American commerce and as time passed I grew relaxed. When people asked me to pose for photographs with them, I did so with good grace, because there I was merely a shopkeeper with a book, comfortable on my own turf, and not a cultural phenomenon. The pressures I had endured on tour seemed deflected by the tiny armies of the dead and plastic animals that stared soullessly from bins and display cases. And by the people of Pershing. Now that they had been put on the map, their businesses thriving, they stepped forward to embrace Therese and me, and often shielded us from the journalists who came daily to the town, forewarning us of their presence and giving incorrect directions to the shop. We took to spending more time among them than we had, stopping in for drinks at Scotty's and, because Therese didn't like to cook, eating dinner at the Mesa Bar and Grille.

Nancy Belliveau, who—as I've mentioned—owned the Mesa, was the subject of my most controversial prayer. A former Vegas dealer and showgirl (and, it was rumored, hooker), she remained, at forty-one, a very attractive woman, going a bit leathery, but having sun-streaked dark blond hair and a statuesque body that she displayed in tight jeans and tank tops. The neon sign above the bar was modeled from her figure and was duplicated in miniature above each of the leatherette booths. She would often strike a pose identical to that of the faceless green neon women when waiting on customers, hands on hips, standing with left leg forward, right leg back and behind, as if in self-advertisement. Outgoing, brassy, and, according to her many victims, a serial heartbreaker, she appeared the polar opposite of Therese, yet prior to my arrival she had been Therese's only friend.

My prayer began with the lines:

> *Not many men in Pershing*
> *haven't had a thought or two*
> *about Nancy Belliveau's breasts*

It went on to contrast the frosty dark space of the bar, the quiet talk, old desertcore guitar bands riffing softly on the jukebox, with the Mesa's hotly spiced cuisine, a culinary analogue to Nancy's sexual home cooking. Though I had intended it to be playful as well as devotional, a number of Nancy's ex-lovers, doubtless in alcohol-fueled critic mode, had objected to the idea expressed in the prayer that they were scarcely more than ingredients in the stew that each night she brought to a boil in her soul kitchen, and so there had been a time when she chose not to put it on display. Now, however, it rested in front of the bar mirror, the liquor bottles ranked like a choir behind it, an artifact of Wardlin Stuart: The Early Days. When strangers asked her what was that thing in the Mexican silver frame, Nancy would not merely show it to them, she would recite it in full, elocuting in a breathy voice those passages in which I described her body or her sensuality.

"That poem's been lucky for a lotta guys come in," she said to us one night shortly before Christmas. Therese and I were at the bar, respectively nursing a beer and a vodka, and Nancy, her elbows on the counter, leaned toward us, flavoring the air with an overdose of Opium. "Oh, yeah," she said. "I see some boy responding to my reading in the right way and he's home free. It's a test, kinda."

"What's 'the right way'?" asked Therese.

"Aw, you know, honey. Like they're dreaming about ya and not looking to fricassee ya and gnaw on your bones." Nancy scooped up ice and chuted it into my glass, then added a splash of vodka. "I'm always on the lookout for a guy who believes it's me who's got the candy and not him." She turned to Marty Cushman, a rawboned young man wearing a Diamondbacks cap, sitting at the opposite end of the bar, close to the window. "Hey, Marty! Am I right?"

Marty glanced up from his newspaper. "Right about what?"

"Who's got the candy?" Nancy asked him.

"You do, babe," he said, and continued staring at her long after she returned to our conversation.

"Don't you think it's maybe a little cruel, rubbing it in like that?" I said.

"I'm not rubbing anything in! Marty knows after Christmas, once the snowbirds start pouring through town, I'll get bored and come back on him."

"It's Nancy's ambition," Therese said with a trace of primness, "to fuck everyone in Arizona."

"Not everyone! Just everyone I *want* to fuck. And don't you go giving me that good-girl shit, T. There was a time you tore it up." She knocked my forearm with the knuckles of her left hand. "She ever tell you about San Francisco?"

"She's touched on it," I said.

"Bet she didn't tell you everything. She rummaged through a lotta drawers, if y'know what I mean?"

"It'd be hard to miss what you mean," said Therese.

Nancy leaned to her and gave her a kiss. "Don't get pissy. You know how much I love ya."

Despite herself, Therese grinned.

The jukebox clicked, the Sand Rubies came on, "Guns in the Churchyard," and Nancy sang along for a couple of lines. "Now if you were unattached, Wardlin," she said, putting a forefinger to the side of her chin and considering me. "If you weren't hooked up with my girl here, I'm not sure you'd pass my test. Sometimes I'll get a bone-gnawer feel offa you. But then I see you puppy-dogging along with Therese, and I'm thinking, that boy's a dreamer."

"The problem with your test," I said, "every guy's got both of those feelings in him. They're liable to change one to the other."

"You don't think I'm aware of that? My test is more subtle than you can comprehend, Mr. Stuart."

"Should I just leave and let you two work things out?" Therese said.

Nancy shot me a look of mock perplexity. "She's in a mood! You keep her out on the desert too long last night?" Then, to Therese: "Okay, honey. You wanta talk about the church social, that's what we'll do." The door opening attracted her attention. "Oh, my God!" she said. "The mouth of hell musta gaped."

Monroe Treat, clad in a gray Western-style suit, was squiring a woman along one of the aisles. He was bigger than he had appeared on television. Six four, six five. The woman was youngish, about twenty-five pounds overweight, and way overdressed for the Mesa in a dark blue outfit that would have been appropriate for a Sunday-morning shout-along. Her makeup looked to have been done by someone who applied glazes to hams for commercial shoots. They settled into a rear booth and were approached by a waitress who wore, as did all the waitresses, clothes identical to Nancy's. The woman sat stiffly, her hands clasped, and let Treat do all the talking.

"Want I should cast the reverend and Miss Petunia into the outer darkness?" Nancy asked me. "I don't mind."

"What the hell for? Guy probably just needs a drink?"

Nancy went to the waitress station and took the order; when she came back she said, "White Russian and a glass of Lillet. You'll never guess who's getting the Lillet! Don't think I ever served it to a man before."

Therese leaned in so our three heads were together. "What do you suppose he wants?"

"A glass of Lillet, apparently," I said. "Forget his ass. If he's got an agenda, he'll let us know."

Nancy idly mopped the counter with a cloth. "Wonder who Miss Petunia is."

Therese had a quick glance at the couple over her shoulder. "That's a good suit she's got on. I wouldn't wear it to a funeral, but it's expensive."

"He's fucking her," Nancy said. "If she's got money, you just know he's fucking her every whichaway, creep like that."

I threw back my drink and pushed my glass toward Nancy. "Can we talk about something else?"

Nancy reached for a bottle of Absolut. "Let's see, now. One of ya doesn't wanta talk about sex, the other won't talk about Treat." She pretended to ponder, poured. "How about the new convenience store out past Cardwell's? I hear construction's going *real* good."

Therese had another peek at Treat's booth. "He's holding her hand!"

"Or maybe past lives," Nancy said. "I ever tell y'all about the time I danced for King Herod?"

"Shit! I'm gonna get drunk in self-defense," I said. "You can start me on vodka martinis after this one."

Nancy and Therese exchanged a look, and Nancy plucked up a bottle of Cuervo Gold. "Tequila!" they both said.

After an hour it got loud at our end of the bar. Loud and happy. Treat, though his presence had put a cold spot at the back of my brain for ten or fifteen minutes, no longer was a figure on my mental horizon. Nancy had hung a string of Christmas lights shaped like cacti above the mirror and I watched them winking on and off with the dazed, happy intensity of a broker watching his stocks all rising on the crawl. Soon our party was joined by Jerry Derogatis, a skinny twenty-three-year-old with stoner hair hanging halfway to his ass who repaired air conditioners for his father's firm. He was a fan of prayerstyle and had written many prayers, claiming they had all been answered, though for the life of me I couldn't see that his basic situation had changed a whit. Trying to ignore his admiring stare made me uncomfortable, but Nancy took to flirting with him and his eyes were all for her after that.

"Looks to me you been working out, honey," she said to him. "Or is that natural manly development I'm seeing?"

"I been thinking about joining the gym over in Solarsburg," he said. "But what the fuck for? Ain't like I got shit hanging off me or nothing."

"I like your attitude. I hate gyms." Nancy finished pouring the round Jerry had just bought. "My last year in Vegas I was in the gym all the time trying to pull this ol' thing together." She identified "this ol' thing" by turning her back to us and patting her tightly packaged ass. "It was like being a chicken in a room full of roosters. I'd go to doing bent rows and there'd be a migration to the machines next to me. I had enough of that crap on the job, so I asked the manager if I could come—"

"I gotta hit the head," Jerry said, and made for the back of the bar.

"We not boring ya, are we?" Nancy called out.

"Naw, be right back!"

Nancy fondly watched him walk away. "So anyhow," she went on. "I asked the manager could I come in after closing some nights and he said sure, but he'd have to be there. Which was fine, except he'd stand at the door and watch me work out. I got ticked off, I said, 'If I'm gonna be putting on a show, I wanta be paid for it,' and he goes, 'Okay. How much?' I was a little surprised . . . not a lot, but it wasn't what I would've predicted. But I thought what the hell and I named a price. It was cool at first, but then he got demanding. He'd tell me to sweat more, to use this or that machine. He had me doing way too much work on my pecs. They were getting massive! I had to switch gyms." She hoisted a shot of tequila. " 'Course that's nothing to the story Therese can tell. Whyn't you tell him about Mr. Kim, honey?"

"I don't know," Therese said.

"Come on! It's just us girls!" She gave my shoulder a buff. "I'm officially making you a girl for tonight, Wardlin. Can you stand it?" She handed Therese her tequila shot. "Drink up, T! Then spill your guts."

They both drank.

Therese was flushed when she set her glass down. "Okay," she said. "My first months in San Francisco, I was mostly doing temp jobs and I never had any money. A girl I knew told me she made extra money posing for nude photographs. No hooking, no touching. Just posing. She said you only needed one steady client. See, the clients paid this Greek guy who owned a building divided up into studios, and he'd provide them with a studio and a girl. Then the clients would tip the girls. So if you got a steady client who liked you, you could do pretty well. I gave the Greek some pictures of me to put in his book and soon I started getting call-ins. It was horrible. I was so shy! None of the clients liked me . . . and I hated them. I got no repeat business. The Greek said things needed to change fast or he wasn't going to use me anymore, so I made up my mind to comply with the next client that came in, whoever he was. A few days later I got a call. I went to the Greek's and I got undressed, I put on my robe. Then I waited in a room that had a couch and a podium, lights, all sorts of props. Eventually an old Korean man came in. I mean he was *really* old! Frail. He had a camera around his neck and was carrying a grocery sack."

"Do I need to hear this?" I asked.

"You shut your mouth!" Nancy slapped my hand. "Go on, girl. Tell it!"

"He put the sack on a stool," Therese said. "And he reached in and picked out a pear. Then he tottered over and handed it to me and signaled he wanted me to hold it. He didn't speak any English. Only his name. Mr. Kim. So I held the pear and I started to take off my robe, but he goes . . ." She waved her hands agitatedly. "Like he's saying, no, no! He comes over again and guides me down onto a cushion. Very gently, his hands all trembly, looking apologetic. And he arranges my robe so it's down off my shoulders but there's nothing showing. A little cleavage was all. Then he took a picture of me holding the pear. He was kind of sweet."

"That's what he was all about?" I asked. "Taking pictures of girls with pears?"

"He had other kinds of fruit in the sack. Oranges and apples, bananas, grapes . . ."

"Okay, I got it," I said. "Bananas."

"No, you don't got it! Do you want to hear what happened?" I told her to go on.

"Don't interrupt me, then!"

I showed Nancy my empty martini glass and she began working on a replacement. Something I didn't recognize was playing on the box, something with a gravelly vocal and a sluggish, swampy beat, and the conversations all around us seemed to be eddying with the music, and I felt part of that eddy, swirled slowly, as if I were not only drunk, but floating in a drink somebody was stirring.

"We met three times a week after that," Therese said. "Each time he'd tip me. Very generously. But it was like we were friends almost. I'd play a game with him. He'd give me a piece of fruit and I'd pretend I was going to take off my robe and he'd stop me. But I noticed it took him a little longer to stop me every time and I knew he wanted to see my breasts. He was anticipating it. That's why we were going slow. He wanted to prolong what he was feeling. Once I understood that, it was okay. I didn't mind him seeing my breasts. I believed whatever he was doing in his head, I wasn't just an object to him, I was a person whose breasts he wanted to see. The next time we met, I let my robe fall open to the waist."

Jerry Derogatis chose that moment to reappear and asked what Therese was talking about. Nancy said if he was good she'd tell him later and gave Therese and I a broad wink.

"It was so strange," Therese said. "When I'd been in the room with other men, it was awful. Ugly and mildewed and rotten. But with Mr. Kim . . . he treated me with respect. He gave me money, but there was respect. Almost friendship, like I said. Maybe it was friendship, at least on some level. I didn't know exactly what would make him happy, but I wanted to do it for him. The way he looked at me when I exposed my breasts, there was nothing lustful in his face. It was like he was remembering, dreaming. I would have liked to ask what he was thinking. If he was remembering his wife or a lover from long ago. I kept going slow, letting him lead me. It was seven months before I began posing without any clothes. Lying on the couch, I'd have these . . . I was going to say dreams, but they were more like out-of-the-body experiences. I felt I was floating up into another place, another plane. I'd hear the click of the shutter, but that was the only thing left of the room. Sometimes where I was, in my thoughts, he'd be with me. And sometimes he was young and handsome. Sometimes he wasn't there and I was alone or someone else was watching me. It was erotic in a way I hadn't experienced before. After each meeting I'd be drifty and spent, as if I'd made love. I'd go home, wander around my room, and think about Mr. Kim. I'd wonder where his home was, what he was doing. I didn't know a single thing about him, though I imagined him in a hundred different lives. Surrounded by family. Alone. With an ailing wife. I thought about him all the time. Not as a man. He was so old, I doubt he was functional. But how I thought about him . . . he wasn't not a man, either." She had a sip of a fresh shot that Nancy poured, then tossed the rest of it down. "We'd been meeting for about a year. One afternoon I was with him at the studio and I knew what he wanted. It was absolutely clear. He was about to hand me an orange, but I didn't take it. I went to the grocery sack and took a banana instead. He put out a hand to stop me. He had that apologetic expression again. But I went back to the couch and lay down. Then I floated up into that place in my head and touched myself, and then I slipped the banana inside me. I kept on touching myself until I came. I'd never had an orgasm that strong before. It was like I'd been waiting a year for it. Like I wanted what he wanted. I realized later that in all those months he had never handed me a banana to hold. Occasionally it looked as if he were going to, but he always moved his hand away. He was just reminding me of it . . . and waiting for me to take it myself."

Jerry Derogatis, confused-looking, made to speak and Nancy shushed him again.

"He always gave me my tip in a sealed envelope," Therese said. "And he always made me open it in front of him—so he could be sure I was happy, I think. Usually he gave me two hundred dollars. The money was sealed in the envelope before he arrived. This time the envelope was very thick. There was ten thousand dollars inside. I couldn't believe it. I could rent a decent apartment, buy clothes I needed for job interviews. I tried to hug him, but all he let me do was take his hand. Then I got it, you know. I understood. He'd put the money in the envelope before he got there. He'd known what I was going to do that day."

"He seduced you," I said.

Therese nodded. "Expertly. I think I knew that's what he was doing, but it wasn't something I dwelled on. I was too caught up in the event. In all the fantasies it evoked. I don't know what it did for him, the whole thing, but I had a feeling my instincts were correct and he was reliving something from his past through me."

"Guy sounds like a sick fuck," said Jerry.

Nancy gave him a pitying look.

"Maybe," Therese said to him. "Maybe he was just a dirty old man. But you don't know, you weren't there. And even if he was, it didn't matter. What I got out of it . . . it was memorable."

"You talking the ten grand?" I asked, and grinned.

Nancy slapped at my hand. "You be good, now!"

"I never saw Mr. Kim again," Therese said. "I didn't really expect to. The money was a good-bye. I figure either what we'd done together had satisfied him or else he chose another girl and went though the same thing with her. Me, I got a little crazy. I started playing games with men. Sexual manipulations. As if Mr. Kim had set something loose in me. Or maybe it was trauma. It felt as if I'd had my heart broken and was into payback. Like this world

I believed in had collapsed. It doesn't seem I should have been that affected. I had a couple of physical relationships during my year with Mr. Kim, but when they ended, I wasn't sad or angry. My true involvement was with him." Therese fussed with her cocktail napkin. "After a while I started to put things in perspective."

"You worked past it," Nancy said.

"Did I?" Therese cut her eyes toward me. "Look how Wardlin and I got together. The letters, the calls, the barriers between us."

I said, "You think I manipulated you the way Mr. Kim did? Or you manipulated me?"

"It makes me wonder."

"Fuck," I said. "I suppose I'm gonna be trying to figure it all out now."

"Don't bother," Therese said. "I've been trying for years and I haven't gotten anywhere."

"That's some heavy shit," Jerry said, nodding soberly. "I mean, y'know?"

"What you think about the story, Wardlin?" asked Nancy.

"I'm with Jerry," I told her. "Seriously heavy shit."

"Naw, you're not gonna get out of this like that! Say!"

I put my hand atop Therese's hand and interlaced my fingers with hers. "Who knows what was on the guy's mind? There was dominance involved, for sure. He was using his power, probably the only way he could. However you interpret what went on, it wasn't that twisted. Just looks twisted because he was old and she was young, and they couldn't have a typical relationship. But that's how people are. Seduction's not necessarily a bad thing." I snagged a Camel pack from Jerry's shirt pocket and tapped a cigarette out.

"For Therese, it was a passage, obviously. Self-destructive . . . but it was empowering, too. Maybe it enlarged her conception of what's possible between people. And maybe it did influence her approach to relationships. Maybe it made her cautious but more hopeful."

Nancy hmmphed, as if amused. "That's one way of looking at it."

"Well, how do you see it?"

"We're all fallen angels, everyone," said Nancy with unflawed sincerity. "And blessed to know these days."

The four of us broke into couples. The Mesa had filled up and Nancy got busy. Jerry lingered by the waitress station, watching her pour. Treat and Miss Petunia were still in their booth. She had loosened up and was laughing at things he said. Therese and I talked more about her story. "The part that's stayed with me most," she said, "is the place I'd float off to. It was cloudy to begin with. Just . . . undefined. Kind of powdery blue. Then I realized that actual clouds were drifting alongside it and I began to see pillars. Like Greek columns. A temple. Like a Maxfield Parrish place. And I'd hear voices. Whispering. I couldn't ever understand them. It might have been the sound of a river. Of course I'm probably embellishing it in memory."

"You go anywhere like that these days?" I asked.

"With you, you mean? I go somewhere, but it's different."

"Different how?"

"It's . . . fiercer, I guess."

"Fierce? Like how?" I elbowed her gently in the side to let her know I was joking around.

She fanned herself with her hand, affecting a swoon. "It's so much hotter!"

"More than you expected, huh?"

"Little more than I hoped for, anyway," she said, and elbowed me back.

About ten-thirty, Dave Gillery, the town's youngest deputy, a big soft-bodied kid with a crew cut, came into the Mesa and told Therese that the shop had been vandalized by somebody who owned a gray minivan. They'd been spotted driving away. We hurried over to the shop and found that an enormous red word—WAR—had been painted on one window and an equally red word with smaller letters—APOSTATE—was painted on the other.

"Treat," I said. "That motherfucker."

"We don't know it was him," Therese said.

"The son of a bitch calls me an apostate, he declares war on me. Then he shows up out of the fucking blue and sits there while a fucking minion does his dirty work. Who else you think did it?"

"You accusing somebody?" Gillery looked as if he were bursting to get all official. Dressed in khakis, slightly pear-shaped, his head only inches higher than the blinking rack of lights atop his shiny white cruiser: an alien visitor might have had difficulty deciding which was the hound and which the master.

"We don't have any proof," Therese said to him; then to me: "Why would he have done it? He must know he'd draw suspicion to himself?"

"Arrogance," I said. "He wanted to watch us scurry around. It was a bad fucking move."

"Don't do anything! It's not like they blew up the place. I'll get it cleaned."

"Naw, this guy thinks I'm a punk. He thinks he can harass me. I know how to deal with that shit."

"Wardlin!"

"You got a suspect," Gillery said sternly, "you lemme handle him. You don't need this trouble, Wardlin."

Disregarding their attempts at restraint, I set out for the Mesa at a fast clip, cold intent building with every step, the street like an art gallery whose paintings of glass storefronts were all variations on the same tawdry Christmas theme. I hit the Mesa's door full stride, pushing into the darkness and music and smoke, and went along the aisle to Treat's booth. He looked startled on catching sight of me, but he smoothed it over and said, "Mr. Stuart."

"You just grabbed the wrong end of the poker, asshole," I said. "Think you can piss in my face, I won't come back at you?"

Treat said, "I beg your pardon?"

Miss Petunia gawked at me.

"Don't fuck with my life," I said. "You go on and preach your dumbass sermons to your dumbass flock. But do not fuck with my life!"

Treat turned sideways in the booth, resting an arm along the back of it, a blissed-out confidence flowing from him. "I don't know what your problem is, Mr. Stuart. If you calm down, I'm sure we can resolve it."

"You're an insane cocksucker, aren't you?" I said. "I mean you must be, speaking this way. I'm a felon, remember? I'm a fucking murderer. I'm not responsible. Caution is required."

Miss Petunia made an aggrieved noise and I believe Treat intended a response, but I flung myself down into the booth beside him, shoving him back against the wall. He tried to push me away, but he was compressed, one of his legs jacked off the floor, the knee jammed toward his gut, an arm locked half-behind him, and I had all the leverage. The physical contact jumped my heart rate.

"You want a war?" I asked him. "We can kick it off right here."

He tried again to push me, but I put my shoulder into him and drove him harder against the wall. I was right into his chest, the point of my shoulder up under his armpit and my mouth close to his head, which was forced to the side. Both his arms were out of commission now. I clamped my free hand high up on his thigh, dug my fingers into the packed muscle.

"Whoops! War's over," I said. "That was easy to resolve, now wasn't it?"

His upper body twisted like a noose-caught snake and I gave his johnson a squeeze. "I'll yank it off," I told him.

His eyelids lowered and I could feel him yearning to resist. I had a quick glance at Miss Petunia. She was petrified, tearing up.

"For a big guy, you're kind of a pussy," I said. "Maybe war ain't your thang."

No reaction. He stared in the direction I forced him to stare: down and to the side at a small wall-mounted plant holder in which a baby cactus sprouted from pale rocks and sand.

"Whatever fantasy you're tripping on, you best get over it," I said. "I survived ten years in a place you wouldn't last ten days. I won't come after you with lawyers. You understand?"

Treat said, "I understand you're threatening me." •

"No. You're threatening me. You're the one came and staked out my bar. You're the one had his monkey boy deface our window. You encroached. What you've mistaken for a threat, if you examine it in context of our splendid American justice system, is considered self-defense. Legally and morally justifiable. Even according to your little black book. You declared war on me in front of a national TV audience. That was unwise, man. It puts you in a bad light, anything should happen."

"Nothing's going to happen," said Treat.

Despite being jammed and shoved and squeezed, he had the air of a man who was patiently enduring a child's tantrum. I thought he might actually be insane, that he was producing too much brain dope and this made him so stupid, he failed to recognize that I wasn't just normal-angry, I was prison-crazy and thus invested with a certain remorselessness. I sensed that people behind me were watching and I guessed that Therese and Nancy were among them.

"Monroe?" Miss Petunia added a quavery extra syllable to his name. "Please, let's go!"

"That sounds like a swell plan, Monroe," I said. "I think you should adopt it."

"This is *your* bar?" Treat asked. "You have a say over who—"

"Questions?" I rapped his groin lightly with my knuckles and he stiffened. "I didn't ask for questions."

"It's my bar," Nancy said, coming up to the booth, assuming her neon-sign pose. "If it makes you feel any better, tell yourself it's me throwing you out."

I slid into the aisle, going shoulder to shoulder with her.

Miss Petunia said, "Please, Monroe!"

He sat up, straightened his jacket, and nodded.

"Don't come back," Nancy said as they got to their feet. "But you tell your friends about us, y'hear?"

Treat's placid mask didn't show a crack. He hadn't seemed so controlled, so impervious to emotion, on *Larry King Live*. I wondered if the days since had done some damage or if this was the true man, unaffected by a nervousness brought on by hot lights and pancake.

Her head down, clutching her purse to her waist, Miss Petunia led the way along the aisle and Treat, taking shuffling steps so as not to tread on her heels, followed. There were a couple of jeers and light applause. The glass door swung shut behind them.

"Jesus, Wardlin!" Nancy whacked my shoulder. "You looking to get thrown back in jail?"

"I knew what I was doing. Guy like that gets after you—"

"Don't tell me! I'm not the one needs an explanation!"

I saw Therese at the bar, sitting with her back to me.

Nancy pushed me toward her. "You busting to testify, there's the judge."

When I dropped onto the barstool next to Therese, she glanced at me sidelong, more a vicious swipe with her eyes than a true glance, and said, "Is that how you were in prison?"

"What?"

She mocked me in a thickened voice: " 'What?' That! How you behaved just now."

"I got angry, okay?" I said. "I'm sorry."

"That wasn't angry. I know how you get angry. Angry's when you blow up real quick and thirty seconds later you feel like a jackass."

"Look, this needed dealing with."

"No it didn't!"

"Yes it did! A guy like that, he starts up with you, you hafta nip it in the bud or he's on you for the rest of—"

"For the rest of what? What were you going to say? The rest of your term? Your time? You're not in prison anymore."

"Coulda fooled me," I muttered.

"What's that supposed to mean?"

I fingered the stem of a martini glass and didn't meet her stare. "I'm sorry. You pissed me off."

"Are you going to come after me like that, now you're pissed off? Are you going to get all stony and hunt me through the streets?" She picked up the Cuervo bottle, which Nancy had left on the counter, and poured a shot. "That's how you behaved in prison, isn't it?"

"Sometimes. When I thought I could get away with it."

"So this tonight, it was premeditated?"

"Maybe . . . I . . . Fuck, I don't know!"

"Was it a reflex action? A patterned behavior?"

Her face was blank, emotions walled up.

"Damn, Therese. Gimme a break, here."

"I simply want to understand if this is how you're going to act whenever you feel something has to be nipped in the bud. This was unnecessary. Even if he's responsible for the window . . . and we don't know that. It might have been someone from his church acting on their own. But even if it was . . ." She shook her head and drank her shot. "You didn't nip anything in the bud. All you did was provoke him."

"Fine. I won't do it again."

"And I can count on that, can't I?"

She poured another shot.

"You're gonna be sick tomorrow, you keep that up," I said.

"Don't worry about it! I won't get drunk enough so I'll go attacking anyone." But she pushed the shot glass away. She looked at me, looked at the mirror, then back at me again. "The cops have been giving you a pass because of the book. Letting you drink and hang out in bars. But if you hurt someone in a fight, they won't have a choice. They'll send you back."

"It wasn't gonna come to a fight. I knew that."

"The hell you did! You're not that great a judge of character, you can read someone from a few minutes on *Larry King Live*. And you certainly don't know what's on his mind now."

"I said I wouldn't do it again. You want me to get on my knees?"

"Couldn't hurt."

I made as if to go to my knees and she stopped me with her hand. "Don't. You've already put on enough of a show."

I could tell her anger was breaking, but I couldn't think what to say that would help the process along. The fact was, I had fallen back into prison mode; but though I could see this and admit to it,

I couldn't rid myself of the belief that I had done the right thing and that the Treat situation had been managed.

Nancy sidled up behind the bar. "You two disappoint me," she said. "I was hoping for a honest-to-God knock-down, drag-out to put a finish on the evening." She fell into a boxer's stance. "Been you'n me, Wardlin, we'd a'gone twelve and you'd be sleeping in the shower tonight."

"That's still to be decided," said Therese.

I didn't feel I had anything to add, so I turned on the barstool and surveyed the booths. The badasses and the bar fighters and the hardcore drunks were down at Scotty's, and the crowd in the Mesa was, generally speaking, of Jerry Derogatis's age. College kids home on Christmas vacation and such. Making merry. Crammed into a back booth, four boys and three girls were singing wildly off-key with the jukebox, which was featuring Neil Young's "Helpless." They hit the line about big birds flying all through the skies and one of the boys made an operatic gesture that spilled drinks and caused two of the girls to shriek and half stand, mopping at their skirts.

"I don't see ol' Jerry," I said to Nancy over my shoulder. "You two have a falling-out?"

"I threw him back. Boy wasn't game limit yet." She rested her elbows on the counter, cupping her chin. " 'Fraid it's destined to be a lonely night for the lady of the manor."

Therese fumbled for my hand. "I'm tired. Let's go home."

"You gonna drink that last shot?" I asked her.

"I thought you didn't want me to be sick in the morning?"

"Yeah, but . . ." I slung an arm about her neck, pulled her to me, kissed her brow. "Maybe it'll make you less grumpy tonight."

"I'm not mad," she said. "But you can't act like this anymore, Wardlin. You just can't."

"I know."

"Too bad I had to kick the preacher out," Nancy said musingly. "Been a while since I done it with a God-fearing man."

Chapter 14

I had found a place in the desert where I would go some mornings when Therese was busy and I didn't feel like working. It was an outcropping of boulders several hundred yards past one of the mesas. The boulders were great lumpy shapes, pale grayish yellow, the indentations on their surfaces worn smooth as dimples, their crests twenty and thirty feet high. At their center was a narrow track of sand and weeds, a miniature canyon winding among stone walls, and I would pace along it or sit and pick up pebbles and fondle them and let my thoughts run out into the solitude, growing empty and content, as prisoners will from time to time, constrained yet somehow nurtured by confinement, pervaded by an almost embryonic sense of well-being. It did not elude me that my visits to the boulders were on some level an attempt to reconfigure a prison mentality. I understood that I needed such consolations, that what had been bred in me during my prison years would likely never be completely winnowed out. But it was a harmless twitch, I thought, and this was not the only thing I enjoyed about the place. I liked the silence broken now and then by the scream of a hawk or the scurry of a lizard, and the striated complexities of the winter clouds, the dry cold air, the mysterious small holes burrowed in the sand where dwelled, I imagined, homunculi with dark wizened faces and beetle-drawn carts and a culture dominated by a philosophy I called Zaharizel—a good desertish, devilly name—which espoused the belief that every creature who had ever existed would one day evolve to become God and rule for a quarter hour on the universal clock, thus inspiring its adherents to live tidy monastic lives, secure in the knowledge that since your fate was inevitably glorious, ambition was inessential, and the reasonable course was to prepare for the Ascendancy by means of contemplation and prayer, because you would not want, as occasionally happened, to go fucking up your fifteen minutes.

Often the beginning to a prayer would come to me as I sat there, and early one morning shortly before New Year's, the sky overhead washing from blue darkness to slate, a chittering noise coming from close by, possibly a bird chortling over a string of flesh it had unearthed from beneath a rock, I had a moment of inspiration and scribbled these lines on a hip-pocket notepad:

> *He is accustomed to great hallucinations*
> *of red and yellow and green curve,*
> *sumptuous signs that advertise fulfillment,*
> *the entirety of promise written in light . . .*

I paused there, not knowing what should come next. The prayers I wrote out on the desert were personal and, now that I had everything I figured to want, I rarely prayed for anything specific and let the words tell me what my hidden desires were. I watched a spider, its body a pale translucent yellow, perfectly dressed for the place, creeping across sand-grain boulders. I scratched behind my ear, wondered what Therese was doing, pictured her breasts. Then I amended the last line and added more:

> *the entirety of promise described in light,*
> *neon angels, Chinese characters drawn on high,*
> *a bowling pin sketched by crimson tubing,*
> *fish, elephants, a glittering nonsensical fauna,*
> *and beneath them, isolate at a sidewalk cafe,*
> *the Lord of Loneliness, indifferent to other diners,*

> *smokes a hand-rolled soul—a cigar it's called*
> *by those unfamilar with the magic of tobacco—*
> *and thinks of Havana, a city to which he's never traveled*
> *yet remembers fondly as having been the home*
> *of his first romance, the love of all his lives*

I didn't like how the prayer was going, because it seemed un-involved with any reward, an ornate doodling without purpose, more fantasy than prayer; and further because I had an uneasy feeling that if it did express a hope, one that hadn't yet become manifest, it might be something I didn't want to examine. But I kept on adding to it:

> *of his first romance, his last meaningful relationship,*
> *the best time he ever had or something of the sort,*
> *the details are hazy . . .*
> *and when He walks home that night*
> *the street above which everything is promised,*
> *returning to the graveyard castle where only He exists,*
> *where He sits forever explaining Himself to Himself,*
> *a little drunk on His own mystery, His nostalgic poison,*
> *He anticipates that someone will be waiting for Him.*
> *He would like it to be a woman, a Colleen, a Desiree,*
> *who will heave gently, incessantly, the calm ocean*
> *of her flesh sustaining Him until darkness folds its ace*
> *and sizes up its losses . . . but He believes it is a man,*
> *or a figure more dangerous than a man posing as a man,*
> *like Him, like His pose, always retreating into mirrors,*
> *too complex to see against a background of reflections*

A scrunching noise gave me a start. It had issued from the other side of the boulders, I thought. Maybe a footstep. My heart quickened. I listened and, hearing nothing, I considered shouting and seeing if that roused a response. It couldn't be Therese—she always called out to me. I pocketed my pen and notepad. Listened. Ten or fifteen seconds passed. It must have been, I decided, scree slipped from the side of a boulder, perhaps dislodged by the passage of a lizard. Then I heard the sound again. Definitely footsteps. Seven or eight of them. When they stopped, I took out my Swiss Army knife and opened the longest blade. The possibilities arranged themselves in my head. Least likely, a solitary hiker. Most likely, someone off the reservation. I was more frightened than I should have been. My chest was tight, my throat dry. I reminded myself that, according to my parole officer, there hadn't been a murder in Pershing for twenty years ("so don't you go committing one, Wardlin"). Nonetheless, I couldn't muster up the courage to shout. I waited there, alert to every sound. The sun was reddening the top of the boulders before I realized I was being foolish. Whoever it was must have moved off, treading across less pebbly ground. Not entirely convinced of this, I climbed the slope of the smallest boulder and scanned the desert in every direction from the crest. Looking northwest, I spotted a figure standing in a fringe of sage eighty or ninety feet out from my perch. The light painted the surrounding desert floor a bloody red and the figure was black against it. Though logic proclaimed it was some-body returning to the reservation from a night in town, the sight put a fresh charge of fear into me and I took a step back. My heel caught a pebble and I teetered off balance for a moment, nearly falling. That got me angry.

"Hey!" I shouted. "What do you want?"

Something glinted in the figure's hand and I thought, gun; then a faint smoke plumed upward from its head. The son of a bitch, I realized, was smoking a cigarette. Smoking and watching me totter about, hoping I'd break my skull.

I gingerly lowered myself to a sitting position and sledded down the side of the boulder, worried that he might have broken into the car; but as I stood on the shelf of dirt at its base, elevated a couple of feet above the desert floor, I noticed that the blackness of the figure was not merely due to an effect of the light. His clothes were black.

I wondered if he could be a Wardlinite. Even now, during the holidays, a few made pilgrimages to the shop. The closest I let them get to me was signing their books, but from those encounters I understood the depth of their zeal. It was perfectly plausible that I was being stalked.

"Who are you?" I shouted.

The man remained motionless, silent.

Trying to see him more clearly, I cupped my hands into a flesh telescope—it didn't help much. "Whoever you are! Keep the fuck away from me!"

The man shifted, though not, apparently, in reaction to my warning—it was more an adjustment in posture, a realignment of weight. Irritated, I moved down off the shelf. I spanked the back of my jeans, knocked stone dust from my hands.

It was in my mind to get into the car and drive home, but distressed by his violation of my solitude and spurred by a burst of anger, I strode toward the man, expecting him to retreat, to react in some fashion. No reaction was forthcoming. He just stood there, smoking. Buffaloed by his show of poise, I stopped after covering about twenty feet, and it was at this juncture I began to associate the man's presence, his demeanor and dress, with the subject of my prayer, the unease I had felt while writing it, and the other, similarly attired man whom I had met months before in Nogales. I had not, I thought, been trying to influence the universe for personal gain. The prayer was an invocation, a summoning, and He Who Had Been Invoked had manifested right on cue, His footstep coming hard upon the writing of those lines that announced His imminence. That coincidence seemed at once proof of the existence of the Lord of Loneliness made flesh and, because I was tempted to believe this, a symptom of, at the very least, severe neurosis. To validate that proof, or to debunk it as mere coincidence, all I had to do was keep walking forward, but I felt intimidated by the man's stillness, by the openness of the desert and the absence of witnesses. I held my ground for several seconds, hovering near the fence of my fear, and then began a sideways retreat toward the car.

By the time I had fumbled out the keys and flung myself behind the wheel of the Suburban, I was in full delusionary stride. I pictured the man in black materializing above the hood, his arms outspread, Christlike. My tension level dipped a notch once I got the engine going, and after I set the car in motion, I had a surge of wild confidence. I would drive toward him, I told myself. Drive toward him and check him out. If he tried anything, I'd use the car for a weapon. Nice. Vehicular homicide. They'd evict me from the joint at the age of sixty-two, a gray leftover now judged too weak to be a menace. Three or four years of steady drinking. Maybe a gig sweeping up at the mission. The young guys would throw shit on the floor and laugh when I stooped to pick it up and keeled over from the heart strain. And that would be that. Another possibility. I would drive past him and he would swoop at the car, a semidivine CGI effect, snatch at me, his hand and arm passing through the glass without breakage, as if it were the skin of a bubble. He would pull me out and draw me to his chest and absorb me into his black all-consuming substance, and when I was one with him, conscious as a star in the galactic sprawl of his unseen inner firmament, he'd light up a fresh smoke, burp, and be off about his business, which I assumed involved the gathering of sufficient soul power to enable him to make a serious move on the big chair of corporate godhood. Doubtless, in a previous existence, he had been one of the monkish homunculi who inhabited my ersatz boulder prison. I sent the Suburban jouncing across the desert toward town, my neck hairs prickling, glancing frequently in the rearview, and I did not feel easy until I saw Therese, still asleep in our bed, and touched her white shoulder, and watched her stir.

I did not cling to my affrighted, half-formed belief in the Lord of Loneliness. When the notion cropped up in my thoughts, I laughed it off. The desert was a spooky place; it could put a person on all kinds of trips. I concluded that the man I'd seen must have been a

Wardlinite and I determined to keep an eye out for him. Then on New Year's Day, sitting with Therese on the sofa, mildly hungover, half watching the Pitt Panthers, Therese's alma mater, being declawed by the Arizona Wildcats in some minor bowl ("the Ginkgo-Biloba Senility Bowl" she called it), I had another look at the prayer, the invocation, and tried to recall what I was feeling when I wrote it, whether there had been a hint of presentiment in my unease, or a sense of my hand and thoughts being directed. That I could recall nothing of the sort only accentuated the feeling that I must be missing something, that somewhere evidence existed to prove I was being watched over—or merely watched—by a presence whom my prayers had helped shape from the uncreate. It alarmed me, this apprehension of the supernatural or, as *Handbook* referred to it, the "ultranatural." (Since prayerstyle was a natural process, I believed, you see, that none of its products, however arcane, should be viewed as magical or inexplicable or divine.) My adherents had achieved miraculous rewards by climbing a ladder with rungs fashioned of answered prayers, small blessings that led ultimately to the large; and since I was the originator of the method, expert in its techniques, I supposed it wasn't unexpected that my own prayers were capable of achieving still more miraculous rewards. The thing that alarmed me, then, was not the idea that I might have summoned forth the Lord of Loneliness, but my reasons for desiring this result. The man in Nogales and the man on the desert had both demonstrated a passive-aggressive menace, and from what I recalled of other less verifiable sightings, fleeting observances such as had occurred in Chicago and the desert behind Jenny's Place, it seemed those men, too, had been surrounded by an aura of reticence and threat. I wondered if my act of creation—if, indeed, that's what it was—had been constructed as a self-punishment. Perhaps I was seeking a judgment on my life. We tend to hide such desires from ourselves, to drape them in costumes that mask their true design. But why would I want to punish myself? I was, I thought, a decent man. A better man, at any rate, than I had been. I had served my time and done good works. This, I realize now, was the thing that should have alarmed me—that I could make so benign a self-judgment.

Wednesday after New Year's, during a lull in business, while Therese was napping, a swarthy, mustachioed man wearing a black jacket, black shirt, black jeans, and carrying a black slouch hat, entered the shop and began snooping about in front, close to the postcard racks. I grew wary, but after watching him browse along the aisles for a minute or two, lent confidence by the fact that I was on my own turf and other people were nearby, I asked if I could be of help.

"I'm just looking around," he said. "Checking shit out."

I had a fleeting fantasy that he might be a stickup artist disguised as a Wardlinite. Certainly his actions were unlike those of the majority of Wardlinites, who would make a beeline for me the moment I came into view, brimming with feverish intensity. He stopped by a stack of *Handbooks,* flipped open the cover of one, riffled the pages.

"I can sign that if you want," I said.

"I'm not big on autographs. Bitch of a book, though. First great book of the new millennium, you ask me."

I hadn't seen the face of the man in the desert, and the long months elapsed since I had encountered the man in Nogales had fogged my memory—my customer had a similar nonchalant manner and border-meat look, but I could not have sworn they were one and the same. I picked up the paperback I'd been reading before he entered and tried to ignore him.

"Mind if I smoke?"

I hadn't heard him approach. He was standing by the register, an arm's length away. NO SMOKING signs were prominently displayed, but I didn't feel I should deny him. I brought forth a ceramic lizard with an ashtray in its back, which I used when things were slow, and set it on the counter. He examined the lizard, petting it with his left-hand little finger—the nail was painted black.

"Nice," he said. He patted his jacket pockets. "Shit! I musta left my lighter somewhere."

I handed him a lighter and he fired up.

"So how's it going, man?" he asked.

I was accustomed to fans calling me by my Christian name, but his familiarity had a quality of intimate association; this encouraged me to be direct. "Didn't you and me have a talk about six months back?" I asked. "In Nogales."

"Possible. I talk to a lot of people . . . and I get to Nogales once in a while."

"But you don't remember?"

"Not offhand."

"You told me a joke. This long, weird joke."

"Sounds like me, but . . ." He shrugged. "Could be some guy resembles me. I've been told I'm a type."

I started to ask if he had been the man I saw out on the desert, but I was possessed by the fearful suspicion that if he thought I was certain of his identity, if his security were breached in that way, he might perform some godlike maneuver and strike me mute or turn me into a baby iguana key chain.

"How's your wife doing these days?" he asked.

"My wife?"

"You know, man. Beauty to your Beast. She to whom you cleave."

In his face was a tinge of attitude, a shadow of smart-ass, but not enough you would notice unless, like me, you were searching for clues, and even then you couldn't be sure. His eyes were so dark, I considered the possibility that he might be a slim black hominid without feature or mark, tucked into a human zip-skin suit.

"Therese," he said. "Isn't that her name?"

I glared at him. "You trying to fuck with my head?"

"Two people in the world, sharing a moment . . . A little head-fucking's practically inevitable." He inhaled and let smoke leak out as he spoke. "Why do you ask?"

"We talked about my wife in Nogales. That joke you told me, you said it was an object lesson concerning her."

"So . . ." He tapped off ash. "So my asking about your wife now, that strikes you as unusual?"

"No, but when—"

"Because that's all you got to tie together this dude in Nogales and me, you got jack. You're a famous man. Your wife's appeared on TV with you. I was inquiring after her. Making chitchat."

"She's sleeping," I said. "She's fine."

He gave out with a grumbly noise such as a doctor might supply when he comes across a puzzling item on your test results. "Two of you getting along okay?"

"That's not a matter of public issue," I said, rankled.

"Hey. Sorry. I guess that is crossing the line, but I feel I know you. From the book, y'know. It's that American royalty thing. Your glitterati lives intrigue us." There was no detectable taint of sarcasm in his flat-affect delivery. "Of course," he went on, "maybe when we met—if we met—you were having troubles with your wife and I'm unconsciously relating to that. That could be another reason why I brought it up."

He was too good at this, I realized. He could keep it up for hours and never fall off the wire. I had no doubt this was the man from Nogales—there could not be two men so elusively literal.

"Marriage," said the man musingly, leaving the word to float in the air with his smoke.

"What about it?"

"Nothing. I was conceptualizing. Playing with the idea. Doing some whither-ing and wherefore-ing. Like if you were speculating about, y'know, a disease or something, you might go . . ." He dropped into a baritone. "Cholera."

"Are you married?"

"Naw, man. I made a vow. I swore I'd only marry if I met up with a woman named Glory Canyon. If I ever run across her, I'm hooked, but for now I'm married to the job."

"What's the job?"

"Self-employed. I freelance in various capacities." Then, before I could continue my interrogation, he said, "I love this place, man. If I was gonna retire, you better believe I'd be setting myself up with a trinket shop. This is the future, places like this."

Bemused, I said, "You mean like for investment?"

"No, thanks. It sucks as a business. Too much competition. I'm talking about entropic process. It's a theory I have. You wanta hear?"

"Maybe another time," I said. "I have to do some stocking."

"Neolithic culture, they didn't have time or the wherewithal to produce anything except what they needed to survive," said the man. "Maybe they carved toys for the kids. Toy mammoths and shit. That's about it. But as societies grew more sophisticated, more technologically competent, the more trivial, whimsical objects they produced. Now we're in the Golden Age of the trivial and the whimsical. Eventually society will produce nothing but trinkets. Everything will have been trivialized. Every resource trashed, every idea reduced to a slogan, every boulderlike edifice crumbled into rubble. We'll inhabit a landscape of lizard-shaped ashtrays and digital crickets and Harry Potter oven mittens. Art will be manufactured, not ripped from the soul. Greatness defined by merchandisers. Love that once inspired poetry, novels, symphonies, and now inspires pop songs . . . it'll inspire some even more vapid form of insignificance. Hell, we're almost there. Your book's a perfect example. You've taken that whole burning-bush, heavenly-glory thing and marketed it as your basic build-a-Jehovah kit. That's why I admire it so much. It's cutting-edge."

Stuck on the "build-a-Jehovah kit" image, I hesitated before responding. "That's some clever bullshit, but I don't know if it measures up to being a theory."

"Well, yeah!" The man butted his smoke on the lizard's back. "That's what I'm talking about. Five hundred years ago it would have occurred to me as a great idea. It would've had some scope, some resonance. It woulda set fire to men's minds. Now . . . clever bullshit."

He strolled off along an aisle, dipped his hand into a bin full of button pins imprinted with snappy sayings and let them sift through his fingers as if they were pirate gold. "That's not the main reason I'd go for a shop like this. It's this stuff, man! All your stuff in here, it's so cool."

"Maybe you'd care to buy some of it," I suggested.

"No way! This place is a like a museum to me. I bought something, be like you plopping down your Visa at the Louvre and saying 'Wrap me up a couple of Monets.' " He cast his eyes around the cluttered space. "A man could be happy here. I imagine you'd be happy if they weren't after you."

"If who wasn't after me?"

"Whoever. You telling me somebody like you, you don't have enemies? Someone who's got it in for you?"

"Not really."

"Come on! Must be somebody out there hates your guts."

"I guess there's this one guy," I said. "This preacher over in—"

"See? That's who I mean. That one guy. He's always around. It's a condition of existence. You know how it goes. Territoriality, man. You don't fuck him up, he'll fuck you up."

Whether this was street logic or advice from a demiurge didn't matter. Confused by his presence, I recognized that I was confused by all things. Those few certainties in my life—Therese, prayer-style—were bobbing on a sea of confusion. I was tempted to believe in oracles, willing to confer oracular status on anyone, and I asked him to expand on what he meant.

"You're asking me for advice?" He took another smoke from his pack, but didn't light it and tapped his chest with his cigarette hand. "Me? Wow. I'm honored, man. Seriously." He came toward me along the aisle. "So this guy, this preacher . . . it wouldn't be the guy you nuked on *Larry King,* would it? That guy from Phoenix? Treat?"

"I'm not sure, but yeah . . . maybe."

"Makes sense. You damn near sank that boy's battleship."

"It wasn't that big a deal."

"Don't you read the papers? Man's losing his congregation. Every day or two up in Phoenix, they print something about him. Some new scandal brought to light. He's got reporters buzzing all around his mess. People coming forward, saying Treat did this, Treat did that. You put the magnifying glass right over that little bug. He's bound to come after you."

"How's coming after me gonna help him?"

He reached over and touched my forehead. It was such a gentle movement, I didn't flinch. His fingertip left a spot of cold sensitivity between my eyes.

"What the fuck was that?" I said, paranoid again.

"I wanted to see where your head was at. It looked normal, but way you're acting, I wasn't sure." He stuck the cigarette into his mouth. " 'Course he's gonna come after you. What else can he do? If he's done crime, he might be going away for a stretch. His fringe people, they'll abandon his ass. But his core congregation, the true believers, he can hang on to them. He needs to give them a cause for belief, and you're it. The man'll blame everything that's happened to him on you. He'll claim you performed a satanic ritual or some crap, and that's what brought him low. He's got to discredit you in their eyes. It's his only play. Won't work, though."

"Why not?"

"For somebody spent ten years behind walls, you ask some dumbshit questions." He lit his cigarette and pocketed my lighter. "Because you're gonna fuck Treat up."

"I doubt it," I said. "I'm not looking to blow parole."

"I didn't say you were gonna act stupid. I'm assuming you've learned a thing or two." He let out a sage chuckle. "I know you, man. I read your fucking *Handbook* and I got a line on how you work, but I can see you're a little confused. It's the fame thing. All those preachers wearing your ass out, it's made you defensive, caused you to adopt a moral stance, and that's just not your thing. Prayer-style was never about morality. It's about gain. Acquisition. Taking care of business. Which is what religion was originally about. Cave people praying for that saber-tooth to turn into a pile of steaks and chops. That morality BS got whipped on it later. Even the Bible says it, man. A time for everything in its season. A time for love, for hate. A time when you need to fuck somebody up. Treat thinks he's colder than you, willing to get more extreme. But you lived somewhere colder than he can ever imagine. You'll be ready for him." The man checked his watch—from where I stood, the dial looked to be dead black, lacking hands and numbers. "Shit, I gotta book. Maybe I'll catch you later."

"You come on back now, huh?" I said as he made for the door, trying to cloak my nervousness with a breezy tone.

He jammed his hat onto his head, tugged the brim down to shadow his face. "Oh, yeah! Next time I'm in the mood for a dinosaur picture puzzle, one of those commemorative Arizona State letter openers, you won't be able to keep me away."

I remained standing at the register after he was gone, so confounded by his appearance, the impression of sinister innuendo I'd derived from his comments, I was almost empty of thought and feeling. Stupefied. Therese came out from the back, rubbing her eyes. "I thought I heard voices," she said. "Was someone here?"

"Might be there's two schools of thought on that," I told her.

Chapter 15

The following Tuesday, a spindly, Lincolnesque young man dressed in a suit and white open-collared shirt staked himself out on the curb across from 'Zona Madness and attempted to thrust leaflets indicting *Handbook* upon everyone who passed. When his leaflets were rejected by loyalist Pershingites, he took to shouting toward the shop—oaths and imprecations and Bible verses, I assumed, though when I went outside to listen, they reached my ears, thanks to the traffic noise, as nonsense phrases ("Jackifrax pecalumer!" "Tangu noribatus!"). Eventually the police made an appearance and he exhibited a series of feints and jab steps that gave evidence he had played some ball in his day, leaving the deputies in the dust, darting about in the street, not trying to escape, merely putting distance between himself and his pursuers, pausing to rail at me—intelligibly, now that traffic was blocked— then darting away again, until Scotty Friedkin, the surly, gnomish presence who presided over the nightly melee at Scotty's Cavern, strode up behind him and knocked him sprawling with a sackful of rolled quarters he had acquired at the bank. As the man was being handcuffed and hauled away, he bleated out a single word over and over: "Treat! Treat! Treat!"

This proved to be the first open engagement of the war. From that point forward, Treat came at us like an army of ants. For the better part of the next two months, not a morning passed without either an assault by a group of gospel shouters waving hand-lettered signs, hurling biblical taunts through bullhorns, or Treat himself, Miss Petunia on his arm, giving television interviews, pointing at the shop and daring the demon Stuart to step outside. His soldiers infiltrated the shop and disrupted what little business we had by committing minor acts of vandalism, screaming for Jesus to take a hand. The phone rang constantly. Along about the second week, the television media picked up the story and the Wardlinites, newly organized on both national and regional levels, came en masse to my defense. They erected a tent city on Robert W. Kinkade's Desert Wind property and staged rallies in the streets. Treat's supporters erected their own camp on the same ground, separated from the Wardlinites by a hundred-foot-wide no-man's-land, and held louder rallies. The town filled up with groups of unsmiling men and women who carried Bibles, dressed in their Sunday best, and would cross the street to avoid groups of men and women, equally unsmiling, wearing black and carrying copies of *Handbook,* an edgy confluence that put me in mind of Westerns in which sheep ranchers and cattlemen scoped each other out on the streets of Dodge preparatory to a range war. Local merchants beamed as their cash registers went *ka-ching.* We cowered in our bunker. Sue Billick called, ecstatic about the entire turn of events.

"We're getting tabloid coverage!" she said. "Do you have any idea what that means?" I said I was beginning to have a fair idea and, yeah, the sales figures were great, but all I wanted was for this to go away.

"It's almost to where we might as well close the shop," I told her. "About our only customers are reporters, Wardlinites, and Christian zealots. It's driving Therese up the walls."

"Why don't you close? You don't need the money. Take a vacation . . . or better yet, come to New York. You can mix business with pleasure. Do some promotion work."

"Therese is nervous about things here. We're not going to be traveling for a while."

Sue started to say something, got out half a word, and then clammed up.

"What?" I said.

"I was going to offer a platitude, something about answering when opportunity knocks. But with you, it's like when you don't answer, opportunity just knocks louder. I guess prayerstyle works . . . though you couldn't prove it by me."

"I didn't pray for this."

"You prayed for success, didn't you?"

"A time or two, yeah. But—"

"This is success, Wardlin."

I took a second to ponder. "It's kinda like one of those stories, isn't it? The ones where the devil gives a guy three wishes in exchange for his soul, and the guy thinks he's got a way to use the wishes to back out of the deal, only the devil's too smart for him."

"It's exactly like that," she said.

I was on the cell phone, standing in the rear doorway of our apartment, staring out at the mesas and the emptiness they seemed to memorialize. It looked like a different world, like if I was to step forward onto the dirt, the connection between me and Sue would be cut and I'd turn around and there would be no store, no town, just mesas and cactus and sand.

"Wardlin?"

"Yeah."

"In Chicago, that night when my prayer wasn't answered?"

"Uh-huh."

"Why didn't you show me what I was really praying for?"

"What do you mean?"

"I've seen you do it dozens of times. You take someone's prayer and show them that what they need to pray for is something simpler than the prayer states."

"I'm not sure there was anything simpler you were praying for," I said. "And I was feeling threatened."

Sue's laugh was a *ha*.

"Why's that funny?"

"Mister Ex-con Sensitive Guy. The inherent humor of the image just struck me."

"That's your label."

"Sure, but it's a good label. It sticks."

"We're getting dangerously close to childish here," I said. "I'm rubber, you're glue . . . all that crap."

Sue adopted her business voice. "Let's say you're right and all I wanted to do was fuck you."

"That's what you claimed, wasn't it? When you asked me to write you a prayer?"

"Right. So let's say it's accurate. Let's say I had a clear sense of purpose. In what sense was that threatening? You had physical insecurities? You weren't attracted to me?"

"I was attracted to something. You. The act of infidelity. A little of both, probably. Maybe screwing up was the main attraction. That's always had great appeal."

"So if it wasn't that stopped you, then it was your thing with Therese?"

"It's not something I want to mess up. I might be able to explain, but you don't want to hear about me and Therese."

"Actually I would. Strange as it seems—to me, anyway—I may be envious."

I went a few paces out into the desert. The phone connection held. "Thing about words, I'm coming to realize, they don't mean a hell of a lot. They're great at creating effects, and that's their true meaning, the effects they create. As a form of communication, they pretty much suck."

"You know, I never saw it before." Sue clicked her lighter and exhaled into the receiver, causing a burst of white noise in my ear. "At heart you're a linguistic hippie, aren't you?"

"Whatever. But what I said's true. If I tried to tell you how it is here, I'd be making shit up."

Sue let that statement hang for a few ticks. "Yeah," she said. "And you wouldn't want to tell anyone a story."

"Not today."

"No, not today. Well, the offer's still open." She left a two-beat pause and went on in an amused tone. "New York. Do some pro-motion. Business, pleasure, some nice dinners. Keep it in mind."

"Oh, I will. I don't have much choice in the matter."

"Because you know I'll remind you? Or because I live in your fantasies? Pick one, Wardlin. Don't give me any cosmic answers."

"How come this is such a big deal?"

"It's not," Sue said. Then, angrily: "It is. But it's not."

When I consider the muddle of a mind, the way your life runs past you all the time on a sort of mental crawl, that little talk we're always having with ourselves, the flippy voice-over that captions our every experience, I realize how difficult it is to be true to oneself, let alone anybody else. Your thoughts are a flowing electric curtain between the world and a place you hope exists inside yourself that houses the real you, the unchangeable "I," a mental asteroid belt of momentary desires and fragmented rationality that hinders self-observation. Being aware of this—hyperaware, in my case—made it tough to answer questions, especially questions of the type Sue was asking. If I could have been honest with her, I would have said there were a couple of occasions when I put myself back in that Chicago hotel, indulged in a hot-pink nostalgia, saw images of breasts and lips and pussy that I'd invented to simulate hers. The effect those words would have caused might have been neglible, but they could not have been less neglible than the fantasies were to me. I don't think I could have explained about Therese and me, because I found the relationship postexplicable. It didn't demand explanation. We had our strains, our periods of alienation, but for the most part we succeeded in dis-missing the confusions of thought and were easy with one another. At times that easiness seemed a sacred alignment. A matter of fate. The mechanism of a purpose we had yet to divine. We may have been fools to believe this, but if so, we were alike in our foolishness, and I no longer wasted any effort in trying to debunk or demystify any facet of the union or my convictions concerning it.

I hadn't been lying to Sue about Therese climbing the walls. Though she had once seen 'Zona Madness as a prison, she had come to view it as our center. She wasn't so inflexible that she couldn't have gone on vacation, but I knew she would worry all the while. And yet staying at our posts was fraying her nerves. The best thing I could do, I decided, was to ride out the siege with her. Day by day, however, it broke us down. If it wasn't a camera crew shooting through our windows, it was a cadre of Wardlinites at the door, inviting me to participate in an event they were holding at the field where the Pershing HS Rattlers played their games. CNN, Fox News, MSNBC, and various other news outlets sent satellite trucks and telegenic women with sultry voices, dressy slacks ensembles, and smooth microphone styles. Despite its triviality, or because its triviality suited some national appetite, the story had legs. Our war was a silly item with which the networks could close their evening reports. Leno and Letterman told Monroe Treat jokes—they told jokes about me as well, but Treat had become the National Villain and got more laughs. Tourists flocked to the area. As a result of the media escalation, our business went from zero to too much. The shop was so packed, we had to hire off-duty deputies as security guards. Mornings were tolerable, but the afternoons verged on riot. The aisles were choked with people snapping photographs, offering business cards, yelling, pushing, asking for autographs, for prayers, for miracles, for sexual favors, and loans. Nights, we shut off the phone and pretended life was normal. We believed that if we persevered, this, too, would pass. But whenever the war appeared to be ending, some half-dead movie star or singer would ride into town and declare his faith in the purity of the gospel according to Monroe Treat, and the Wardlinites would then deliver up a brighter celebrity, a Hollywood babbler who would endorse *Handbook* as a work of inspired genius, and the battle would rage again. Now show biz was involved, politicians began to circle, scenting a dead First Amendment issue upon which they could legitimately and safely feast. Pundits debated spirituality, legality, morality, personality, and, ultimately, their own culpability in boosting the ratings of the country's hottest reality show. Our president declared severally that Monroe Treat had not contributed to his campaign, that I was representative of the Great American Spirit of Ingenuity, that he believed in God and, indeed, held frequent converse with the Big Guy. A Wardlinite patrol engaged a Christian contingent in the no-man's-land between their campgrounds, a skirmish of rock-hurling and brawling that resulted in half a dozen arrests and seventeen hospitalizations. Our bunker mentality hardened. We rarely left the shop, ordering in groceries, eschewing meals at the Mesa Bar and Grille. I became convinced that Sue Billick was stirring the pot, tossing a spicy bit in the PR mix however she could. Her calls and e-mails were poorly disguised gloats that said, in essence, One way or another, I'm fucking you. "I understand this must be a nightmare for you and Therese," she wrote once. "But you'll be grateful in the morning."

Therese was planning to attend a trade show in Phoenix at the end of February and, admitting defeat, we seized the opportunity to close the shop and booked a suite at the Adams Hotel under the name of Mr. and Mrs. Clay Callison (this the name of a wholesaler in Tucson who supplied our geodes and other mineral items), the idea being that we could sustain a better quality of life in Phoenix and still be close to Pershing should the need to return arise. We hoped the town would return to normal, absent our presence, and, though the media would surely sniff us out, it would be easier to elude them in the city. We left Pershing in the middle of the night in order to avoid leading an exodus of journalists and Wardlinites— as it was, a van full of print media followed us beyond the city limits, where they were picked off at a roadblock manned by Dave Gillery and a fellow deputy, Bobby Goines, whom we had persuaded to provide this service. That drive across the desert felt as liberating as had our drive south from Walla Walla, because the prison term from which we had escaped, though less a durance vile than a dime for manslaughter bought in the state of Washington, had been harder to bear in some ways—I suppose the freedom it had curtailed was more valuable to me than the freedom I had lost that long-ago night at the Galley.

The first day of the trade show, I split off from Therese and wandered about the crowded convention center, a whitely encaverned hubbub soothed by cool breeze Muzak, booths offering bobblehead dolls, Arizona Barbies, beer mugs and bottle openers bearing laminated sunsets, a trillion bright and useless things, all purveyed by sexy sales models and men with rows of buttons affixed to their lapels. Twice I was recognized, but managed to shake free of my admirers and lose myself among the herds of gift-shop owners, browsers, senior citizens, bored children, and plainclothes security that constituted the body of the crowd. I took special note of a booth that sold little plastic mesas with feet that would hop about when you wound them up—I bought several, charmed by the vision of an actual Hopping Mesa migrating about the Southwest and crushing cities in its path. Done with shopping, I was looking for Therese, hoping I could pull her away from business for some lunch, when my cell phone played its annoying symphony and, thinking it must be her, I answered by saying, "Hey, sweetness."

"Not sweetness," said a man. "It's me. The guy come into your store around Christmas. You thought we'd met before . . . in Nogales. You remember."

"How'd you get this number?" I asked.

"I've got something to show you. Something that'll get Monroe Treat off your ass. Meet me at the concession stand east end of the center."

He broke the connection.

Curiosity overcame paranoia. I threaded my way through the throng to the concession stand. He was leaning against the counter, dressed in his customary Wardlinite drag and drinking a milkshake. White driblets clung to his mustache. He sipped vigorously as I walked up, making the straw gurgle, and tossed the cup into a trash bin. His skin looked darker, not the adobe color I recalled, as if a shadow inside him had grown large and muddied his complexion.

"Let's go," he said.

"Whoa!" I said. "Go where?"

He wiped his mustache clean with the back of his hand. "You think I've got something in my pocket that'll get you clear of Treat?" He jammed his hat down over his eyes. "Maybe I do. But we need to find him first. We'll have to use your car. Mine's in the shop."

"Hang on a second. Who the hell are you?"

"Man whose mind works like yours should know better than to ask that question."

"And just how is it my mind works?"

"Don't you know? You might oughta take a peek at *Handbook*. It's on plain view."

I intended to push him on the issue of his identity, but he cut me off. "I haven't got time for this shit," he said. "There's two ways you can fly. You can decide I'm a deranged fan who's going to spirit you away to a jail he's rigged up where you'll write prayers for him the rest of your life. Something like that. Or you can tell yourself, this guy seems somewhat rational. Maybe I should see what he's got to offer, because right now Treat's making my life hell and I could use an edge." He hitched up his belt—it had a buckle of black onyx. "Pick one."

I stood there, unable to choose.

"How about I give you a name," he said. "Darren. That help?"

"You don't look like a Darren."

"It's my favorite name."

"Yeah, but is it your real name?"

"I could haul out ID with the name Darren on it."

"What would that prove?"

"See what I'm saying?" He gestured toward the crowded aisles, the booths. "Now we got that settled, let's get on up outa here. The temple's starting to feel oppressive."

I constructed a theory about the man as we headed for the exit. I had written a prayer, several prayers, describing the Lord of Lone-liness. Then, coincidentally, I had met a man in Nogales who roughly fit that description. A hustler of some sort. He had read *Handbook*—probably even before meeting me—and had taken note of the description and become sufficiently intrigued to involve himself in my life for a purpose I could only imagine. Perhaps this involvement tapped into some personal mythology, or perhaps he perceived himself to be a secret master, a magus of the streets, and here was his opportunity to practice mastery. It sounded remotely plausible, more plausible than the alternative view, and, given that it did, I wondered what possessed me to accompany him. That I could not detect a trace of enmity in his behavior was not a cause for confidence. My instincts in this regard had never been sure. Nor was I all that desperate to find a remedy for Treat—being away from Pershing had lightened the pressure on Therese and me. Though he had driven us from our home, we remained firm in our belief that time would put an end to the war.

I collected the Suburban from the parking lot and, following the man's directions, drove out into the suburbs, an exclusive area of ranch houses and Spanish colonials with decorative fencing, vast sunstruck lawns green as hope, swimming pools like immense square-cut aquamarines, all set along winding, untrafficked roads. The place had an air of deluxe vacancy—it looked like Robert W. Kinkade's vision of paradise. No people visible, all inside enjoying their AC or having battery-powered sex, whatever it was that floated their boat. The man kept up a line of wry chatter about the trade show—"the temple" as he called it—and at one point fished a plastic mesa from my shopping bag, scrutinizing it the way a miner might examine a chunk of ore for color.

"Outstanding choice," he said. "A true refinement of the inessential. Makes you wonder, though, doesn't it? Like maybe the trinket-o-verse might somehow be reflective of other spheres? Like there could be a dimension out there where hopping mesas menace human society?"

This comment stepped so close to my own whimsy, it pricked up my ears; but I was bored by his exaltation of gift-shop garbage and, not wanting to encourage him, gave no response. Rounding a bend, I saw a ranch house with a number of oddly shaped smaller structures populating the lawn. A miniature golf course. The man instructed me to pull over at a trash collection point beyond the house. The golf course was more ornate than most, the obstacles being large play-through replicas of famous foreign edifices: Taj Mahal, a pyramid, Tower Bridge, Parthenon, and so forth. Nine holes, nine replicas. All glistening as if freshly painted. Parked beside the Taj was a shiny red chopper, its chrome wheels aglint. The man pointed to it and said, "There's your boy."

"Treat?" I said. "That's his bike?"

"He's a Harley man. You pegged his ass on *King*. The guy's a low-rent Elvis imitator. Him and his woman are inside. They usually fuck in the Parthenon. Must be in the mood for a little Kama Sutra."

"Who's the lucky lady?"

"You've seen her. Lucy Reiner. Chunky little item dresses like her grandma. She's worth about a hundred kazillion apples. Less now that Treat's got hold of her."

"She gotta be whack, putting a goddamn miniature golf course in her front yard."

"Rich people, they like big toys, that's all that is. Her daddy was a golf course salesman. Sold courses to the Japanese, the Arabs. All over." He removed a black leather case from his inside jacket pocket. "You imagine wanting to grow up to be a golf course salesman? What sort of ambition is that?"

"Bet her neighbors fucking love it," I said. "These kind of people want their everything smooth. No lumps. No circus tents."

The case turned out to hold opera glasses. The man peered at the Taj through them. He laughed dryly and offered the glasses to me. "Care to watch your boy work?"

"Not hardly."

"Man's got his kink on today." He refitted the glasses to his eyes, regarded the shadowed interior of the Taj for a few seconds more, then patted the steering wheel. "Come on. We got about a half hour to get where we're going."

"Isn't this what you wanted to show me?"

"This is Site A. Now I'm going to show you Site B."

"Darren," I said. "I'm going try calling you Darren, okay? Even though I know it's not your fucking name."

He inclined his head as if I had honored him.

"So what am I supposed to think, Darren? About you checking out Treat? What's your payoff?"

"It's a complex question. Why don't I answer as we drive?"

He directed me to proceed out into the desert and I did so without deliberation, leadfooting the Suburban along a two-lane state road that wound uphill through steep cuts of yellowish rock and then down across an ocean of sage and cactus.

"This thing about payoff," said Darren. "That's not what's happening here. Not in the sense you mean."

"Yeah? What sense is that?"

"The prison sense. My interest is not so pragmatic. You've got yourself a situation and I want to be of assistance. You're someone I think highly of, someone whose work I believe in."

"You know," I said, "I've heard that song. A guy comes along, helps you out with a situation just because . . . hey, he's just that kind of guy, y'know. Next thing, he and a couple of pals catch you in the showers and ask you to do them a little favor."

"Stay with me, okay? Listen." He turned up the AC a notch. "I get no satisfaction from good works. I'm not trying to say I do. For me, this is all about an aesthetic. About history. The rise of a new American church. I desire to be part of it."

"Uh-huh. Right."

Darren made a frustrated noise. "Thing you don't seem to get, prayerstyle's not a shuck. You've never been able to accept that. You dip in and out of belief. That ambivalence is worked all through *Handbook.* It's part of why you're a success. People have grown tired of evangels who claim they've got all the answers. They're not searching for another man of faith, they're searching for a man of doubt. A man who'll tell them this *might* work, this *might* be the way. Somebody who offers everything the ol'-time religion offers. The prospect of salvation on every level, material to the spritual. A preacher who's sinned and gotten past it. A new text, a fresh gospel. They like all of that. But what really seals the deal is you give them a disclaimer. You're saying 'I don't know. Maybe. Could be.' That tells them you're honest and they fall to the faith more easily. You've tapped into the mother lode of American skepticism. You've come up with a scam that doubts itself in public. You've roped in doubters of every age, race, and denomination and made them believers by marketing holy cynicism. And here's the beauty part—your product works. You're living proof of your theory. Your own man-in-the-street commercial. That makes you my fucking hero."

What he said may or may not have been an answer to my question, but it blurred my focus—his affectless delivery seemed to run counter to the explicit flattery, to countenance what I had done as something less than the sum of his statement, reducing words like *hero* and *genius* to clinical distillates, giving the impression that he considered my accomplishment inadvertent, a small thing, the heroic genius of an ant who wanders from the nest and brings back a new and glorious food stuck to its feet. My suspicions satisfied on some level, I asked how Treat's affair with Lucy Reiner, a woman with whom he was occasionally seen in public, would help resolve my problems. He put me off, saying that I'd understand once we reached Site B, and fell silent, staring out the window at the sand. Once in a while I glanced over at him, not so as to encourage conversation or see how he was doing, but to make certain he was there. Though the mere sight of him had caused me unease in the past— if, indeed, he was the same man I'd encountered in the desert behind 'Zona Madness, at Jenny's Place, and elsewhere—now, close to him, I realized that he had less presence than anyone I'd ever met. Not an ounce of gravitas, no fume of energy. Vibe-impaired. A human-shaped sack of emptiness. I had the idea that whenever I turned my eyes away he thinned into a mist, that the pressure of my gaze was holding him together. Thinking about him in that way reinvigorated my suspicions that he must be a psycho, a stalker, or something darker and more improbable. I saw myself slowing for a curve, doing a shoulder roll out the driver's side door, scrambling up to watch the Suburban passing through a circular gateway of flames that had materialized above the road.

Just short of twenty miles into the desert, a dirt track angled off to the left. Obeying Darren's instructions, I followed the track and parked a quarter mile in. We walked another hundred yards to the crest of a brush-covered promontory that overlooked a stretch of tawny sand dominated by a pinkish flat rock shaped like one of those couches you see in the orgy scenes of movies about decadent Rome. The rock appeared to be fifteen or twenty feet long. From where we stood, we were able to look almost straight down on it— like the view from the top of a three-story building.

"So?" I said.

"He'll be along."

"How do you know?"

"It's his routine. He fucks Miss Lucy, then he rides out here and does his thing." Darren lit a cigarette and exhaled with gusto. "Grab yourself some ground. You don't want to be standing where he can see you."

We sat facing each other on a rocky patch close to the crest. There wasn't a breath of wind; the sky was cloudless. It was as if the universe had been edited down to that patch of rock, an expanse of blue, a scatter of dusty shrubs, and the two of us were spirits who'd been isolated in a private piece of the afterlife and were about to have a palaver. I flicked crumbs of stone aside with my forefinger and studied the grain of the rock. Darren smoked. Finally he said, "Don't you have any more questions?"

"Questions? Oh, yeah. Tons," I said. "Like who was the twisted motherfucker came up with the idea for credit cards?"

"A New York accountant who didn't get credit for it."

"Those new twenty-dollar bills with the yellow in them . . . are they ugly or what?"

"Seriously ugly."

"All right. Ben Affleck and Jennifer Lopez. They break up, they get a gun license together, they show up at a Red Sox game, they break up again. What's the deal? Did we almost witness the first celebrity crime spree?"

"Two truly dumbass individuals were gaming each other. No, it wouldn't be the first." He gave an annoyed sniff. "What I meant was, did you want to ask questions about the Lord of Loneliness."

A chill swallowed me up. Like on *Star Trek,* when the captain beams down and his body is gradually transformed into glittering particles—that's how that chill took me over. I didn't want to look at him, but I did. He offered a cigarette. I accepted and married the end of it to his smoke and sucked until the tobacco caught.

"You must have noticed the resemblance by now," he said, and made a show of displaying his profile.

"You mostly resemble a Wardlinite."

"But you know I'm not a Wardlinite."

"Suppose you tell me who you want me to think you are."

"It's not important—I thought it might be an interesting topic for discussion." He flicked his cigarette over the edge of the cliff. "Nothing can be proved, anyway. We've already established that."

"You're fucking with me again," I said.

"Well, you do pose a temptation."

"You see me as a hick, do you? A chump?"

"You are a hick. A famous hick, but a hick no less. But that's not important, either."

I sat and smoked for a few ticks. "Who do *you* think you are?"

"You know the bit in the Bible about God making man in his image? Most people take that to mean God resembles a hominid with opposable thumbs, but what it mainly means is our minds are made in the image of God's. He may hear every sparrow fart and be familiar with our deepest thoughts, but he doesn't have a clue about his own nature. Just like you and me."

"That's cute," I said. "Extremely deft. But I'm not buying it."

"Buying what?"

"That you're the Lord of Loneliness."

"Well . . ." The man tapped out another cigarette. "At least you managed to express it in the negative."

"Here's a news flash, Darren. You're not the lord of fucking anything."

He lit the cigarette and his smoke was snapped up by a puff of wind that came out of nowhere. "Not even of this moment? That's weird, because I feel very much in control."

I was torn between the urge to flee and the desire to assault him—as a result, I did nothing.

"You have to be drunk to believe in shit," he said. "Like with love. You're not drunk on it, you can't believe in it."

I chose not to respond. I would get through this, I told myself, whatever it turned out to be. Then I'd go home and climb back into the world where Therese and I lived together. The patch of rock on which we sat was cut by dozens of parallel grooves, as if something with tiny runners had been dragged across the surface while it was hardening. As I stared at them, the grooves deepened into mighty canyons wherein a submicroscopic army wandered, starving and lost and invisible to everyone but me. For a time I lived their tragic story. When I glanced up I saw that the air had acquired a pellucid luster. We might have been encased in crystal, a snow globe with an arid blue sky and sand instead of snow. The sun a blazing cubic zirconium hidden by glare. A digital vulture soaring overhead. My thoughts scampered this way and that, like rabbits newly freed from a hutch, not knowing which way to go or why, unsure of this wider wilderness. Each of the nearby shrubs enclosed a host of scurryings and munchings I hadn't previously noticed. How would a spider's breath sound, I asked myself, if it were fifty times bigger than you? And imagined I heard a rapidly recurring, whistly noise. I studied my half-smoked cigarette, realizing that I felt happier and more relaxed than I should have.

"What am I smoking here?" I asked.

"Magic cigarette. Little designer something I whipped up. I call it"—he performed an Arabic gesture, the equivalent of a trumpet fanfare—"the Perfect High. TPH."

It crossed my mind to toss the cigarette away, but I didn't feel it was worth the effort.

"I was going to call it My Essence, but that sounded too much like a perfume," Darren said. "I thought you could use a perspective on what's about to happen."

"What's that?" I said, finding it difficult to speak.

"The heart of your enemy will be revealed."

I wondered if he smoked this brand of cigarettes all the time. That would explain a lot.

"You're probably feeling sluggish," he said. "Don't get tense. It's just the rush. You'll perk up."

I barely heard him; I was appreciating the heat, how it warmed me from the inside out, as if I were being microwaved. "How long we been here?" I asked.

"Not long in terms of time, but relationshipwise . . . we're a ways toward becoming history."

I understood this, then did not understand it. A more crucial question occupied me. "If you're the Lord of Loneliness . . ." I said. "I mean if you're really him, let's see you prove it."

"This is good. This is very good. We're doing Bible stories. Who was it asked Jesus to perform a miracle as proof? What did he say? You recall?"

"The devil, I think. And Jesus said for him to fuck off."

"Yeah, yeah. I remember now. But more to the point, what would I say when offered such a challenge?"

I tried to work that problem out in my head, coming up with several possibilities, but Darren interrupted the process by saying, "I guess I've already said it. You can't rewrite history. Shit! I could have done something more eloquent than 'This is good. We're doing Bible stories.' I could have said, um . . . How you feeling, man?"

"Hell, I can come up with something better than that!" I said. "How about this? 'Proof? What do you want? A sunflower to sprout from my ass? I'm not that kinda guy.'"

His smile broadened, worked into a chuckle. "No, man. I was asking how you were feeling for real."

"Oh." I tested the force of my well-being. "Not bad."

"Troubles pushed aside? You're centered in the moment?"

"Yeah . . . matter of fact." I had another toke off the magic cigarette. "I like your suggestion, the sunflower thing. Wish I'd thought of it."

"What can I tell you? It's a gift."

A distant chain-saw sound gnawed at the silence.

"That'd be the subject approaching on his Harley," the man said. "Best get down on your belly so you can look over the edge at him."

You could just see the highway from the promontory crest, a strip of mottled gray like a stretched rattlesnake hide. Coming toward us, Treat's motorcycle laid a curving track across the sand, his rear wheel spitting up a dusty wake. The grind of his engine evolved into an explosive disruption. He pulled up by the flat rock, gunned the engine twice, switched it off, dismounted, shook out a kink in his leg, and started unbuttoning his shirt. He draped the shirt on the edge of the rock, stood scanning the desert, the sky. The vulture was still circling. He ran his hands through his hair and rolled his shoulders, loosened his neck. Then he unbuckled his belt and skinned down his jeans. He was wearing lime-green bikini underwear.

"What the fuck's he doing!" I asked under my breath,

Darren put a finger to his lips and signaled that I should keep watching. Treat boosted himself up onto the rock and took a stand at the lowest end, facing off into the desert. After a second he lifted his arms above his shoulders in the manner of a priest supplicating his god. Whether he was addressing his invocation to the sky or the vulture—which had dropped lower—or a figment of his imagination, it was impossible to say. He held the pose for a good thirty seconds, then stripped off his underwear and lay down, his head pillowed by a bulge at the high end of the rock. He fumbled with his crotch and began to masturbate. The stillness of the desert was such, I could hear him faintly and profanely urging on an imaginary lover.

Before my revulsion kicked in fully, revulsion directed both toward him and my voyeuristic posture, there came a moment when it seemed I was actually looking down into his heart and understood what I saw to be no ordinary wanking but a perverse form of worship. I'd been wrong about him, I thought. He was, after all, a man of faith. Eccentric though it might be, the arc of his daily rounds— the dalliance with Miss Lucy, the trek into the desert for a spot of self-abuse—was marked by the obsessiveness of religious practice. I imagined the god to whom he devoted this peculiar service to be a black vinyl creature living in a cavern underneath Las Vegas, a glamorous, neon-eyed, showbiz version of evil incarnate whose exhalations were a mingling of gasoline fumes and Elizabeth Taylor's White Diamonds, and who had sent its familiar, the vulture, to receive this bizarre tribute. My greatest misapprehension concerning Treat, I recognized, related to the depth of his insanity. His greed and amorality masked a more disturbing corruption. It stood to reason that I had underestimated the danger he presented. I had underestimated him in every other way.

I inched away from the crest. Darren caught my arm, but I shook him off and scooted on my butt toward the patch of rock where we had waited. There I renewed my acquaintance with the grooved lines in the stone, the canyons and the lost army. Birds flew low above their heads, speaking in the voices of their women, goading them with piteous cries that told of rape and mutilation. Their child-general, he of the pupil-less yellow eyes, had been misled by visions sent from an unknown source within Bazar-Anglot, the city they had razed, and their sole hope was that his steed, the witch Samari, entrapped in the body of a white mare, would break free of a binding spell and restore his sight. I should, I thought, seed their story with prayerstyle propaganda, make it a parable for kids of all ages, type it up and send it to Sue Billick.

Darren joined me and offered another cigarette. "I'm still wrecked," I said.

"You can't OD on this stuff. You smoke more, it just tunes you up. That's one reason I call it . . ."

He waited.

"The Perfect High," I said without enthusiasm. "What's Treat doing?"

"Having a little pillow talk with himself. He hangs out for twenty minutes or so after he's done. However long it takes for the stuff to dry on his belly."

"Christ!" I plucked out one of Darren's cigarettes and lit up.

"You get what I'm saying about Treat? He's not your typical Jesus lizard. He's working off some sick shit. He won't quit coming at you."

"Maybe."

"No maybe about it. You think because you and Therese left Pershing, he'll find something else to do? Not gonna happen."

"Let's say you're right," I said. "What's driving his weirdness?"

"Childhood trauma, I expect."

"No, I mean what's he fucking doing? This isn't Christianity at work."

"It's prayerstyle."

That set me back on my heels. "Yeah, sure."

"I'm telling you true. You don't think he read your book? Why's he so set against you? Ever ask yourself that? He's jealous. You came up with the divine weapon he's been hunting his whole life."

"You told me before it was because he needed to keep his people in line. His congregation."

"That's some of it. The rest is, he can't be the creator of prayerstyle. He's been denied that claim to fame and it torments him, because it's such a sweet hustle. Why couldn't he have come up with it? That's what he's asking himself. It fucks him up, you beat him to it. So he's devoted himself to becoming a master of the art. The motherfucker's writing prayers day and night. What he does with Miz Lucy, what he does out here? That's just him dressing up prayerstyle to suit his needs. Giving it trappings. Frills and feathers."

"That's crap! You don't know what's going on with him."

"Yeah I do. It's my place to know." He sat up straight. "You ever consider that when you came up with prayerstyle, it was similar to the guy who came up with the idea of harnessing the atom for power?"

"No. I never considered that, because it would be stupid."

"That guy didn't see the downside. He couldn't imagine using atomic power for evil purposes. He never figured on North Korea. That's who Treat is. He's your North Korea."

"You're nuts," I said. "Fucking insane."

"You bet I am. So are you. The entire human race is out of its fucking tree. Prayerstyle itself is an act of insanity. That it seems to work is insane. Its primary appeal is to the insane." He reached out and gave my head a soft hit with the flat of his hand, as if to jog my brain back on track. "Ever wonder who else has tapped into prayerstyle? It's not such a complicated theory—other people must have thought of it. Could be they practiced it without realizing it. And that could be why the world's so fucked up. Because of prayer. Doesn't it seem like everything's being run by someone who's gone spectacularly insane? What if the certifiably insane are in charge? What if the world's character reflects their character? Prayerstyle's obviously an idea someone locked away is liable to stumble across. It's a natural fantasy for the powerless, that they can change the world by means of words. So it's possible, maybe even likely, that thousands of schizos, all drooly from their meds, are praying chaos into being. They're offering up mumbling, demented prayers twenty-four seven that each create minute changes and in sum produce famine and terror. Unending slaughter. They're your forerunners, dude. And you're the prophet foretold. The one who puts it in a package and sells it on the cheap. Christ or AntiChrist, now . . . the jury's still out on that."

I felt disoriented. It wasn't that I bought into his bullshit, but that what he said seemed evidence of a mental infestation that had poisoned everything, even the mind of God, in whose image our own minds were cast.

"I'm betting you're Christ," he said. "It would suit my theory of reductionism. Remember? We talked about it in your shop?"

I said, "Yeah."

"You know how the incarnations of Buddha are supposed to manifest various aspects of the Buddha nature? I think it's the same with Jesus. The original was the Lamb of God. You . . . you're Celebrity Jesus. Trinket Jesus. Check it out. If Jesus came back right now, what would we get? Jesus in concert. Jesus preaching on Pay Per View. Ten trillion Second Coming Web sites. Jesus awarded a star on the Hollywood Walk of Fame. Another Mel Gibson movie, maybe a documentary. Personalized Jesus items on eBay. Jesus on *Larry King* and *Oprah*." He dropped into interviewer mode. " 'So tell me, what was it like growing up by the Sea of Galilee? As a Jew, how do you feel about Israel? Are you dating?' Books, too. A shitload of books. Jesus Christ's Fasting Secrets for the slim, trim Christian in you. *Savior!* The truth about Gethsemane. Pontius Pilate: mensch or supervillain? What really went down with Mary Magdalene? It'd be damn near the same as what you've been experiencing. And if that's how things are, if I'm right, this alley fight between you and Treat might just be the ultimate showdown. Diminished incarnations of good and evil going to the mat while the world looks on as if it's an entertainment and not destiny playing out. Fits in perfectly with the way news has become entertainment." He snapped his fingers by his ear, like a gambler putting a lucky charge on his dice. "I'm feeling this, man! Seriously. It's got a ring. Plus it fits another theory of mine. See, I figure Jesus doesn't just drop in on the planet every two or three millennia. He's coming back all the time, but not many people notice, because we're not looking for him to slip in without the last trump sounding. We're waiting for the big finish, the final incarnation. All the interim incarnations more or less fly beneath the radar. They cause a ripple, get a little media exposure, and then sink back into the stream. They're probably unaware they're Jesus. It's not necessary for them to wake to their Jesus natures. They're here to perform some minor Jesus function—like putting a bug up the ass of organized religion, tossing a few money changers out of the temple. They don't rate being scourged and killed . . . or if they do, they get beat up in an alley, maybe shot by some asshole. It might not even make the front page."

Contrary to what Darren had told me, a couple of hits off the second magic cigarette had an extreme effect. Every element of his features grew ultrareal, so sharply defined that the rest of the world looked false, like one of those painted carnival façades behind which you stand and have a funny photograph taken of your head superimposed above a cartoon weight lifter's body. He reached inside his jacket and produced an automatic pistol with a flat black finish and held it out to me.

"Now's your chance," he said. "You can get rid of that nasty North Korean problem."

I laughed. "Opera glasses, a piece . . . What else you got in that jacket? A petting zoo?"

"It's an easy shot. A fucking snap. Thirty feet maybe. This little kitten doesn't have any kick. Like firing a BB pistol."

"You can't be serious!"

"Do I look like I'm joking?"

"I'm not shooting anybody."

"You'll save yourself a lot of grief, man. Right now it's just you and Treat. Baby Jesus and the Devil. You don't take care of him now, meaner sharks than Treat are gonna come snooting around."

"What's meaner than the Devil?"

"Someone hails from a colder place. The Devil's a creature of heat. That causes him to make passionate errors. There's them out there who could take the Devil for a stroll and come back gnawing on his shinbone. Same goes for the Baby Jesus . . . especially if we're talking Trinket Jesus. Problem for avatars is, they attract a special class of predators."

I had a moment during which I knew he was right, that Treat was the kind of trouble needed killing. "And I'm sure you wouldn't tell anyone. You won't use it against me."

"I wouldn't make a good witness." He gave the gun a waggle. "Going once."

"Even if wanted to kill him, I don't have the stones. Not in cold blood."

"Oh, you want to kill him. Just think back to when you did Kirschner. You didn't intend to kill him. It was a drunken impulse. That's what you tell yourself. But when you swung that bottle, I bet a little extra juice went flowing along your arm. Some part of you loved killing his ass. You might want to let that part out for exercise about now." He waggled the gun again. "Going twice."

The moment when I might have taken the gun had passed, the body of the urge pushed aside by memories of prison, the dregs of it rinsed down the drain by moral justifications. "Put that thing away."

"You know, I think a great deal of our problem has to do with my manner. It causes you to distrust me. You feel I'm playing you. What's really going on, I'm playing myself. It's how I stay interested in things. I suppose I could stand to retool the ol' personality. Stop being such a smart-ass. Let me assure you, though. My involvement with you is far from whimsical. I want this for you, man. Doing Treat will open you to whole new levels."

I shook my head. "Put it fucking away."

He shook his head dolefully and then said, "You ever write a prayer to get rid of Treat?"

"Couple of times, yeah."

"Didn't work, did they? You know why? Because Treat's down there right now praying for some evil to get rid of you. Two of you are deadlocked, like wizards with opposing spells."

"I'm not hearing this."

"The world is full of magic, man. Magic cigarettes. Magical circumstances. Sympathetic magic. The pagans had it right. We tend to overlook their contribution. What this is"—he jiggled the gun in his palm—"it's another magical form. An answered prayer that makes people disappear."

"No sale," I told him.

"Gone." He set the gun down. "I'll catch you later."

I was uncertain of his meaning.

"Get outa here," he said.

"Don't you need a ride?"

"I'll find one."

Hesitantly, I came to a knee, then stood. "What're you going to do?"

"Get the fuck gone, will you? I gave you a warning, and if you won't listen, the hell with you."

I looked toward the edge of the cliff. I couldn't see Treat on his bed of stone, but I saw the track his motorcycle had carved in the tawny sand, curving out toward the highway, like the shape an immense talon might have made as it was swiped across the desert.

"Everything that's happened today has been what you might call a teaching tool," Darren said. "A little lesson in reality. But I can tell you're not going to learn it until it bites you in the ass."

Chapter 16

Leaving Darren alone on the promontory was my second murderous act. Though I later pulled back from this self-judgment, I was at the time almost certain that he had stayed behind to do what I would not; thus my abandonment of the scene constituted tacit approval of a homicide. As I drove, I half expected him to pass me from the rear, riding a red Harley. My head was atingle with his bullshit. It was seductive bullshit, very much in accord with my own brand, with my "magical view of opportunism" (this the phrase used by a London *Times* critic in addressing the essential content of *Handbook*), but I was unable to dismiss it as such. The demented idea that I might be an unawakened avatar tugged at my mental sleeve, begging to be acknowledged, and when I did acknowledge it, it demanded to be embraced, tempting me to perceive myself as a man whose message had touched the souls of millions, whose wise counsel changed lives. This being the case, I wondered, was it so ludicrous to imagine that my actions had been guided by a strand of divine will? Most of my brain cells jumped up and down, screaming, "Yes, you asshole!", but they were outvoiced by a choir of gospel shouters chanting, "We believe! We believe!", and during the weeks that followed, now and again I would sink to partial belief, accepting the possibility, at least, that I might be a crucial element in the Universal Plan. Cynicism undermined belief, sparing me a complete immersion in the irrational, but even at my most cynical, the idea would creep in and I would begin to speculate with unhealthy fixity on the topic of my essence.

I scanned the paper the next morning for news of Treat's death, but found no mention. Later that day I switched on the TV and there he was, giving a live press conference from Pershing, asking his parishioners to forgive the DA who was promising to indict him for fraud, counseling them that instead of reviling the man, they should pray that the demon possessing him be cast out. Relief contended in me with disappointment. Disappointment gave way to conjecture. How had the man, Darren (the name had never worked for me), gotten back to Phoenix? Hitchhiked? Stepped into a wormhole? On the back of Treat's bike? This last possibility had special appeal. It had been a trap, I conjectured. The gun full of blanks. Blue uniforms hiding in the brush, waiting to violate my parole the instant I accepted the gun. Logic told me that there were problems with this scenario, but it suited my mood and it took me almost a week—a week free from contact with either Treat or Darren—before I stopped expecting to hear that telltale police knock on my door.

Not a day passed without news of Treat. Fresh indictments loomed. Forlorn men and women were thrust forward to testify for the cameras how their childlike faith had been violated by the reverend's duplicity, how they had been dispossessed of money, virtue, and good sense while under his spell. In the face of these accusations, Treat's claims about me grew increasingly strident. I was an instrument wrought by the Lord of the Pit to lead the mighty force aligned against him, an evil axis of lawyers, drug dealers, and satanic dupes. Demons were whispering in the ears of sleeping congressmen, influencing them to adopt anti-Treat stances, and more insidious demons were seducing the souls of his followers with false promises of redemption. Television reports documented grim patrols of Christians and Wardlinites confronting one another in the streets of Pershing. The local merchants no longer beamed. When interviewed, they expressed a chary ambivalence whenever my name came up; none would speak directly against me, but it was obvious they'd had enough of a good thing. Even our staunchest ally, Nancy Belliveau, was less than wholeheartedly supportive.

"I love Therese and Wardlin, but Lord, there's times I wish he never published that book," she said. "Pershing used to be a nice, quiet little town. Not too prosperous, maybe. But now we got prosperous, I come to appreciate the value of quiet."

This statement, given to a journalist from Fox News, angered Therese. I reminded her it was a sound bite taken out of context, but she felt betrayed.

"Nancy knew what she was doing," she said. "She's no fool. She knew we'd see it."

"She didn't say anything that bad," I told her.

"Yes she did. You're just not hearing it."

Thereafter she began to talk about traveling. I doubted she was serious. She was tied to Pershing in ways I didn't understand and leaving was merely something she liked to talk about, a game she enjoyed. I played along, hoping she might be trying to break free. Sue Billick was in process of arranging a foreign tour and I had received permission to leave the country. I wasn't yearning to meet the European, Far Eastern, and Australian chapters of my fan club, but a tour would place us beyond range of Treat and so I pushed the idea. I went so far as to secure passports for us both.

The Adams became our home. Security kept journalists and Wardlinites away. The front desk screened our calls. We felt insulated and not imprisoned. We slept in, ordered room service, watched Spectravision. We had time to talk, the kind of time we hadn't had since shortly after my parole. Mainly we talked about leaving. There was, as I've suggested, a lot of "let's pretend" in our conversations. Let's pretend we're going to go to Mongolia, to Egypt, the Turkish Riviera. Whenever I got serious, she would put me off or switch subjects. One night about a month after we had checked in, as I lay on the sofa and Therese sat cross-legged on the floor beside me, sifting through travel brochures, we discussed where we would like to wind up, if not in Pershing. Pittsburgh was her choice.

"When you come into town from the I279, you go through a tunnel and onto a bridge," she said. "It looks like Oz."

"Pittsburgh looks like Oz? It's green? Big emerald palace . . . all that?"

"You haven't seen it, so don't make fun."

"Yeah, but Oz . . . Come on! We're talking about Pittsburgh here. What did Carl Sandburg say? City of big slag heaps?"

"I'm not the only one who says it looks like that," she said with utmost seriousness. "It's a widely held opinion."

"They do some heavy drinking in Pittsburgh, don't they?"

She spread open a brochure, studied a picture of Balinese temples. "You have to see it before you judge. The first time I saw it, I was floored. Michigan had offered me a big scholarship, but they were out of the running after I saw Pittsburgh."

"You think maybe you had a taste of London, Paris, Rome, places like that, you might—"

"No."

"Okay, it looks like Oz. Is that it? That's the attraction? I know you had fun there when you went to school—that doesn't mean you'd have fun there now."

"You don't think we could have fun in Pittsburgh?"

"You don't think we could have fun in Rome?"

"Not as much as in Pittsburgh."

"Why?"

"Because I'd have more fun in Pittsburgh, and if I have more fun, by extension, so will you."

"Explain what I'm going to be doing to have so much fun."

"Just being in Pittsburgh."

"In other words, just standing around inhaling the Pittsburgh mixture is more fun than, like, going to Roman nightclubs and art galleries, the Colosseum, the Trevi Fountain. . . ."

"All that is is sightseeing. Pittsburgh's got sights."

"Like for instance?"

"The Cathedral of Learning."

"I thought that was in ancient Alexandria or somewhere."

"Nope. Pittsburgh."

"So at the Cathedral of Learning, what I'm getting, they must brainwash you about believing Pittsburgh's Oz."

"I can't rule it out. But if that's so, then it works."

"For real," I said. "Pittsburgh's where you'd want to go?"

"What do you think?"

"I guess anywhere's good with me, except for where I've been. I don't have a Pittsburgh in my past." I reached out and rubbed her shoulder. "When you went out to San Francisco, how come you didn't go to Pittsburgh instead?"

The phone rang; Therese wrinkled her nose. "Shit."

"Leave it," I said.

She let the ring sound two more times, then jumped up and went for the phone, which rested on a table by the bedroom door. "Hello," she said, and then, "Hi, Dave." She listened for a while, responding now and again with a hushed "Yeah" or "Okay." After hanging up, she stood a couple of seconds with her hand touching the receiver. "That was Dave Gillery," she said in a colorless voice. "Somebody firebombed the shop."

I sat up. "What?"

"I need to get back home." In her face was a blankness that I'd come to recognize as a prelude to tears; she fussed distractedly with her hair. "Can you drive? I don't want to drive."

I stepped up behind her, put my hands on her shoulders. I'd been too startled by the news to absorb it, but touching her seemed to infect me with her portion of shock. "They catch who did it?" I asked.

"They arrested some guy," she said. "But he claims it wasn't him started the fire, it was the Lord God of Hosts."

I can see now that much of my life has been an angry gesture and yet I've never thought of myself as being a particularly angry man. I suppose I've been able to disguise anger, at least to my own eyes, but it's clear that the decade I spent in prison and the period thereafter when I achieved fame and fortune comprised a single violent act that mimicked the arc of the blow with which I struck down Mario Kirschner—those years were, in effect, a slow-motion version of that blow, delivered with the same offhandedness, the same apparent lack of guile, the same insolent dismissal of any right or principle other than my own. I came to believe that everything I felt during that time—ambition, desperation, hope, self-pity, lust, fear—was an articulation of that sweep of bone and muscle toward its inevitable conclusion, and that if I could relive the moment when I murdered Kirschner, if I could experience the act nanosecond by nanosecond, I would learn that I had passed through flashes that expressed each of these emotions and more. I suspect that for a brief instant I must have loved Kirschner, loved his suitability as a victim, loved the fact that he was a person I prized so little, I could hurt him without a qualm. I have considered what this says about my feelings for Therese, but I can't, spiritually speaking, afford to speculate on the matter. Nor do I speculate on the origins of my anger. I am satisfied to think of it as a relic of childhood or a color that's been attached to my soul throughout my various rebirths. Understanding it more completely would profit no one. It's enough to understand that I am, like the majority of my kind, a relatively untalented killer who spends his days trying to hide from his true nature, often doing so by persuading himself that he is embarked upon good works or a voyage of self-discovery.

Eventually I used the anger I felt on seeing the ruin of the gift shop to justify another murderous exercise, but my initial response was spontaneous, untainted by any agenda. The apartment had suffered only minor smoke damage, but the shop was gutted, the aisles awash with black water and garbage, walls and ceiling charred, roof beams exposed. Under the glare of the television lights arrayed outside, looking into the place was somehow unseemly, like looking into a ghastly wound. A few display cases were partially intact, but the glass was shattered and the contents beyond salvage. Upon the remaining shelves were melted figurines, fused-together earrings and key chains, scorched mineral specimens, warped joke license plates, unidentifiable globs of plastic—exhibits in a museum of damage. The postcard racks were twisted wire trees. Therese and I mutely prowled the aisles, poking at the debris, inhaling smoke and chemical retardants, while deputies kept journalists, the curious, and Christians and Wardlinites at bay. We heard reporters taping their reports, probably the third or fourth that day for each, bursts of contention between Treat's fans and my own, and peremptory shouts from the police. Yet it seemed quiet where we were. The plips and plops of water dripping from the shelves and ceiling had a more pronounced value than did any of the sounds from outside. Therese was stunned, incapable of talking about what we might do, but my connection to the shop was not so strong as hers, and I was already thinking how the disaster would change our lives.

We'd been sloshing around for fifteen minutes or so when a Wardlinite knocked on the doorframe and entered: a slight fiftyish man with neatly trimmed gray hair and mustache, wire-rimmed glasses, and a tanned face that brought to mind the faces of regional anchormen: handsome, but not sufficiently striking to warrant a network gig. He had overall a fussy authoritarian air, presenting in his black clothing the appearance of a Nazi optometrist or a junior high school principal whose hobby was adjudicating witch trials. He carried a black laptop case embossed with the silver initials *GB*. Speaking with a clipped precision that I assumed to be an affectation, he introduced himself as Galen Brauer, president of the Wardlinites' L.A. chapter. I told him to get out.

"That's the kind of reaction demonstrates why your shop was firebombed," Brauer said. "You've rejected us. You've failed to use us as a resource. We could have protected you."

"How'd you get past the cops?"

"You have friends everywhere, Mr. Stuart. Not all of them wear *black* uniforms."

The smug implication of that comment, floating the idea that he had inside information to which I wasn't privy, covert influence with the Pershing police force—it pissed me off, and it also caused me to imagine clandestine Wardlinite cells, prayerstyle terrorists, cult-programmed policemen with paperback copies of *Handbook* in their pockets, a great cabal enjoined in my cause. "That mean you slipped Barney Fife a fifty?" I asked. "You sleeping with one of the deputies?"

Brauer stepped toward me along the aisle. "You've called an army to your side, yet you refuse to engage the enemy. That has to change."

From an adjacent aisle, Therese said, "Can't this wait?"

"Here's where waiting has brought us, ma'am," said Brauer, directing her attention to the ruin with an orator's sweeping gesture. "Considering the result, do you truly think more waiting is what we need?"

He was salesman smooth in his use of the inclusive *us* and *we,* and he didn't give off a zealot's radiation as did the typical Wardlinite. He had a con man's glib self-possession and I suspected that was precisely what he was. And there was a distance in him that most might have seen as flat affect, but that I connected with the way cons seem to shrink back inside their skins when they're sizing you up. His presence sparked a professional curiosity in me. I wanted to watch him work.

"Treat wouldn't be a problem if you hadn't let him become one," Brauer said to me. "Unless you deal with him in an organized manner, you're inviting worse problems."

"And you're going to help us," said Therese.

"I have some suggestions you may want to consider."

"You think I'm blind to what you're trying to do?" I asked.

"I hope not. . . . because what I'm trying to do is persuade you to notice what's going on around you. You're successful enough now, you're bound to attract fish with bigger teeth than Treat's."

"Present company excepted, of course."

Brauer smiled as if to acknowledge a hit. "It's time you started getting aggressive and not just reacting to threats. That's all I'm telling you."

"I've seen this dance step before," I said. "You offer yourself up as advisor, counsel . . . whatever. If I say yeah, then you're in close. You'll know my weaknesses, every mistake I make. If I say no, you'll undermine my authority with the Wardlinites. You'll try to make me irrelevant. You either worm your way in or you co-opt. It's a pretty crude power play."

"When a business grows so large people start to depend on it—lots of people—it's incumbent upon them to take matters into their own hands if the CEO fails to protect their interests."

"You're showing us your teeth now," Therese said. "You're threatening us."

"I can't stop you from characterizing it that way, but I'm simply stating a business reality. Wardlin Stuart's becoming a brand name. You have agents, publicists, lawyers, what have you. They take care of the money. But this . . ." He waved at the torched ceiling. "They're not equipped. You can file all the paper you want against Treat. The man doesn't give a damn how many times you sue him."

Therese came around from the other aisle and stood at my shoulder. "I don't understand what else you think he can do to us."

"Burning you out doesn't convince you he's dangerous?"

"The key question isn't what Treat intends to do to us," I said to Therese. "It's what Mr. Brauer intends to do to Treat. Want to fill us in on that, man?"

"Let's just say that I know how to keep Treat occupied."

I took Therese's hand. "You see, that's the other danger here. Mr. Brauer is liable to involve us in criminal activities without our knowledge. Activities for which we nonetheless might be held repsonsible."

"Every caveat you raise is legitimate," Brauer said. "But if you're not going to handle the problem yourself, you'll have to trust someone who will. It might as well be someone who believes in you."

"You're a believer, are you?"

"This . . ." Brauer plucked disdainfully at his jacket. "I'm not so much into the trappings. That's just to get me in a few doors. But I'm a devout believer in prayerstyle. I wouldn't be where I am today without it. As a matter of fact, I wrote a prayer about this meeting tonight."

"Did you now? How's that going for you?"

"So far so good, but I'm still working it." With a forefinger, he prodded a melted lump of metal resting on a shelf—part of what had once been a display of piggy banks—and said, "I've been concerned I might have prayed for too much. But circumstances dictated I take the chance."

"Because of the fire? You figured we'd be vulnerable."

"I hoped the fire might make you more prone to listen, but no, that . . . that wasn't what spurred me to act."

"I can't . . ." Therese pulled her hand free and folded her arms; she was starting to tear up. "I'm going in back. When you're done, let me know."

"I'm done now," I said.

"No!" She looked at the floor. "No, you sort this out. I'm . . . I have things I need to do."

Watching her hurry along the corridor into the apartment, I knew she was angry at me for allowing the conversation go on so long. I turned back to Brauer, fully meaning to hustle him on out and then make things right with Therese. He had set up his laptop on a scorched shelf just below eye level and now he switched it on with a soft *bong* and handed me a bound folder that contained, I saw, a résumé of sorts. I told him I had things to do and not to get comfortable.

"The same goes for you, Mr. Stuart," he said. "It's crucial that you not get comfortable. To make that point, I need to show you two pieces of video. After that, if you wish, I'll be out of your hair."

I tried to return the résumé, but he told me to hang on to it.

"You might want to look at the first few items," he said. "The rest can wait."

The top two lines of the résumé testified that Brauer had spent the years between 1975 and 1979 at Chico State Prison in California, serving time on multiple charges of conspiracy to commit fraud. "Guess you made a few youthful missteps, huh?"

"If you read on," he said, "you'll notice there are no further convictions. No indictments. Only crimes that no one can prove were committed."

I skimmed the pages; each one detailed several complicated swindles. "Yet you're confessing to . . . What? Twenty, twenty-five major felonies here? Is this something you hand out to everybody?"

"It's for your eyes only. I wanted you to understand that we have common ground."

I thought to raise an objection, but realized that if Brauer was, as the résumé claimed, a master of the big con, there would be no point in denying a certain similarity between us. He punched a key and a jiggly image of Treat's church materialized on the screen. I'd seen the building dozens of times, but given this amateurish frame, it looked less architecturally stylish, a mound of opaque glass blocks heaped into a form that roughly resembled a fortress with a single turret. The crudity of the camera work lent the footage an unreal, science-fictional aspect, as if it were covert footage of an alien hive.

The scene shifted to the interior of the church. After a flurry of quick cuts, views of ceiling and pews, and audience pans, the camera steadied on a shot of what passed for an altar in Treat's Jesus Lounge: a stage fronted by baskets of flowers; a hundred-soul white-robed choir halved (boys on one side, girls on the other) by a red carpet that led up an incline into a cloud of fog-machine fog from which lifted a forty-foot glass cross, bathed in serene blue radiance, seeming to suggest that following an awards ceremony and a cloudy passage, the saved would enter heaven and be exposed to lethal levels of radiation. At stage left stood a conversational grouping of sofas and easy chairs where sat three elderly men and a thirty-something blonde with big hair and a trophy-sized rack, wearing a yellow suit with a perilously short skirt. The men held open Bibles and the woman's head lolled as if she were being transported by the noodlings of an invisible organist. The choir swayed and hummed tunefully, reminding of those slave choirs dressed in mammy clothes seen swaying and humming in 1930s movies set in the antebellum

South, conveying a honeyed nostalgia as Massa Treat strolled forward to deliver his oration at the lectern, a spike of polished pinkish stone (the same shade as the stone on which Treat had practiced self-abuse) adapted to that purpose, thrusting up from the floor like the claw of some subterranean-dwelling cuddly pink predator whose attack against the citadel of the Lord had been blunted, just barely, by the armor of faith. Treat gripped the lectern, gazing down, his lips moving, then threw back his head and sang out in a husky tenor, "Jesus!" The choir fell silent. The old men muttered affirmations and the blonde, closing her eyes and lifting her arms, gave all her good stuff a shimmy as if she were working into a lap dance. The audience was hushed.

"Like all men I am adrift on the tide that ebbs back and forth between the paradise coast of Jesus love and the shoals of Satan's wildfire shore." Treat spoke these words rapidly, without dramatic inflection, as if they were unimportant, something he mentioned merely as a formality. He let a few seconds pass and shouted, "Like all men, I have been accused! Like all men, I have been raised on high and brought low! Like all men, I have been broken and I have been healed! Like all men—"

Brauer fast-forwarded, stopping every so often to show me that Treat was still shouting fifteen minutes, thirty minutes, an hour after he had begun. "That piece was recorded last weekend," he said. "He'd been riding the up escalator for a while and that was the peak. I thought he was going to lose it. It took them another half hour to get him offstage. Now this . . ." He double-clicked on an icon. "This is two nights ago."

The image that appeared was wavery black-and-white, with a time signature running in the right-hand corner, all shot from a fixed camera at an angle that had to be no more than three feet above the floor, because someone was pacing back and forth in front of the lens, and all I could see were thighs and buttocks clad in a pair of plaid trousers. The sound was muddy, as if recorded underwater. Wearing briefs and a bathrobe, Treat was slumped on a pale couch, his feet propped on a coffee table. A floor lamp was positioned to the right of the couch, shedding so much light, it transformed his face into a radiant, almost featureless oval—I could only see his expression when he turned his head to the left. The blonde who had been onstage, now wearing jeans and a T-shirt, her hair loose about her shoulders, came to sit beside him: Degan Mellory, acording to Brauer; a longtime associate of Treat's who owned a string of gentlemen's clubs. A man's voice, no doubt belonging to the plaid trousers, rumbled unintelligibly, and the blonde said to Treat, "Bob's right. You have to concentrate on defending yourself."

Treat fingered the sash of his robe.

"You hear me?" The blonde punched his shoulder with the heel of her hand. "Everything we've talked about is going to be for shit unless you pull it together."

Treat's chin dropped to his chest.

I heard the other man talking, but wasn't able to make out what he was saying. Treat kept fiddling with his sash. It looked as if he were trying to fit the end of it to his belly button. The other man moved in front of the camera and sat in a chair to the right of the couch. It was Robert W. Kinkade. I realized that I should have recognized his trousers. He patted Treat's knee and muttered what might have been an encouragement.

"What's he doing there?" I asked, and Brauer said, "That's a toughie. He's working for me, I think. But you never know with Mr. Kinkade."

I asked Brauer for a further explanation, but he urged me to watch the rest of the video. Degan pressed Treat on the importance of participating in his defense against the charges brought against him, saying the lawyers were offering assurances that if he got off his ass and made a few mea culpas, the sentence would be light, perhaps probation and community service.

"We've got him right where we want him," said Kinkade. "But we can't close the deal until we know what's going to happen to you. That affects our timetable."

Treat remained unresponsive.

"What's it going to take to get you behaving like a man again?" Degan asked. "Let me know, all right? Because I'm sick of having to change your diapers."

"Get rid of him," said Treat dully. "Now. I want him out of my life."

Kinkade seemed apalled by the prospect. "We can't do that! We'd have to change everything!"

Displaying animation for the first time since the video had begun, Treat sat up straight and glared at Kinkade. "Then change it! I can't abide that son of a bitch walking around and smiling."

"If we do anything now," Degen said, "there'll be chaos. You know that. We're not ready to move."

"I'm not saying hurt him. Discredit his ass! Do what he's done to me."

Degan and Kinkade exchanged glances.

"Look," Treat said. "Doesn't it make sense he's got to have a reason to kill himself?"

"He's depressed," Kinkade said. "That's all the reason anyone needs."

"Is that *your* reason, Bob? That why *you're* thinking about killing yourself?"

"I'm not going to kill my—" Kinkade broke off and stared anxiously at Treat.

"Guess I never saw the death wish in you before," Treat said. "I can sure see it now."

"Why don't you keep it in mind who's stuck by you through this?" said Degan. "You asshole! We're not changing a damn thing! We're not going to fuck things up just because Wardlin Stuart hurt your feelings."

Brauer shut the recording down. "That's the gist of it."

I must have been tightly focused on the video, because suddenly I could hear the sounds of the people outside, the water dripping, the passage of a car on the street. Brauer was watching me, his head tipped to the side, like a bird trying to make certain that a twig wasn't actually a worm, waiting to see if it would move.

"What were they talking about?" I asked.

"Can't you figure it out?"

"They were talking about killing me, weren't they?"

"They don't come right out and say it, but yes . . . that's some of it."

I thought with regret about my man Darren and his offer of a gun. "There's more?"

"They're planning to take over your ministry. Once you're dead . . ." Brauer closed his laptop. "They'll put forward a reformed and chastened Treat as your successor."

"Oh, yeah! That'll work."

"You know better than that. Look at yourself. The reformed sinner as minister. It works every time. Christians love a fool for Christ."

"I'm not a minister."

"You're being disingenuous now. You may not be ordained, but you serve the purpose. You fit the cliché." Brauer took his laptop down from the shelf. "Here's the scenario they've concocted. You commit suicide. Involuntarily, of course. And then after an appropriate time, Treat resurfaces. He celebrates you and your work. He confesses that he was wrong about you. Tells everyone you were a great man. Yet he also puts forth the notion that your suicide was due to the absence of God in your life. Prayer without God may get you earthly rewards, he'll say. But not a heavenly one. Treat's a decent actor. He'll do a beautiful Wardlin Stuart impression, with a dab of Jesus thrown in here and there. He'll pick up the torch you dropped. He's got people embedded among the Wardlinites. And he's got associates like Kinkade. So when he begins to preach about prayerstyle, his own copyrighted version, they'll help push your audience to him."

"You said Kinkade was working for you."

"We've never met, but I have a hold on him. It's shaky, but it's paid off. I invested anonymously—and fairly heavily—in his Desert Wind property. My agent's been able to squeeze some information out of him. In a crunch, though, I believe he'll flip back toward Treat. Degan has her hooks in him. With an old fart like Kinkade, a piece of ass like Degan is a powerful motivator."

"She's fucking him?"

"It's the way of the world," Brauer said.

"What about Treat? She doing him, too?"

"They have a platonic relationship. Like brother and sister cobras. I can't get an accurate line on what's going on there. Maybe they fucked once and it didn't work out. Anyway, what I have isn't enough to convince a DA to indict. That's why I haven't gone to the police. I'm afraid that all I'd do would be to give Treat and his people a heads-up." He shifted about so he was standing with his feet braced wide apart, holding the laptop case in front of him with both hands. "The reason I showed you the first video was to make the point that Treat is unstable. Despite what Degan and Kinkade told him, they expect him to do some time. Probably a year or two. They need to keep you alive until he's ready. But he's a loose cannon. He might act precipitately. In fact . . ." Brauer waved at the wreckage. "It appears he already has."

As Brauer had been speaking, I thought with some regret about Darren and his offer of a gun. "This is fucked! What am I supposed to do? Beat him to the punch?"

"I don't expect that'll be necessary."

I waited for Brauer to offer a suggestion. He made a clicking sound with his tongue, dug a business card from his breast pocket and handed it over. The dark blue face bore his name and phone numbers. Hand-lettered on the back was a list of names, among them a judge, a banker, and a member of the state securities commission.

"Check me out with these people," he said. "I'm not giving you their numbers, because they're all in the book. That way you'll be sure you're calling them, not someone I've set up. They'll provide you with access to records that should convince you I'm not after your money. Then you can decide if you want me to take a hand."

"If you're not after money, what are you after?"

Brauer's hiccup might have been a laugh. "When I began to explore the situation, I told myself it was all about protecting your interests. I thought they needed protecting. As I said, prayerstyle's been a help to me. It's something I want to get involved with on a more intimate level. I feel I can bring something to the table. But once I started investigating Treat, I realized I was having fun again. I've been legit for almost ten years, and I missed the action. That may sound ridiculous, but there it is. Now don't get me wrong. I expect to be compensated if I get involved, but I'm flexible as to how."

"If you keep up the surveillance, one of them's bound to say something more. Maybe that's all we have to do."

"Maybe. I've had Treat under surveillance for a couple of months now. What you just saw is all I've gotten . . . except for what Kinkade told my agent. And I doubt he'll talk to the police. I'll keep it up, but the time element worries me. I'm one hundred percent sure that what happened here was Treat's idea alone. I doubt Degan or anyone else knew about it. If they can't control him, he's going to continue being a problem in the short term. There are some things we can do immediately, very simple things, that will derail this whole business. Things that will remove every element of risk to you and your wife. But it has to be your call. I'm not going to take further steps unless they have your approval."

I considered the pluses and minuses. "You may be a little too slick for me, man," I said. "That's the sense I'm getting."

Brauer hitched up his shoulders in a half-shrug. "I am what I am. The way I see it, too slick's exactly what's called for."

A chunk of plaster crumbled away from a flap of wallboard that the firemen had hacked loose as they hunted for hot spots, alerting me once again to the disaster amid which I stood. I kicked at a wad of charred paper, the remains of a road atlas, and a wavelet of black water spread along the aisle. The weight of the sodden atlas had felt good against my foot, nourishing a hot spot inside me, and I wanted to kick it harder.

"Tell you what. If I go that route, I'll give you a call in a day or two." I flourished his business card. "This number where you'll be at?"

"My ranch. If I'm not in the house, you can reach me on the cell."

"All right. I'll call and we can set up a meeting."

"Perfect," Brauer said.

Chapter 17

O ne thing I've learned about prayer is what not to pray for. On TV, you're always hearing people, a good many of them jocks, saying they've been praying over some decision, whether to re-sign with their old team or whatever. Maybe the Divine Advice channel is subscription only and, not having accepted Jesus as my personal savior, I'm getting a scrambled signal. It's a possibility. But I am dead certain that asking the universe to influence your brain waves is not something prayerstyle was designed to do. Prayerstyle is an act of will. It exerts influence, it doesn't seek to be influenced. And so I had no impulse to write a prayer concerning my decision about hooking up with Brauer. Truthfully, I didn't even think about him for the rest of that night. I had enough to do taking care of Therese's head. It wasn't until the next morning that I gave the idea serious consideration, and then it took me less than a minute to decide that I should meet with Brauer. If I didn't like the smell of things, I could walk away, but if there was a chance he could keep me from having constantly to look over my shoulder, I wanted to hear what he had to say. I called the people listed on the back of his business card. Some offered proof that he was obscenely wealthy; others testified to his dependability in a crisis. Strangely enough, this evidence made me less interested in dealing with him—the too-slick factor again. But a meeting, I told myself, was far from a commitment.

"Give me a time," Brauer said when I called him that evening. "My place is down on the border, across from Altar. I can drive up to Pershing, no problem."

"Maybe not," I said. "I don't want to tell Therese about this. It'll upset her."

"We don't have to meet at the shop."

I was standing out behind the apartment, looking at the last of the light limning the mesas, the stars bright and sharp against the dark blue as gems in a DeBeers ad. Dead quiet, except for now and then the yip of a coyote. "Yeah, this is a small town, though. It'll get back to her. And if we're going to do business, maybe we shouldn't be seen together."

"Nothing will be traceable back to either of us. That much I guarantee. It's the upside of being too slick. But whatever suits you."

"How about Nogales?"

"Nogales is good. You familiar with Alvina's, on the Mexican side?"

"Yeah, I know it."

"Tonight, tomorrow . . . ?"

"Mid-afternoon tomorrow."

"I've got a couple of faxes coming in around then that I'll have to respond to. Let's make it a little later, shall we? Say five-thirty, six?"

When I ended the call, I turned and saw Therese standing in the doorway, giving me a dirty look. "Was that the man from yesterday you were talking to?"

I nodded. "Yeah, I'm going to scoot down to Nogales and listen to his pitch."

"You weren't intending to consult me about it?"

"I'm not commiting to anything!"

"How will I know? You might not want to upset me."

"Jesus, Therese! I think we can use some help. I'm willing to listen to anyone at this point. But if you don't want me to go . . ."

She leaned against the doorframe, arms folded; her face was shadowed, her hair haloed coppery red in the lantern light behind her. Our electricity was out and we were using candles and oil lanterns, camping out in the ruins—she refused to stay in a motel.

"I'll call him back and cancel," I said.

"I don't care."

"The hell you don't."

"No, really. Do what you want."

I tapped out a cigarette from my pack. "Okay. What *should* we do to protect ourselves? Leave? That's what you want, let's leave. Let's not just talk about it."

She rolled her neck, working out tension, and let her head fall back against the doorframe, her eyes angled away from me. "I look at you sometimes, it's like the first time I saw you walking toward me. Edgy and desperate. Glancing side to side, like you were afraid of being mugged. And I said to myself, What the fuck was I thinking, coming here?"

"I'm not gonna fight with you."

"What the fuck was I thinking, believing this criminal is who he claims to be? That was my reaction. Then when you came close, I didn't see that desperation anymore. All I saw was how you looked at me, and I thought, he can change. But now, every once in a while, even when you're close, it's like I go to that first distance again. I see you doing that yard walk and I know who you are. I mean, I can see everything about you."

Hearing that, I didn't want to deny it, I wanted to say, Please, tell me what you see, because I believed in that moment she could do what she said, she could look right inside me and explain a few things; but I guess I didn't want it that much. I lit my cigarette and exhaled profusely, a smoke signal conveying, I hoped, impatience with this unworthy debate, and I said, "So you gonna lay it on me or you want to stand there and act superior? Either way I'm fine."

"You don't need me to tell you anything. You spend enough time navel-gazing, for all the good it does. What's it matter how much you know about yourself, if all you do is file the information away?"

"Therese," I said. "Come on! Let's not do this."

"This is your favorite tactic. You start a fight, then you want to make up right away. It's annoying."

"I didn't start this."

"Oh! I see. I'm the duplicitous one."

"Okay. I started it. All right?"

"Of course if you want to be technical, I did start it." She affected a sugary Southern voice. "You provide the tinder and I the spark. It's the story of our love."

"This is your goal here? Fucking with my head?"

"Why waste time with discussion? No matter what conclusion we reach together, there'll come a moment when you have a flash about what's the right course of action and that's what you'll do. Even if it's totally contrary to what we decided. It saves time to skip ahead to the recriminations."

A shooting star cut a silver track as it zipped down behind a mesa. I hoped for an enormous burst of light that would illuminate the desert, so bright it would give pebbles a shadow, and that the subsequent crater would disgorge a host of spidery-limbed invaders from whom I would rescue Therese, thereby preserving the union.

She stood up straight and jammed her hands into the hip pockets of her jeans. "It's kind of comforting knowing in advance how you'll react. This way I don't get so upset. See, now you don't even have to worry about that. You're not going to surprise me. I know—"

"This isn't you being upset?"

"If you want to be technical," she said with heavy sarcasm. "But it's not a full-on case, because I expect you to behave like this. I have absolute confidence that whenever a chance to screw up presents itself, you're gonna be all over it. One day you'll find a way to screw up that'll drive me away."

"Maybe this is the one."

"Who can say?"

"Beats me."

I strolled a short ways out into the desert, staring at the mesa behind which the shooting star had vanished.

"I used to believe you'd get rid of that guy," Therese said.

"The guy who screws up? Why would you think that?" I dug my toe into the sand, trying to uproot some sage.

"I was just hoping. But I smartened up. You have this twitch that kicks in when you feel pressured. It sets you off in the same direction every time. Maybe it's more like a seizure than a twitch, because the effects last for days. Weeks. And after you get back to normal, it's never long before the twitch kicks in again. So that's what you end up being, mostly. That twitch."

"It's not all on me. If we could get away for a while . . . I mean far away . . . maybe we'd find out we don't have any serious problems. But you're stuck here. Pershing's your La Brea tar pits."

"Changing addresses won't change what's happening to us!"

"How would you know? You're never gonna try it. And what's this shit about 'what's happening to us'? We were having a fine ol' time in Phoenix."

"Were we? I'm never sure what's going on with you. I . . . Oh, fuck!"

I glanced back to Therese. She was pushing her fingertips against her brow as if trying to suppress a headache. I had the urge to fetch her some aspirin. The dry savagery that had crept into our dialogue over the past months, it hadn't yet gone bone-deep and inoperable, but I worried it might be verging on that terrible a malady.

I went to dislodging the sage with my toe once again. "You remember saying I might not be ready for the bullshit that went along with *Handbook*? You pegged that one. But before New York, when it was mostly just you and me, we were doing great. We need to take some time for ourselves and we can't do that here. We have to go somewhere there's not going to be a reporter or a Wardlinite turning up on our doorstep every five minutes. Someplace we can figure things out."

I was about to say something like, I love you, Therese. I admit there are times when I lose track of what that means, but there's other times when it's the one thing that makes sense. I was further going to say I'd give up prayerstyle, I'd not only give it up, I'd trash it, I'd confess it was one hundred percent a lie, a gimmick, and every miracle it had performed was simply an affirmation of the gullibility of the American consumer—I would confess all of that and decorate the confession with a demon laugh and pledge my soul to Satan on

Oprah if that would be the glue that held us together. I had a whole long speech cued up, but when I looked to the doorway, ready to deliver it, fat with sincerity, I found Therese had retreated into the apartment and this made me suspect that she must have X-rayed my sincerity and perceived at its core a tumor of fundamental falsity.

Aggravated, I walked out beyond the fringe of sage and onto the flats. Gravel crunched under my soles, loud as popcorn in that big silence. The wind or something more clever made a skittering pass at my heels. I smoked the rest of my cigarette and thought how I might look to a sniper lying on the hardpan, peering through his scope at an orange face blooming bright and simple, then shrinking to a dim point of fire, trying to decide whether he wanted to watch blood leak from a forehead wound or merely to extinguish the cigarette. The wind steadied, flowing east to west. I heard a faint humming, as if the desert were vibrating, and embedded in that humming, the way it happens when you're drowsy, listening to the sound of your tires along a freeway, I began to hear a dimly stated choral music, as of some classical madness devoted to the splendor of God. I tried to isolate the melody from the white noise in which it was embedded, but it was too elusive, like a golden thread worked into a magpie's nest, a glint showing among a weave of dirty twigs. I hated the tendency I had developed—a byproduct of prayerstyle, no doubt—to assign universal significance to every dumbass thought that stumbled through my brain; but I was persuaded then to believe that there was a moral and structural equivalence between that ephemeral music, that imaginary thread, and the constituency of creation. Fragments of purity glinting from a chaotic ugliness that both obscured and supported them. I flipped my cigarette away and the wind bore it to the side, scattering sparks. In that brief arc of light I could have sworn I spotted someone standing off to my left. The sight gave me a start, but I wasn't afraid, and not because I took it for an illusion. I'd become so accustomed to little dark figures on the periphery of my life, I was losing interest in them, beginning to take for granted their ineffability, their insubstantial nature. It seemed that half the world was populated by such flimsy, indefinite demons.

Chapter 18

lvina's was a tourist place situated close to the customs buildings that guarded the border, a location that guaranteed it heavy gringo traffic. On the wall above my booth was a photograph of Benicio del Toro sitting in the very same booth, looking sly and grizzled. According to a caption beneath the photograph, eating at Alvina's had been for him "an experience that will remain with me for the rest of my life," a testimonial that impressed me as being ambivalent, perhaps a kindness bestowed and not an exuberant tribute. Whatever Benicio's true opinion of the food, dozens of Americans, nearly half of them senior citizens, appeared to have taken an optimistic view regarding the meaning of his words and were shoveling in chile colorado and gazpacho and chicken mole, their conversations underscored by *ranchero* Muzak played at a low volume. In the Mexican manner, the frames of the windows and doors were painted a different color (red) from the walls and ceiling (avocado green), but this scheme was overly bright, and there were large red squares painted on the walls, as well, so the atmosphere achieved was less that of an authentic traditional restaurant, which Alvina's claimed to be, than the mad simplistic cheerfulness of a set designed for a TV show whereon lucky children are invited to frolic with a host costumed as a goofy-looking purple bear. The bottles behind the service bar held great appeal, but I limited myself to coffee while waiting, a fast that caused my waitress, a sharp-faced woman named Delimar, to treat me with the coolness due a small tipper.

It had occurred to me on the drive down that Brauer was making more or less the same offer Darren had made atop the cliff. That I hadn't rejected Brauer's pitch out-of-hand sponsored the notion that I was becoming a model citizen, someone who endorsed killing so long as it was cloaked in efficiency and distance. I had smelled blood on Brauer and I believed his "very simple things" must involve some form of violence. Try as I might, I could think of nothing short of murder that would stop Treat in his tracks. As Brauer pointed out, Treat was litigation-proof and it would be a distinct challenge to embarrass him after the embarrassments he had already suffered. Brauer and Darren were remarkably alike, I thought. The most salient difference between them was that Brauer affected a direct manner, yet was indirect in stating his intentions, whereas Darren affected a mysterious persona and was crystal clear about his intent. They were the yin and yang of murder boys. As for me, if there was any significant difference between the Wardlin Stuart of Lopez Island and the current incarnation, it was that I had grown more calculating, that I was willing to contract out my anger. I wasn't quite ready to put the job in the hands of a pro, but what with Therese refusing to leave Pershing, I felt action was justified.

Six o'clock came and Brauer did not appear. I took out my cell phone, but decided against calling him. If he stood me up, then fate would have spoken. I brought a smile to Delimar's lips by ordering two vodka martinis, and drank them in swift succession. The cell phone rang. Brauer, I thought. "Where the hell are you?" I asked.

"I'm here," Therese said. "Where the hell are *you*?"

I told her I'd thought she was Brauer.

"He called," she said. "He misplaced your number, so he called me. He's caught in a snarl at the border. They're checking everybody. He says he'll be there soon as he can."

"Why didn't you just give him my number?"

"I thought you might want to talk."

The connection crackled.

"Well," she said. "I've given you the message."

"How are you?"

"I'm okay."

"Just okay?"

"You expect jubilation?"

"I'm sorry about last night. I was an asshole."

"Me, too. I'm sorry."

Delimar approached and I pointed to my empty glass, sending her veering toward the service bar.

"I've been thinking over what you said, about me not being able to leave Pershing," Therese said. "Maybe you were right. Maybe it is neurotic."

I started to respond, but she talked through me.

"I did a walk-through of the shop this afternoon with Lyle Gallant. Going over the claim."

"Is there a problem?"

"No, he was very sweet."

"*Sweet's* not a word I'd associate with Lyle."

"You don't see that side of him unless you're a woman. But anyway, while I was looking around the shop, I started to feel disconnected from everything. From the shop, from Pershing. It was weird. More like something I wanted to feel than a real feeling. But it seemed like a sign."

"Yeah?"

"It got me to thinking. Maybe we should go."

"Go?"

"Right. Not make a plan or anything. Just head to the airport and pick a place . . . a destination."

I stirred this around for two or three seconds. "Is this tactical? You telling me this because I'm meeting with Brauer?"

"Of course I am! I don't want you doing anything crazy. That doesn't mean you're not right about me being neurotic."

"I never said you were neurotic."

"Pathological, then."

"Whacko," I said. "That was the term I was going for."

"So what do you think?"

"This is really what you want?"

"It'll be months before the shop can reopen. And I'm not sure I want to reopen. It might be better to give it some time and then see how we feel."

"The thing is," I said, "I don't know if I can just up and go. The tour's not arranged yet."

"Sue could set up some immediate dates. And your parole guy, he's halfway to being a Wardlinite. He won't be a problem."

"Yeah . . . Yeah, that's true."

"You don't sound enthusiastic."

"I'm stunned is all."

Delimar set a fresh martini down on the table; I had a sip and perhaps I made an appreciative sound, because Therese asked what I was drinking.

"Martinis."

"Don't get too drunk."

"I'll eat before I drive back."

"Okay. We can talk when you get home. Or maybe it's best not to talk at all. Just do it."

At a table adjoining my booth, two pasty, white-haired, crepe-throated women in pastel slacks and embroidered peasant blouses, *huipiles,* were watching with hawkish intent as a third woman fed an old man a bite of something on the end of a fork. He chewed and made a sour face and pretended to choke. The women chortled and put their hands to their cheeks at this outlandish display; the old man made a playful grab for the one who had fed him, a parody of lechery that caused her to squeal and cross her arms over her breasts.

"Wardlin?"

"I'm here. I got distracted by something."

"Where are you?"

"Alvina's."

"Oh, right. God, maybe you should drink more."

After ending the call, I worked on the fresh martini. Though flying off with Therese was the best possible result, I realized I was a little disappointed, that I'd been anticipating interacting with Brauer. The old man at the nearby table kept up his roosterish behavior, grabbing at the other women. Watching this depressing vignette put me on edge and I looked out the window. Darknesss had settled over the town. A stream of headlights, cars bumper-to-bumper, were proceeding from the border, moving no more rapidly than would a procession of pilgrims carrying torches. Vendors walked alongside them, holding out tacos, bunches of flowers, beads, dolls. I imagined Therese reading a magazine, drinking a diet Coke, sitting in an orangely flickering cell that was embedded in a globe of stars and painted stone and sand. I felt a crazy longing to be with her, as if she had become suddenly unattainable and we were separated not just by miles, but by the regulation of a cruel providence. My mind refused to stick on one subject. I considered hitting a drugstore, loading up on OxyContin, then recognized what a primitive idiocy that would be. I contemplated the prospect that there would one day be a George W. Bush Presidential Library and decided it would be stocked with volumes such as *The Little Golden Book of Trees.* I wondered if Darren was in town. I recalled a conversation from my high school days, the subject of which—if you found out you had a fatal disease and could kill one person, who would it be?—I had taken seriously. I'd been unable to come up with anyone whose death would have made a difference to the world. Knock down one villain, another snapped into view. That had once been my opinion, at any rate.

I didn't recognize Brauer when he entered. Wearing a Houston Texans cap, jeans, a denim jacket, and a gray T-shirt, he could have passed for a worker in a maquiladora. He hustled up to the booth, all apology, and insisted on buying me another drink, which Delimar fetched, along with a margarita for Brauer, giving him much less attitude than she had to me. He spoke to her in Spanish and she nodded toward me, said something and laughed.

"She says you're more handsome than Benicio," Brauer said, indicating the photograph above the booth. *"Muy guapo."*

I didn't think that was what she had said, but let it pass. "You two know each other?"

"Delimar's worked at Alvina's since Pancho Villa, and I meet with clients here on occasion. The food sucks. Mexican food for morons. Grease and salsa. But it's easy to find and people want to see the place because the cast of *Traffic* ate here when they were on location."

"I don't much like it myself."

"Well, hell. There's a great seafood place a few blocks away. Why don't you let me have a couple of drinks and then we can walk over." He took a pull on his margarita. "That was a hellish crossing. I thought I was going to be stuck all night."

"What was the problem?"

"Who knows? The Office of Homeland Stupidity doing its ridiculous thing. It's still a mess. You might have trouble getting back."

"They're checking in both directions?"

"Seemed to be." He sucked on his straw again. "So. Where should I begin?"

I drank deeply, pondering whether or not I wanted him to sell me. "Therese and I . . . we had talk when she called to pass on your message," I said. "We're gonna abandon ship. Take an extended vacation. I appreciate your offer, but we decided the best course is to back away."

A ripple of annoyance surfaced in his face.

"If you hadn't been most of the way here, I would have called you. I figured I'd make it up to you some by buying you dinner."

"I'll never say no to a free meal." Brauer removed his jacket and laid it on the seat beside him. "You know, you're likely to be in the same pickle when you return. Treat won't be brought to trial for months, maybe more than a year."

"If that's so, we'll deal with it then. I know how to get in touch with you."

"Always willing to lend a hand. You might want to think this over some more, though. If you change your mind, I haven't got anything pressing the next few weeks."

"That's not gonna happen."

"Whatever you say." He lifted his glass in a toast. "Here's to crime."

"Yours, not mine," I said, and drank with him.

"This vacation . . . where are you planning on going?"

"Europe, maybe."

"Europe's America with better food and older buildings. You can do better. What are you looking for? A big city? Peace and quiet?"

"Peace and quiet. A place on the water."

Brauer appeared to be searching his files. "Patagonia," he said firmly. "Lots of small coastal towns. They're used to tourists, but not overrun by them. Clean. Spectacular scenery. Friendly people. You've got civilization if you need it, but an hour from the coast you can be in the middle of nowhere."

"You been there."

"I was down last year about this time. It's the perfect time to visit. End of summer, beginning of fall. There's a national park called Los Torres. In Chile. It's as close to being on another planet as you can imagine. Natural rock towers standing hundreds of feet high. A forest of them. Absolutely surreal-looking."

We finished our drinks, ordered another round, and Brauer filled me in on his Patagonian holiday. From the way he described his travels, I pictured him posed dauntless-explorer style against a backdrop of snowy peaks, wearing North Slope and Land's End gear, digital camera in one hand, steel-tipped hiking staff in the other, like an ad from *Outside* magazine. Yet he made the place sound attractive. I saw Andean glaciers, ice floes, Pleistocene verdure, cold deserted beaches with whales in the offing. It seemed like a place where Therese and I could hide a while, a place that provided clean lines of sight. Midway through my fourth drink I began to feel light-headed, my thoughts flurrying like dust before a broom. I told Brauer I might have hit my limit. Maybe we should head on over to the seafood place.

I had hoped the air would clear my head, but as we walked along the narrow, crowded street, breathing in neon-colored heat and gas fumes, an evil-smelling sweat broke on my face and neck and chest, and I began producing saliva in prodigious amounts, having to spit every fifteen or twenty feet. A mural fading on the façade of one of the stucco buildings that lined the street showed 1950s-style men with greasy hair dancing with big-haired women in calf-length dresses, celebrating the explosive emergence of an ice-cream sundae from the center of a silver star: their glossy smiles broadened when they spotted me. In a bright storefront window a black and red plush insect with the words *Spanish Fly* printed in gilt letters on its belly beat its fuzzy wings. Eyes that gleamed like chitin swung toward me—shopkeepers leaning in doorways; skinny guys who opened their mouths to display crack vials nested within; young women walking arm in arm, chubby cakegirls with pink icing melted on their faces; shrunken widows in black shawls sitting on the curb, cardboard boxes containing cigarettes resting on their laps. Brauer chattered and asked questions, distracting me to some degree from what I was feeling, but the night was overpowering me. The grumble and honk of stop-and-go traffic, outpourings of jukebox love, machines whirring in a tailor's shop, the babble of pedestrians as they pushed past—it all combined into a rush that seemed to be accelerating toward me like the *whish* of a leathery tongue whipping forth to curl about my waist and snatch me into an enormous maw . . . and then that rush fragmented into a million separate noises, a chaotic sound-track of shrieks, breakage, blurts of song that served to orchestrate the visible world into an alternation between normal stretches of time and moments of frozen light and arrested motion, all strobing in and out. My stomach grew queasy, my heart felt out of rhythm, and there was bile in my mouth. I told Brauer I had to sit down, I was messed up. He took my arm and said, "You'll feel better once you eat." The thought of food made me gag. I tried to pull away, but Brauer tightened his grip and steered me toward the mouth of an alley. When I continued to resist, he pushed the barrel of a gun into my side.

"Y'know what these fucks will do if I shoot?" he said. "They're not going to come after me. They'll steal your clothes, your wallet, and leave you to bleed. When the smell gets too strong, someone will drag you away. Until then they'll step over you and make jokes. So if you don't believe I'll shoot, you keep it up."

His complexion had gone blotchy and the blotches shifted over his face like amoebas; his pores were the size of pencil leads; his body was stringy, jointless. A snake man, dying from his own vile secretions. His head weaved slightly from the venom sloshing about in his brainbox.

"What do you want?" I asked, baffled by his transformation, by his motives, and by the quavery, liquid sound of my voice.

A woman with a grimy bandage covering one eye, a freakish medieval face, a Dürer etching made flesh, stretched out a hand to us and arranged her features in a piteous grimace. Even her dress, a once-white, sweat-stained thing imprinted with grungy roses, was a form of suffering. The sallow infant cradled in her arms was either dead or unconscious, its eyelashes like sewn stitches. I smelled its fetid diaper and knew its guttering life as an inconstant pressure on my skin. Brauer cursed at the woman and she moved away with the crowd.

"I want you to walk on ahead of me," he said. "I want you to do it right now."

The relative darkness and quiet of the alley allowed my thoughts to cohere. I'd realized long before that I had been drugged, but the drug was so strong, the sleet of noise and smell and light so overwhelming, from moment to moment I had lost sight of the realization. Now I was able to trace the physical and mental distortions I felt back to their infancy, the inability to think I had experienced after Delimar served my first martini. A multilayered stench captured my attention. Spoilage so advanced, it yielded a sweetish odor compounded of rotten fruit, feces, vomit, cat death, all aged in one another's' flavors. Shadowy lumps of garbage bobbed on a cement-colored channel. Sparkles flourished in the air like camera flashes from a distant audience. I debated making a grab for Brauer's gun and decided it would be foolhardy—I could barely keep my feet. Fear jetted through me, then hilarity. Nothing bad could happen. I was protected by the chemicals in my blood, by the cosmic immunity they bestowed. A beatific wave swelled inside me and I understood that I had special powers, an irresistible gift for diplomacy. I would engage Brauer, tell him I knew he was operating on orders . . . but whose? Treat's? Didn't matter. I'd demonstrate to him the asburdity of the situation. At the end of the alley, parked in a vacant lot littered with flattened cans and cardboard trash, a white SUV glowed pearly and tremulous, a white horse trembling with the anticipation of being ridden. Beyond it, a deeply rutted street and tin-roofed houses of concrete block with dirt front yards and candleflames flickering in their windows like souls trapped in gray skulls still wearing the tarnished silver wigs they had worn in life. The curdled sky above Nogales, clouds of pollution sealing off the stars, was a muddy orange, eddying sluggishly like unwholesome sea life. The street noise, diminished by half, seemed festive, and the garbage smell had been replaced by an intricate chemical bitterness, a chord of acids and sulfides. It was all very beautiful. Beautiful and horrid at once. I stopped walking, intending to steep myself in the energies of this border vision. Brauer rapped the back of my head with his gun butt. My vision shorted out. I staggered forward, pressing the heel of my left hand against the injured place. Pain spread across my scalp as if following the tributaries of a crack. I heard a thin singing in my ears and realized that I had gone to my knees. Brauer hauled me upright and slung me at the SUV. I fell into the rear door, my face close to the window. Smoke-gray fluid slopped against the inside of the glass.

"Open it," Brauer said, and then a more resonant voice said, "We're not on *Larry King* now, are we, shitball?"

I wobbled about in an ungainly turn, leaned on the SUV and saw Treat standing at Brauer's shoulder. I wasn't surprised to see him— no more, at any rate, than I was surprised by everything else—but I was shocked by how he looked. His head was enormous, an Easter Island head with Elvis hair and hooded eyes.

"You stupid cocksucker!" Brauer went chest to chest with him. "I told you to keep out of my business!"

"Calm down, man." Treat's grin seemed to mirror the curving track his Harley had left on the desert sand outside of Phoenix. "I came to watch you work your magic. I'm a fan."

"You're not going to rest until you're neck-deep in shit, are you?" Brauer had regained control. "You're fucking incorrigible."

"Think I'm gonna miss this?" Treat chuckled, then stepped close and head-butted me. My vision whited out again. I slumped down against the tire, holding my forehead. He kicked me in the thigh and, when I turned away, in the small of the back. I had a confused appreciation of the next few minutes. Somebody picked me up and slung me headfirst. Gradually the world reassembled around me. I became aware that I was lying facedown on the floor in the rear of the SUV. We were moving rapidly over bumpy ground. Treat was talking. I discovered that if I rested my head on my arms, the pain lessened. I understood that I was going to die. The carpet had been recently shampooed.

"How you doing back there, Wardlin?" Treat called. "You comfy? Can we get you anything?"

Brauer said something that was drowned out by the noise of our passage and Treat laughed.

"Do you think you're indispensable?" Brauer asked. "You're not indispensable."

He said more, but the car hit a pothole—I was flung about and for the next bit I was too rattled to listen. The nap of the carpet fascinated me. Like looking down from a plane flying over a gray forest. I tried to summon a sense of urgency, but was sidetracked by a ridiculous philosophical speculation concerning the legitimacy of action.

"You seem to think fucking up is part of your charm," Brauer said. "You know, like we're going to look at your fallen-down, fucked-up ass and giggle . . . like we would over a toddler taking a spill."

Though this was surely addressed to Treat, I was enthralled by its relevance to the condition of my own soul, and thus missed the better part of Treat's answer, catching only the words *hired help*.

"That's what you believe? You're my boss?"

"You need to look at our relationship in terms of Hollywood business structure," Treat said, his voice rich with good humor. "I'm the talent. The talent gets what it wants."

"You're kidding?"

"You see things different, do you?"

"Oh, yes! Very different."

Suspended against a field of blue and white upholstered padding, a Sunday-school color scheme, the colors favored by the coolest people in heaven, was a vibrating silver wishbone—the door handle. It was either within easy reach or at a telescopic distance, depending on my fluctuating point of view. Moved by animal reflex more than actual hope, I gave it a nudge and felt the locking mechanism shift.

"You're like a clown at a birthday party," Brauer said. "You're a fairly effective clown; you're proficient at doing certain clownish things. It's not like there are no other clowns."

"You just don't appreciate me."

"It's not like you don't need to be cognizant of the fact you're pissing people off. I want you to be clear on that."

"Am I pissing you off?" Treat said this merrily. "Bet I am, aren't I?"

"You're making me reassess my commitment to you."

"And that's a bad thing, huh?"

"I wouldn't feel good about it," Brauer said. "But then I'm not a clown."

I could no longer be certain that I had felt the mechanism shift. In fact, I was so addled, my overall conception of locks had suffered, and I wasn't certain what such a shift signaled, whether locked or unlocked; but Brauer had been disconcerted by Treat's appearance—he might, I thought, have forgotten to secure the doors. Without any sense of desperation, more like, Oh, okay, why not?, I gave the handle a second, harder try. The door opened and I half crawled, half flung myself out into the street.

I hit shoulder-first in the dirt, flipped into a roll, then went head over heels down an embankment—a transit of pinwheeling lights and darks, sharp objects jabbing me—and crashed through something, fetching up on my back, dazed, staring at the corrupted sky, photic flashes dazzling my vision. My neck and shoulder ached. Blood had soaked through the knees of my jeans, and I had pain in my left wrist. Yet I could detect no serious damage, and the shock of my tumble had overridden the drugs in my system with a shot of adrenaline.

"Ay, Dios!" A voice shrilled behind me and I scrambled up to all fours. Fat and affrighted, her filmy nightdress plastered to her body, mapping her pudenda, causing her belly button to resemble a lunar crater, a woman cowered in the doorway of a tin-roofed shack with a Pisa-like lean; two big-eyed children clung to her legs. None of them looked quite human. Clever insect fakes. Intelligent beetles were invading the human sphere, eating our poor and taking their place. Some were already sitcom stars. One day they would rule the plenum. I tried to stand and slipped on a piece of shattered wood. A board fence lay in splinters around me. My gaze snagged on the crown of a banana tree at the corner of the shack. Its ragged fronds twitched feebly, fitfully, like the legs of a stomped spider. Watching them move made me feel stoned again.

"Rodolfo!" the woman shouted. *"Ayudame!"*

I heard a soft pop that, even in delirium, I recognized for a gunshot. The woman must have recognized it, as well—she dragged the children inside and called out once more to her Rodolfo, who likely was sleeping off a drunk or else he would have made his presence known. Silhouetted by the red glow of taillights, a man was aiming a handgun from the crest of the embankment, some unguessable distance above. Pretty and unreal. The black figure, the bloody air smoky with exhaust. If I'd had a camera, I would have been tempted to snap a picture.

A round chewed up dirt in front of my knee—that restored me to survival mode. I staggered to my feet and lunged against the flimsy rear door of the shack, knocking it off its hinges, and went reeling inside. Shrieks in the dark; the piping outcries of children. Something heavy struck my shoulder and clanged against the floor, this followed by a hoarse Rodolfoesque curse. I smashed through the front door and onto the street. At my back, a trollish hairy-chested man in briefs and a wife-beater lumbered out of his castle, brandishing a machete. My diplomatic skills seemed inadequate to the task and I ran.

For a patch of time that may have been significantly shorter than I believed, I ran without apparent effort. It was as if I were less running than borne along by the turning world. My stride was fluid, my breathing easy—I believed I could run forever, outdistance any pursuer, and, freed of this particular physical concern, I was able to get my bearings and see where I was headed. On every side were adobes with caved-in roofs; solitary standing walls of larger structures that had once housed small businesses and now stood windowless and doorless on darkened streets: a sampler of ruin that spanned the range between demolished and unfit for human habitation. Barrio Esquina del Sol. "Sunny Corners" in American. It was the worst part of the worst part of town, occupied by hungry dogs and the living dead, the barely alive having emigrated to public housing (a benefit—and one of the ironies—of NAFTA!) after too many pollution babies born with their skulls embedded in their chests. About two hundred yards straight ahead, rising like a yellow and white cake from the ashes of the oven wherein it had been baked, sat the cause of this desolation: the United Products maquiladora. A brightly lit three-story building with wide glass doors and faced with plastic paneling, it covered several square blocks and was surmounted by chimneys from which pale smoke roiled up to commingle with the older poisons in the sky— under the wan glow of roof lights, the separate columns looked faintly green and ectoplasmic, not smoke at all, but extrusions of morbid, crepey tissue that had been leached of vitality and were being squeezed out through tubes, produced in the manner of sausages from some gruesome raw material.

Noticing where I was affected my running style. I began to labor and stumble. A stitch developed in my side and the bruises I had accumulated were throbbing. Except for my wrist. The wrist felt numb. My breath grew short and slobber filmed over my lower lip. I searched about for a place to hide, to rest. Nothing offered itself. I sensed a single bleak presence everywhere, a bitter magic at work, a pervasive menace. An oily black meniscus bulged from each broken window and unhinged door. Within the wrecked houses, the darkness was being compressed into great black birds, heads tucked underneath their wings, nearly crushed by the clay shells from which they would soon burst, shattering the silence with their flights, soaring up and screaming their hatred of the world, joining wing to wing to obscure the sky and form an apocalyptic night, starless and final. I slowed and leaned against a stucco wall, trying to shut my mind against the pyrotechnics of thought. My heartbeat was scarily irregular; my limbs felt alternately cold and warm, as if my blood were flowing in spurts, the veins snarled and twisted. This close to the maquiladora, I could hear its insides thrumming. Its light cast heavy shadows that appeared to have the potential to become blades, to slide scissor-quick across the ground and snip you off at the ankles; the vacancy of the street, of the entire barrio, was profound, such a lushness of absence, it caused rustles and scuttlings to sound like dice rattling across a Masonite board. Each tiny bump of stucco was pointy and ultrareal. Colors glistened; patches of gravel trembled as if they were simmering in a frying pan; crumbling ledges teemed with detail. I was unable to explain my perpendicularity in the face of so much complexity, a complexity in which form and direction were dissolving; I was afraid to step away from the wall, thinking I might have misapprehended my position relative to all else. Someone had spray-painted a slogan on the wall across the street, drippy crimson letters like the titles of an old horror movie. Left-wing haiku, I figured. A howl of social protest. It took me a while to bring the words into focus: "Long Live the Devil!" In Esquina del Sol, at least, the universe had taken that cry to heart.

Chapter 19

It wasn't prayer that saved me then, but instinct or chance. An instant before Treat and Brauer came into view at the far end of the block, I felt exposed and, catching sight of a gap in the wall on my right, I stepped through it, spotting the two men out of the corner of my eye as I did. The ruin in which I'd taken shelter had a partial second floor accessed by stone stairs; the roof above the lower floor was missing. In the dimness I saw broken roof beams resting on dirt the color of cigar ash. A rusting car fender lay against an interior wall. I peeked out at the street, not convinced that I hadn't imagined Treat and Brauer. There they stood, talking in angry voices, too far away for me to hear what was being said. Treat turned his back on Brauer and strolled ten or twelve feet toward my vantage point. His face looked swollen, squashed into an oval, and held a glabrous shine. Ranus Treat. He said something over his shoulder to Brauer. Scornfully, I thought. Brauer barked a challenging reply. Treat ignored him, jamming his hands into his pockets—he may or may not have spoken. I remembered my cell phone and reached into my inside jacket pocket. No phone, only a ballpoint pen. The phone must have fallen out when I tumbled down the embankment. Not having it made me feel more imperiled, even though I had no solid idea of whom to call.

Fear was only one among many mental attractions vying for my attention. My thoughts were traveling a circuit that serially disposed me to amusement, an aesthetic appreciation of the weird and the beautiful, confusion, illumination, and back to fear. As Treat moved a couple of steps farther away from Brauer, gazing up into the sky as if unconcerned with the things of this world, perhaps prospecting for a cloud with a pleasing shape, I passed into the illuminative phase and observed that the alignment of objects and shadows in the street was inauspicious, a pattern of jagged shapes at whose center two human pieces were facing in almost opposite directions, evoking the idea of an unsustainable tension, of cross-purposes, and implying the need for an immediate correction. Accompanying this insight was a shudder provoked by queasiness and a chill. I was concentrating on calming my stomach when Brauer walked up behind Treat and, shielding his face from the blood spray, shot him in the head. Treat crumpled onto his side. Brauer stood over him, his stance wide, as if he were about to take a leak, and fired three additional shots into the body. I froze, not letting myself make a sound, but from my rear there came a metallic screech. The rusted fender was shifting, scraping against the stone wall, and then the boy who had been curled beneath it, his flesh perfectly adapted to the form, like a crab to its shell, emerged, kicked the fender aside and fled up the stairs toward the second floor. I didn't dare look out onto the street again—I knew Brauer must have heard the noise—and I hurried after the boy.

The corridor at the top of the stairs was pitch-dark and I was forced to grope my way. My hands encountered filmy structure—like cobwebs, but stickier. Veils of petrified odor, maybe. The stink was so cloying, it verged on the material. Each time a board creaked underfoot, I stopped and listened for Brauer. I reached an open door and eased through it, stood with my back to the wall. Now that death had been removed from the plane of the purely conceptual, I was even less committed to a course of action. Brauer was bound to search the place. I needed to locate an exit, but I felt enervated, physically ill and mentally incompetent. Then I heard a sharp *snick* from close by. The sound dug a cold notch in my spine—I pictured a switchblade opening. I held my breath. Another *snick*. A miniature spearpoint of flame materialized, illuminating a corner of the room. Enshrined in its glow, sitting cross-legged, holding a lighter and a glass pipe, was a jaundiced creature, scrawny and bald, clad in a ratty work shirt that covered its body to the mid-thigh. No trousers or shoes. Except for yellow rims, yellow as the seepage from an infected wound, its eyes were red. I couldn't tell if it was male or female, but I chose to consider it a man, because it would have been too awful to think of it as a woman. He stared at me and made a fussy, fuming noise before applying fire to the bowl, but offered no further acknowledgment. As he sucked on the glass tube, his cheeks hollowed and his skull flattened and his ears elongated, becoming the demon of the pipe. He snapped the lighter shut and vanished. The bowl burned ruby red in the dark. Imagining that he was evolving further, mutating into the bestial, I backed out of the room and went as quickly as I could along the corridor, no longer worried about creaking boards, more rattled by this apparition than by Treat's death.

At the end of a second corridor was a window crossed by two nailed-up boards. Through the gaps I could see the flat stone roof of an adjoining building below and the glare of the maquiladora beyond. One board was loose. I pried it off and began working at the other. The nails shrieked as I pulled them free. My mind steadied and I felt confident that I would escape; but when I tried to hang by my hands from the sill, preparing to drop onto the roof, pain lanced through my left wrist and I lost my grip. It wasn't a long drop, but I landed awkwardly on my side. My wrist was swollen. A fracture, I figured. And once I regained my feet, I realized that I had injured my left knee. I hobbled toward the retaining wall at the edge of the roof. Confronted by another hang-and-drop situation, I straddled the wall in a way that would favor use of my right hand. Two soft *pop*s issued from the building I had vacated—I couldn't move any faster, but my thoughts accelerated. I wondered whether Brauer had killed the fender boy, the demon, or some other wretch. Maybe they had killed him and he'd gotten off a couple of rounds before dying. That I doubted. The decisiveness he had displayed in taking out Treat spoke to his efficiency as a killer, though the last three shots had been excessive. I recalled what Therese had said, that I wasn't that great a judge of character; yet I had called it with Brauer. It was my own character I had misjudged, my ability to handle men like Brauer. In prison I had been lucky to last a decade. And that was my basic problem, I thought. With a flash of that zowie, rhinestone-studded, unearned enlightenment such as comes only to the mightily stoned and the easily confused, I accepted what I had previously merely understood: that I was still trying to prove myself, to create circumstances that would test my jailhouse people–skills, working behind some adolescent urge toward mastery. The simplicity of that revelation astonished me. I made a vow never to forget what I had learned—this would by God be a red-letter day in the life of Wardlin Stuart—and lowered myself over the edge of the roof. A bullet threw up a puff of concrete dust next to my fingers. I let go, taking the brunt of the landing on my right foot, and went at a limping run toward the maquiladora.

Workers were streaming in and out through the doors as I approached, a shift change in progress, and about three hundred of them, mainly young women, some carrying shopping bags, were walking in a group toward the heart of town. I fell in among them, holding my wrist to my stomach so it wouldn't get jostled, hunching my shouders and ducking my head to hide the height difference; but I must have appeared as beat-down and grubby as they did—or else they were too exhausted to care—because nobody seemed bothered that a gringo had sneaked into their midst. The group stayed packed together, not thinning as you might expect. I remembered an article describing how rapists had a predilection for picking off women as they returned home following their shifts. That would explain the herd mentality. Even ducked down, I was tall enough to gaze out over the top of the crowd, and I became entranced in watching their heads bobbing—it looked as if a curious animal with a flat, flexible body and hundreds of heads was floating on a choppy river that flowed between ruinous banks. I came to understand that this was not a metaphor—we were united by our auras, individual Kirlian bodies that merged into a single all-encompassing aura, a transparent sac upon whose soap-bubble surface myriad glints of color shifted. We were an island nation in the most literal sense of the term, constantly adding new citizens as more workers were absorbed into the group. My hallucinations, I noticed, were evolving away from the jaggedness of an LSD-type trip, growing less chaotic and spastic in their onset and passage, acquiring an organic character that I associated with peyote and mushrooms. I supposed I had ingested some designer dope that combined the best of both worlds. The worst of the physical discomforts caused by the drug had dissipated—if Brauer hadn't been trying to kill me, I might have enjoyed the experience. I kept an eye out for him, but there was no sign of the man. I suspected he had a general idea of where I was, however, and I decided to peel away from the crowd before we reached a congested area, where it would be difficult to see him coming. I thought this was a canny strategy, a real savvy move, dismissing the fact that for a very long time now, I had been consistently prone to do the wrong thing.

Twenty minutes and perhaps three-quarters of a mile after I had joined the off-shift exodus, the crowd, its ranks swelled to double its original size, began passing a black building roughly the width and length of an airport hangar, though not so high, having only two floors. It was situated on the edge of Barrio Cielo, another desolate neighborhood, albeit upscale by contrast to Esquina del Sol, the majority of the houses being inhabited, a few of the streetlights functioning. The façade of the ground floor was fabricated of black plastic that had been molded into the form of six trees, intricately detailed, with thick trunks and interlocking leafy crowns, and these formed the arches that framed five entranceways—there were no doors. Smallish white neon words, LA VIDA ES MUERTO (Life Is Death), partly obscured by plastic leaves, were suspended above the center entrance. The interior was crowded, smoky, noisy. The police were present in strength, doing rent-a-cop duty, guarding the entrances, eyeballing everyone who passed beneath the arches. Well-dressed men of various ages stood in groups outside, smoking, drinking, laughing, taunting the maquiladora women who left the crowd and went into the club. Those who did so carried shopping bags or some sort of carryall. I pushed to the perimeter of the crowd, bided my time, and when half a dozen women near me waved good-night to their friends and headed for the club, I attached myself to them, shielding myself behind a short busty girl in a sweated-through white top and a pink skirt, and entered La Vida Es Muerto.

Chapter 20

Anyone who has done their share of psychotropic drugs, or experienced a chemical imbalance that causes mental illness, or been afflicted by visions of other planes, has no need to be told that consensus reality is a one-size-fits-all proposition. If you happen to wear a size 24 shoe, you can dig all day through a bin of flip-flops at Kmart and never find a pair that will validate your humongous feet—it's an analogy that might well be applied to altered states of consciousness and how they are characterized by the authors of our consensus. One of the standard arguments against the existence of things-not-seen is that an abnormal chemical constituency in your bloodstream invalidates those formerly invisible things that come to light when you're high, whacko, or spiritually possessed; and yet since our perceptual bias is determined by a chemical constituency, fueled by a mix that undergoes slight changes from day to day, it strikes me that this contrary argument is unreasonably assumptive in taking the stance that extreme variances from the norm have less validity than do other, lesser variances. For instance, can a solid citizen, a person with acceptable responses to the events of his or her life, be deemed sane strictly on the basis of our judgment of those responses? Isn't it possible that these responses were arrived at through a sequence of irrational determinations? By similar rule, should the opinion of a mental patient who examines, let's say, the American (or any) political process and perceives it to be the insane manifestation of a delusionary, power-mad culture be considered—albeit accurate—irrelevant simply because that culture so judges it? Lots of holes can be punched in that argument. I'm not claiming an institutionalized schizophrenic is correct when he tells you that Saint Francis is sitting on the mantelpiece, threading a necklace of human teeth—I'm just suggesting that the things you only think you see may have some influence on the things you swear you saw.

I say this to justify the propositon that, although the chances are excellent I was only tripping, it's not inconceivable that some of what I experienced during my time in La Vida Es Muerto may have commented upon and perhaps even exposed to a degree the underpinnings of a world whose essential nature is hidden from our sight, and whose ultranatural (supernatural) adjunct has frequently been misconstrued, made glorious or fearsome, when in fact it's no less trivial and mundane than any of the rest. Passing through the entrance, wide as a castle gate, I felt a sense of dislocation, and my initial impression was that I had stepped into a dimly lit yet gaudy oblivion, a realm of smoke and shouts and dancers and drunks and throbbing music as distinct from its surroundings as swimming beneath the surface of an ocean is from floating atop it. The arboreal conceit stated by the façade was further developed within. Thick support posts of black wood were carved into the semblance of trunks, many with circular bars built around them, and the ebony ceiling was a relief of branches and leaves, and from the floor sprouted realistic-looking stumps that served as tables, buttery lamps cupped by depressions at their centers, underlighting faces, hollowing cheeks and eye sockets, transforming womens' cleavage into shadowy abysses, and, also rising from the floor, formations shaped like the crotches of oaks and serving as love seats, occupied by entwined heterosexual couples, some of whom were obviously having sex, others working up to it—in sum, the room had the aspect of an evil forest in which elvish flames pointed up the dark and revealed the secret frenzies of a bacchanal.

Toward the rear of the building was a stage where a rock-and-roll band performed under purple and crimson spots; the music was loud, but conversation was possible near the front. I claimed a stool at a bar close to the entrance, sitting behind a support post so I could keep watch for Brauer and not be seen. On the countertop, slightly raised as if they were natural productions of the wood, were chains of symbols that made me think of molecular diagrams and equations. I expected them to vanish, to flow away into the grain of the wood, but they did not. The bartender, a wizened old man with gray hair and serpent eyes (vertical pupils, gold humors, nictating membranes), brought me a Dos Equis. People thronged the entrance, squeezing past one another, slipping in and out. Fifteen or twenty minutes before, I would have been unable to cope with the movement and noise, but I felt solid now, attuned to the drug that was orchestrating my systems, and I had no difficulty in focusing. Seated on my left, separated by a gap of two stools, two middle-aged men with pomaded hair and gold on their wrists and fingers, were chatting amiably; on my immediate right, a tanned blond woman in her mid-thirties wearing a sundress, American by the look of her, attractive but starting to go a little leathery, was stirring a parrot-green drink with a swizzle stick. She seemed familar. My eyes stuck on her and she said in a surly tone, "That's right. It's me. Now get over it!"

"Excuse me?"

"I said you're right. Your unasked question is resolved. It's me."

Still nonplussed, I said, "Me, too."

She gave me a flat stare, then laughed. "I guess that makes us even."

I scanned the entrance for Brauer.

"You've got this where-the-fuck-am-I expression," the woman said. "I bet this is your first time in La Vida."

"You come here a lot, do you?"

"You know, if this was a script, I'd demand a rewrite." She adopted a sultry manner. "Do you come here often?"

"Naw. Taking care of the orphans eats up most of my time."

She shook her swizzle stick at me, like a priest shaking out a few drops of holy water onto a baby's head. "I'm pretty sure I've never seen you here . . . but I know you."

"I don't think so."

"No sir! I've seen you somewhere. Your smart mouth strikes a chord, too." She put on a hick accent. "You famous or something?"

"I was wondering the same thing about you."

"Could it be we're both celebrities and don't recognize each other? What a hoot! It's almost like an existential dilemma."

"I don't get it's a dilemma."

She sipped, stirred. "Not yet."

No sign of Brauer. I was starting to believe I might have lost him. I did see, however, transparent figures eight and nine feet tall, thin and cylindrical, given substantiality by a washed-out greenish tinge, the color of cucumber slices. They wavered and vanished and reappeared in the midst of conversations, moving from one group of talkers to the next, like eavesdropping vegetable ghosts. And then I noticed a man hanging near the entrance dressed in a black jacket and jeans, black hat. The flow of the crowd hid him from view and I half stood, peering about the room. An ally, even one as irritating as Darren, even if it were only a stray Wardlinite, was something I could use.

"You gonna tell me who you are?" the woman asked.

"I don't want to spoil the mystery," I said, sitting back down, unsuccessful in my search. "How about you?"

"Not unless you go first." She fished a cigarette case and a tabloid newspaper out of her purse, then set the purse on the floor. A banner low on the tabloid's front page proclaimed that Rodney Dangerfield wanted to be cloned. "Gee, if we're not gonna talk about how famous we are and all, what's left?"

"The bartender. We could talk about him. See, I'm thinking he might just be the Navajo Serpent Guide of legend. Check out his eyes."

She checked them out. "Extremely reptilian."

"You see the pupils?" I asked, uncertain whether she saw what I did or if she thought I was trying to amuse her and was playing along. "The membranes?"

"It's not surprising. The management here are snakes."

A game, I decided. "You know the management?"

"I am the management." She lit her cigarette and angled her exhalation toward the ceiling. "An investor, anyway."

I said I thought this might explain why every other woman in view was being groped and drooled on, whereas the blonde was high and dry and solitary.

"The night is young," she said. "You meet who you're given to meet."

"In life . . . or just here?"

"Especially here."

"I see. We're talking about a destiny thing. La Vida Es Muerto, it's kinda like a vortex, a crucial spiritual nexus."

"It's precisely like that."

A scuffle broke out by the entrance, an event that attracted the interest of several of the tall transparent things and also brought some cops over to investigate. The transparent things, I realized, bore more than a passing resemblance to cacti. Cactus ghosts. Looking at them put a sour taste in my mouth. The sense of relative physical well-being I'd acquired after joining the crowd at the maquiladora was beginning to crack. My joints ached and the skin on my face felt oily, grimy. With Brauer apparently out of the picture, it was time to start working on a way home. The room rippled, as if time were dilating or the barrier between continuums had been breached. Driving would not be a great idea. I presumed that with some slight effort I could make this flirty blonde my new best friend. If she had a car, the bond of celebrity, the fraternal regulations of the rich and famous, would compel her to help a fellow celebrity in distress.

"Bet you're an actress," I said. "A comedian, maybe."

She smiled.

"So why would a famous actress get involved with a place like this?"

"Have you seen other places like this?"

"Okay, I admit it's a cool bar, but—"

"There you go!"

"But Nogales? Come on! Nogales is a shithole."

"Name me somewhere's not a shithole."

"If you put it that way . . . Yeah."

"What other way is there to put it? People are people, right?"

I was having nerve twinges across my shoulders; I tried to work them out by rubbing the nape of my neck. "Man, I'm seriously fucked up."

"You have a specific complaint?"

"Somebody slipped drugs into my drink. Acid, maybe."

"Somebody here?"

"No, it was back downtown."

"You seem fine to me."

"That's good, because I feel like I got scales growing on me."

"I have Valium at the hotel, but that doesn't do you any good."

"A couple Valium would work," I said eagerly.

"Wish I could help."

She crossed her legs and cast her eyes elsewhere, a clear indication of dismissal, and I realized I must have pushed too hard or leaked an odor of desperation, and she had determined that I was attempting to enlist her sympathy, playing her—which, of course, I was—and by doing so I had violated the celebrity code of behavior or made her suspect that I wasn't a celebrity after all, just someone who wanted something from her, and thus was beneath notice.

"You know Sharon Stone?" I asked.

I could see her thinking, Boy, did I misjudge this creep! Her face a slack mask, she said, "No." She hauled her purse up from the floor and began picking through the contents.

"Sharon and I did Larry's show together," I said. "Nice lady."

Doubt sharpened her features. "Larry King?"

"Yep. Last fall. When I was touring."

She quit looking through her purse. "You're a musican?"

A simple admission ("I'm Wardlin Stuart.") and I'd have her back, we'd soon be heading for her car; but I had a flashback of the old Wardlin, a shot of Lopez Island contempt, and I wanted to mess

with her, to tell her a story—in a cruelly roundabout fashion—
about a famous actress who was starting to hag out and had persuaded herself that now she was into kinkier action than A-list
industry parties could provide, hanging out at a rococo Mexican
brothel where you could fornicate with giant beetles and drink
snake-venom martinis and mingle with violent degenerates who put
their Hollywood cousins to shame.

"She was planning a party for me, but I broke off the tour," I
said. "I had a family emergency."

The blond gave me a canny look. "She has wonderful parties.
You've been to her Santa Barbara place, I assume?"

How fun, I said to myself. A test. There were so many good
answers, answers that would yield a high score, I couldn't choose,
but I was most tempted by, No, I've never been to Santa Barbara,
but did you know she's got a birthmark on her ass shaped like a little
rooster? They had to slather make-up on it for *Instinct*.

"Remember that dilemma we were talking about? This may be
it," I said.

As I was debating what would be the most hurtful way to twist
the blond woman's brains, a Mexican girl in a low-cut blue cocktail
dress insinuated herself between our stools, her back to the blond
woman, and whispered in my ear, "You don' wanna fuck that wore-
out bitch! I give you better pussy than her!"

Pretty and round-faced and black-eyed. A white cactus flower
pinned in her long dark hair. Her perfume had an astringent under-
tone. I pulled back in order to get her all in frame and saw a diminutive, plump hooker with peacock-blue eye shadow and shiny black
lipstick and breasts pushed up so high, with a slight effort she could
have rested her chin on them. The tightness of her dress made her
appear about four months pregnant. She also seemed familiar. Two
familar faces in a row. What were the odds? "Are you famous?" I
asked her.

"Oh, yeah!" She rubbed her chest against me. "Wan' I should tell
you what I'm famous for?"

I stared at the blond woman, but spoke to the Mexican girl. "Are you an actress?"

"Best you ever seen, man!"

"Way I hear," I said, "you seen one, you've seen 'em all."

Without a word, the blonde climbed down from her stool and went off to meet whomever she would be given to meet. I resisted the urge to say something vile. The Serpent Guide approached and asked the hooker what she wanted to drink.

"Something she can afford," I told him.

"What's the matter wit' you?" She hooked my wallet out of my jeans with her forefinger and opened the bill compartment. "You got plenty of money!" I tried to grab it from her, but she turned away and inspected my driver's license. "Warrd-leen Stu-art. That's you, man? My name, Incarnación." She pronounced it as if it were the name of a proud country and ordered a tequila from the bartender.

I snatched the wallet from her hand.

"Don' be so rough, Warrd-leen!" she said. "You don' gots to be rough wit' me."

I had a burst of rudimentary yet instructive insight, recognizing that I was far from home, that I should put Nogales in the rearview and do it in a hurry, and also thinking how badly I wanted to see Therese, if for no other reason than she was the only person who could restrain me from being a total asshole.

Incarnación tugged at my arm. "Why don' you come up in my room, lemme be nice to you?"

"Where's your room?

"Upstairs . . . in the back. Come! I show you."

Upstairs and in the back worked for me. There would be stairs, a fire escape, a rear exit of some kind. A plan of action took shape. Brauer was almost certainly off somewhere on the wrong trail and, since Barrio Cielo wasn't far from a more civilized quarter, I could risk a dash across the wasteland. Then a phone call and a cab ride to the border. But as Incarnación led me deeper into the club, into the false black forest, as the noise swelled and we were engulfed by lithe, cat-assed dancers talking in Polynesian hand-speak, writhing and folding into each other, stained purple and red by the stage lights as if drenched in wine, singing along to a monster rock tune, music to stomp someone to death by, propelled by mastodon-like bass footsteps, the thought of escape was crowded out of my head by the mutant noise and thunderous energy and the words of the song:

> . . . . *the protons ripple, the neurons scatter.*
> *The neon flickers, night's a dagger.*
> *The flies are singing, end of illusion. . . .*
>
> *Black angel! Evil answer!*
> *Black angel! Evil answer!*
> *Perfidioso.*

Incarnación was dancing with her head down, fists clenched, her breasts jerking, flopping, sweat flying off her in crystal droplets that sounded a pure sad tone before being swallowed up and sizzled into nothingness by the great brazen din of the guitar Satan who ruled for the moment in the world, and if it hadn't been for my wrist, my knee, I might have danced with her. I was subject to primitive compulsions, to spasms of savage emotion, as if the lyrics of the song, those overly theatrical, meaninglessly menacing lyrics, embodied a dollop of actual evil and were the Mexican perversion of an Aztec curse that turned men and women into animals, and I found myself bellowing, *"Perfidioso!"* along with the singer, a slender teenage kid whose ugly, guttural, lust-thickened voice was the voice of a demon twelve feet tall with a barrel chest and goat horns, crouched and howling into his mike, while the rest of the band, with the exception of the drummer, a blue-haired gnome hunched over his kit, stalked the stage with the elegance of demented princes, whirling, nearly falling, righting themselves and posturing, sometimes going face-to-face, exhorting one another to new heights of foulness, driving guitar spikes into people's forebrains and inciting them to perfidy. The dancers enclosing us seemed design components of a living tapestry, like one of those medieval pieces depicting a forest primeval among whose leaves and branches and trunks are hidden the faces of beasts and devils, and between the dancers' bodies, in an aperture partly obscured by arms and legs, I spotted a panther slinking along, its black coat agleam, eyes pointed with crimson, and, shortly thereafter, a bearish animal with tusks, perhaps a huge boar, shouldered past, knocking two couples into a clumsy spin, though it was no less graceful than most of the moves being busted, and then a crepe-throated iguana man, walking upright, switching his dragonlike tail, sauntered into view, his head swinging toward me, his long bone-colored face shifting toward the human as if he were absorbing the particulars of my shape, and just as I began to think the dancers were in fact turning into animals, because there seemed fewer of them now and more animals were appearing all the time, birdwomen, erect serpents, monkey girls, dog boys, cockroach men, and even the people who had not been transformed displayed signs of incipient change, their teeth curving, faces emptying of character, becoming stylized, simplified versions of themselves, it was then I caught a glimpse of Treat, the dead version, hair matted with gore, skin gone gray, escorted by a handful of cactus ghosts— it looked as if they were conveying him somewhere, maybe back to his desert rock. In an instant he was lost among the dancers, vanished so quickly, I could not be sure I'd seen him, and I had no appreciable reaction other than surprise and a reminder that I could not be seeing any of this, that it was all a chemical pageant, a Mardi Gras event in my blood, sexy young corpuscles tossing beads out of windows and exhibiting their hallucinatory breasts to the celebrants below, and then another avenue opened in the wall of dancers, and standing twenty, twenty-five feet away was the first anthropomorphic monster I had encountered that evening: Brauer. He wasn't looking at me, but he was scanning the crowd, and before he could turn in my direction, I dragged Incarnación toward the stage, shoving people aside, shouting at her, asking where the fuck was her room, did she know a way out? She made placating gestures and mouthed, Okay, okay, and directed me to the side of the stage, to a door mounted in the wall, almost invisible because it, like the wall, was black and carved into leaf sprays, and once it had closed behind us, the music muffled, I asked if there was a rear exit.

"You don' wan' to leave now, macho," she said, setting foot on a stairway leading upward from the door. "Just when things 'bout to get hot."

I pinned her against the wall and repeated the question.

"What the fuck's wrong wit' you? You scared of somebody?" She twisted away. "Don' worry! You be safe in my room. Nobody gon' find you there."

"I'll give you money. . . I'll give you money now. But I want to get out of here."

"Then you gon' have to get out the way you come. You don' wan' to see what's back of here, anyway. Just rats and bones, man. Barrio Cielo."

"Is there a back door?"

"I tol' you, man! No! They bring everything through the front. Supplies, liquor . . . everything!"

I believed she was lying, trying to keep me inside the club so she could milk me for money, but I thought that once we reached her room, we could carry on a more definitive negotiation, and I told her to lead the way. The corridor that opened off the stair was not quite wide enough for two people to walk abreast and lit by red bulbs mounted on the ceiling, spurring me to recall World War II submarine movies, the SS *Decrepit* or whatever, having barely survived a barrage of depth charges, running under emergency conditions. There must have been a hundred doors ranging the corridor; a few stood open, revealing windowless rooms not much bigger than walk-in closets with black plywood walls and, under stark lighting, men and women in various degrees of undress engaged in pre- or postsexual activity, haggling, having parting conversations, money changing hands. In one, a naked plus-size woman was lying facedown on a bed—scarcely more than a cot, really—and her trick, a sixtyish man with a trucker wallet chained to his belt, was securing the woman's tail, a scorpion tail with a prominent sting, the same pale brown as her skin (though opaque), by means of a manacle that appeared to have been bolted to the wall for that very purpose. I discounted the notion that I had truly witnessed this, yet was relieved to discover that Incarnación's room did not come equipped with a manacle, being furnished with a bed and a wooden chair and a TV—every room had a TV and they were all switched on in order to drown out the sounds of amor that otherwise would have been heard through the walls, so that as I'd walked along the hallway I caught snatches of pop music, sitcoms, soccer games, political discussion groups, gossip and quiz shows, the entire entertainment spectrum in review. The staleness of degraded lust seemed the smell of an unspeakable sorrow, not merely a residue of commerce, and it, too, was part of the furnishings.

Incarnación went to switch on her TV. I told her we wouldn't be making much noise, but she switched it on anyway, keeping the volume low, and started to remove her dress. When I advised her that would be unncessary, she said, "Relax! Maybe you change your mind, eh?" She pulled the dress over her head, folded it, reached under the bed and brought forth a shopping bag that held a pink skirt. I understood why she looked familiar—she was a maquiladora girl, the same one behind whom I had hid when entering the club. Moonlighting to make a living wage. She cupped her hands beneath her breasts, lifting first one and then the other as if comparing their weights, smiling at me. Her panties were baby blue with a yellow flower placed above home plate. Her chubbiness was baby fat. I doubted she was older than sixteen.

I slipped two hundred-dollar bills from my wallet and showed them to her. "Where's the back door?"

She scowled at me, her brows knitting together, her black lips pouting. "Don' you hear what I tell you? Ain't no back door!"

I added another hundred.

"I'll tell you a lie, that's what you wan'," she said. " 'Cause I wan' that money. But there ain't no back door."

"What the fuck kind of place doesn't have a back door?"

She seemed to struggle with the question.

"The corridor," I said. "Is there a stair at the other end?"

"Yeah, but it's blocked, you know. They don't let nobody come in that way."

I fixed her with an accusatory look.

She shrugged. "That's how it is. I don' know why they do it that way."

My mood had alternated between fear and stoned distraction since leaving Alvina's, but now panic slammed into me. I couldn't be certain I had seen Brauer on the dance floor, having also seen a panther, a giant boar, and a dead man, but neither could I rule out the sighting. I had allowed myself to be trapped in a cul-de-sac, and if Brauer was in the club, he would be methodical in his search. I sat down heavily on the bed, unable to muster thought. Incarnación, taking this as a sign I was ready for love, tried to put my left hand on her breast, but I fended her off. I patted my pockets, thinking I might be carrying my Swiss Army knife. All I found was the ballpoint in my inside jacket pocket. I couldn't imagine it would be much use.

My panic eased, or was chemically suppressed, and I became aware of a familiar voice issuing from the television. Our president was giving a speech. He'd say a few lines, there would be a shot of an applauding audience, men in tuxedos, women in gowns, sitting at tables with white cloths and wine bottles and shiny cutlery, and there would follow a shot of the president smirking, an expression that made him look like a twelve-year-old dressed in a man suit, mightily pleased with himself for having gotten off a good 'un, and I speculated on the possibility of whether one could use prayerstyle to influence politics—would you have to start at the level of affecting the reelection campaign of Mary Jo Grundy to the town council, or could you step right into presidential politics?—and that caused me to remember the ballpoint and my own predicament, and to wonder if at this late date I could write a prayer that would keep Brauer from killing me.

All I had to write on were hundred-dollar bills, eight of them, and when I started writing, Incarnación strenuously objected, but calmed down after I told her the money would still be good. "What you writin'?" she asked.

"A prayer."

Out of respect for my devotion, I assumed, she sat next to me with her hands clasped and head bowed, letting me proceed.

> *Oh, Lord of Loneliness,*
> *border Jesus of the barbed wire*
> *and the rusted water,*
> *Caretaker of rats and silences . . .*

"What you prayin' for?" Incarnación asked.

"My fucking life."

"You still scared, huh? I tol' you nobody gon' find you here." She peeked at what I had written. "That's another name for Jesus . . . the Lord of Loneliness?"

I said, "Yeah," and asked her to keep quiet, but quiet was not to be had. A jolly laugh track could be heard coming from behind the wall at my back, and behind the opposite wall a mariachi band was harmoniously lamenting, and on Incarnación's television, our president was murmuring what passed for knee-slappers in GOP circles—I couldn't concentrate and I thought how weird it would be if a case of writer's block wound up being the cause of my death.

> *Caretaker of rats and silences,*
> *whatever words you need from me tonight,*
> *I have no strength to speak them.*
> *Whatever aces you hold . . .*

I had no feeling for what I was trying to write, no sense of being connected to anything. The right words were there, in my head, but I couldn't corral them into lines and images.

"You finish?" Incarnación asked.

I have no strength to speak them.
When I drive the Southwestern highways,
a rattlesnake turns to a crack in the road
and as I approach, the crack gets wide,
no way I can make it to the other side.
The world is that sort of puzzle now,
a puzzle with a central missing piece,
a mystery in which one dangerous thing
is always becoming a more dangerous thing,
and I cannot penetrate its confusions.
Exempt me from ritual this night
and accept my imprecision
as though it struck the perfect tone.
Whatever aces you hold, employ them
against he who seeks my death—
kill him for me.

It was the shortest and most incompetently framed prayer I had yet written. On top of that, it embraced an unsuitable reward. Had I been asked to write such a prayer for someone else, I would have refused. I should have asked for escape—asking that a life be taken was not merely morally unsound, it pushed the limits of the form, strained prayerstyle's capabilities. It was too big a step, too large and sudden a demand. I thought about giving it another go, but either the words satisfied my true desires or else more and better simply weren't in me. Staring at the bill on which I had written, I felt like a fool for having succumbed to my own sales pitch.

"Hey," Incarnación said. "You think somebody's gon' to hurt you here? That's what scarin' you?"

"Yeah."

She tapped the bill on which I had written the prayer. "How much money you got?"

"Eight hundred and change."

"If I'm gon' help you, I need more," she said after a pause.

"You know a way out?"

"I sneak you out of here, I can't come back. So I need more from you. Up in El Norte, you got lots of money? Don't tell me you don', 'cause I know this 'bout you."

"Oh, I got money. I didn't bring my checkbook, but I have credit cards."

She pooh-poohed this idea. "I don't wan' so much. Gimme the pen."

Using the seat of the wooden chair for a desk, she made writing look like labor, squinting, slowly printing words on both the back and front of the bill; then she told me to read what she had written.

> Wardlin Stuart promise he pay Incarnación Barrera eight hundred dollars she shows him how to get out of La Vida es Muerto. He also promise he get her a job in the USA and help get a green card and give her the more money so she's live until she gets paid.

"You sign," she said. "And write the day, too."

She removed her pink skirt and sweat-stained top from the shopping bag and began to dress. I asked what she was doing.

"Soon as you sign, we leaving, man. They find out what I done, they gon' hurt me."

"Just because you showed somebody the way out?"

"People like hurtin' people, they don't need much 'scuse, you know."

I signed and dated the bill; I passed it to her, along with the rest of the money. Incarnacion stuffed it into her breast pocket. "That's a contract," she said, staring fiercely at me. "You don' keep your promise, I sue your ass."

"How do we get out?"

She picked up the shopping bag, went to the door, checked the corridor. I repeated my question.

"Back door," she said. "What kinda place it is you think don't got no back door?"

Chapter 21

Behind La Vida Es Muerto was a tract of land large enough to support a second nightclub of equal size, an acreage of rubble and weeds and depressions filled with rainwater and crooked little bushes sprouting from heaps of garbage. A portion of the sky had cleared and a few stars were visible overhead. The wind hissed and slithered. Ambient light and my ensorcelled vision combined to paint the area with a sinister gloss, as if it were a battlefield where witches had fought with wolves and black blood had rained down from heaven and things lay buried that would never die. The end of the tract merged with a dirt road that led straight toward the center of town and about a quarter mile along the road was the edge of a well-lighted district where there would be shops and telephones, maybe even taxis. We picked our way over shattered concrete and glass, mats of soggy plaster and sheets of buckled cardboard, over empty cement sacks and broken boards. I had expected Incarnación would stick with me until we reached the street, but she kept so close on my shoulder, I derived a feeling of something more than a utilitarian attachment and asked where she was going.

"Wit' you, man."

"Yeah, but like, are you going home?"

She stopped walking. "I'm goin' to El Norte! Wit' you!"

"The States? You need a visa."

"You gimme enough money, now I buy a fucking visa."

For a moment I was at a loss. "You talking about a forgery?"

"A what?"

"A forgery . . . a fake."

"Yeah, yeah! That's it! Don't worry, they won' check me close, I'm ridin' wit' you."

I had an impulse to tell her the contract she had written would be no chore to break—she had taken advantage of me and I didn't feel I owed her. But I had to admire her hustle, her opportunism, and the money was not a real issue.

"We'll see what happens," I said.

It was too dark to read her expression, but from her tone of voice, I assumed she was giving me her brow-knitted, pouty scowl.

"I got you in writin', man!" she said. "You ain't goin' noplace 'cept I goin' wit' you."

Somewhere up ahead of us, a thud and what might have been a grunt of pain. I dropped into a crouch and pulled Incarnación down beside me. She appeared to think I was assaulting her and clawed at my face. I subdued her, whispered for her to be quiet and told her there was someone hiding out in the rubble.

"You think it's that guy . . . the one's after you?"

"I don't know," I said, but I knew it was Brauer, that he must have spotted me fleeing toward the second floor and supposed that I would use the rear exit. I couldn't tell where he was hidden or what kind of angle he had on our position. To our right was a garbage heap. I pointed it out to Incarnación and, keeping low, we moved behind it.

"It's him," she said. "That guy, right?"

"He can't see us. We're all right for now."

She began to talk rapidly under her breath. I heard the word *Virgen* and realized she was praying.

Given the inversion layer that blankets Nogales, I estimate the odds against the moon doing a flyby must be way up there, and the odds against it happening when the moon is full or nearly full are higher yet; but that night we hit the lunar jackpot. No more than two or three minutes after we took refuge behind the garbage pile, a lopsided fat moon, yellow as a wheel of Gouda, rolled out from the clouds and appeared to stall directly above us, turning dark-and-mysterious into a no-man's-land lit by flares. Every detail was sharp; the quiet seemed to have deepened. It was like a day with a black sky and a strange-looking sun at zenith. Incarnación clutched my arm and cast me a frightened glance. I signaled her to stay calm, but my heart rate was out of control, verging upon hamster-on-a-tread-mill numbers. Then I saw Brauer standing about twenty yards ahead and to the left. The washed-out blue of his denim jacket was clear, and so was the gun in his hand.

"I know you're there!" he called. "I saw you when you came through the door!"

Incarnación restarted her prayer.

Brauer held the gun muzzle-up beside his ear. "This is how you want it . . . Okay!"

Glancing behind every obstruction, he began to negotiate a path through the litter. Waiting and trying to jump him was not a good bet. Nor was running. I looked around for something to use for a weapon. The best prospects within reach were a couple of empty paint cans. Waiting and trying to jump him, it seemed, was the way to go. I thought Incarnación could throw a paint can, blind him for a second, and then I could take him low. But Brauer had closed the distance by about a third, when she chose to bolt. I tried to catch her by the leg, but she eluded me and went scrambling over the uneven ground toward the rear door of La Vida Es Muerto. A bullet took her high in the back and drove her forward—she flew into a two-legged construction of wood that might have been the remnant of a carpenter's bench, flipped over it and vanished behind some loosely stacked concrete blocks.

Death put a charge in me. Despite having witnessed the fool-hardiness of running, I jumped up and sprinted for the door, taking a different track from Incarnación, angling toward one of the taller piles of rubble, thinking I could make the run in stages, going from pile to pile, or that I might find a concrete chunk to use as a weapon. Five or six steps into my run, however, I tripped and fell into a ditch filled with rainwater. I floundered about, trying to stand—my injured knee buckled and I splashed onto my back. Water covered me to the collarbone. I had an uncanny, hallucinated moment when I looked down at my chest and saw a blanket of black silk and reflected stars. Brauer loomed above me, his face masked in shadow beneath the bill of the Texans cap. The thought of dying in a star-spangled ditch in tumor town bred a cold wide terror in my chest, as if a door into some subzero place had opened there, but part of me was all right with it, weary, uncaring . . . until I remembered Therese and then I wanted magic to save me, to dissolve, mist away and rematerialize north of the border an easy walk from 'Zona Madness.

"We can make the same deal you had with Treat," I said. "It'll be better. I know the business. You won't have start-up problems. You can sit back and watch it flow."

"It's been such a disappointing evening." Brauer seemed genuinely distressed. "A confusing evening. I'm not sure what I want anymore. But if it's prayerstyle, I'm going to have to find a way to work without you."

"Listen, man! I can make you—"

"I really don't have time to talk," he said.

He aimed the gun at my face. A wordless thought flashed through my mind that seemed to embody all the things I wanted and loved in an instant of fiery regret. Then a shot, not a soft *pop* but a flat *crack,* and Brauer cried out. He flopped onto his belly beside the ditch, grabbing the back of his thigh and cursing. I crawled up out of the ditch, away from him, and collapsed among some weeds.

"Was that some serious nick-of-time shit or what?" said a dry, affectless voice.

I rolled onto my back, bracing on my elbows.

Darren was standing over Brauer. He tipped back his hat and looked down at me. "No thank you? You not even gonna say 'Nice shootin', Tex?' " He waited for me to speak and finally said, "Well, I can see you're all tore down. At a loss. Guess I must have seemed like the answer to your prayer."

"Motherfucker!" Brauer said. "I don't know who the fuck you are, but you—"

Darren dug the point of his right boot into the bullet wound and Brauer screamed. "Jesus! Aw, fuck! Christ!" he said between clenched teeth and spent the next couple of minutes dealing with pain.

"I told you so," Darren said to me. "Didn't I?"

I was afraid of him, I believed him to be the black angel of my invention, a menace to his creator.

"I did," Darren said. "I told you you'd get your ass handed you. People won't listen to me, usually I just say fuck 'em. But in your case I'm making an exception . . . this once."

"Thanks," I said.

"It's nothing, man. *De nada,* you know."

A veil of whitish smoke or poison gas drifted across the moon, cutting its light by half, and Brauer groaned, and a gust stirred a faltering breath from the weeds and crooked bushes that sounded like a giant uneasy in his sleep.

"Know who this is?" Darren squatted by Brauer and tapped him on the shoulder with the barrel of his pistol. "He stands in relation to Treat as I do to you. Not that you could prove it. But basically he's the answer to one of Treat's prayers. What you think about that?"

"I don't want to think about it."

"Fair enough. But here's something you need to think about. You gonna kill him, or is it up to me? 'Cause we can't let this one live. You know that, don'tcha? This one, he'll come for you hard. He'll find a way to bring you down."

On his stomach, still holding his thigh, Brauer darted his eyes toward me, then at Darren.

"I got a theory." Darren lowered himself to a sitting position, resting the gun on his knee. "If someone abandons their life . . . and

I'm talking about anyone, no matter they're a bum on the street with a few greasy dimes to their name, or Trinket Jesus with millions in the bank. If they abandon control of their life at crucial moments, if they let somebody else carry the weight, they forfeit control for the rest of their days. They're in the wind, at the mercy of the wind, and wherever it blows them, they're stuck with it. Some folks say control's an illusion, but you and me, we know different. At least I do. You only allow yourself to know it every so often." He offered me the gun. "You willing to forfeit control? Maybe you already have forfeited it, but there's a chance you can regain it. This here's that chance."

"I have a thought," Brauer said. "May I speak?"

"Cool with me. Better ask Jesus here, though. God knows, he might be able to come up with an opinion on some subject."

I nodded to Brauer. "Yeah, speak."

"You're concerned I may pose a threat," Brauer said. "But let me point out, you've got me cold on a murder charge, and I—"

"Two murder charges," I said.

"Right! Two murder charges. I'll be in prison a very long time, if I survive it, so there's really no substance to your concern."

"I'll take this," Darren said. "First place, you'd be doing time in a Mexican prison. You can buy your way out of the joint down here with a lifetime supply of salad dressing. Second. I know you. Except for the fact you're no ways as much fun, you're me. Me . . . but you got a dead lizard, a ribbon, and some beads stuffed into the cavity where the soul usually resides. You're a fucking zombie Monroe Treat conjured up, and I'm not listening to your bullshit. You could drop a hundred million on us, the world's supply of pussy . . . Wouldn't change a thing. Sooner you accept that, the better it'll go for you."

Brauer said, "You haven't thought this through," and Darren said, "You want me to knock you out? 'Cause if you don't shut up, I will knock you out. You just lay there and think of some other way to wiggle out of this. I bet you come up with something."

The clouds closed in around the moon, sealing us off from its glow, and once again the acreage behind La Vida Es Muerto acquired a sinister aspect, darker and less still than previously. The wind kicked up strong, fluttering the cement sacks, the cardboard flaps, the torn packaging, making a sound like hundreds of tiny mouths licking at one of the black puddles that dappled the ground. The lights of town looked farther off. Darren, reduced to a partial shadow, said, "If I pull the trigger, it's gonna be you who killed him, man. You might as well take control."

"Please," Brauer said, and stiffened when Darren pressed the muzzle to the back of his head.

"A deranged fan desired to please me," Darren said. "You can sell that story to the papers and the TV, but not to yourself. If I am a deranged fan, you can stop me. I'll give you the gun. You just have to ask. Once you have the gun, no one's forcing you to use it. You can leave things as they are. But I don't believe that's in the cards."

I had a Pontius Pilate moment. Brauer's eyes were on me and his thoughts, perhaps his prayers, were beaming into my head. I felt the power of his pathos and his hate. I wanted the moon to return, to reveal his true face and abolish the Kabuki mask I saw melting up from the shadow—grooves gouged down his black wooden cheeks and hooded glowing eyes and mouth partly open onto a flickering red inferno.

"You really piss me off," Darren said, and fired.

The flash lit Brauer's head and I saw bloody shrapnel and his hair flattened and the wincing expression that would remain on his face until someone fixed it for the funeral, and would be stuck in my head a lot longer. The detonation shocked my heart. I had heartily offended a god in whom I only believed at times such as these, and the fear that there would be spiritual consequences for what I had done stabbed into me, and I was certain it left a single black-red droplet to seed a tumor in my flesh that could never be excised unless I found a redemptive product whose gothic grandeur would drown out the voice of my reason. Or maybe not. Maybe it would fade away, as it had with

Kirschner. The body gave off a faint hiss that I hoped wasn't Brauer's demon escaping. After a second I realized it was my caught breath shuddering out.

"How'd that feel?" Darren asked. "You not being drunk this time, you musta felt that one." He hopped up and shook out a leg, as if his knee joint were troubling him. "I tucked the gun down there by his foot. Don't touch it! It's evidence you didn't shoot him."

He walked away a few feet and stood with his back to me. It had gotten so dark, I could barely make him out against the sky. "The way things are now," he said, "you're going to wonder about this night for years. You'll wonder about everything. Take my advice and spare yourself the effort. You won't figure it out. You had a chance to know everything, but now you're never gonna know squat."

I could hardly wait for him to be gone.

"Goddamn it!" he said. "Are you just gonna fucking sit there? You're not going to say a word? We were working on a relationship, man! I could have shown you some shit! Jesus!"

I hadn't heard him move, but he must have walked farther off, because I no longer saw him. "Good-bye," I said, feeling I needed to say something in order to soothe him.

No answer came.

I levered myself up, leaned on a solid section of the garbage heap, and took stock. With all my aches and pains, it would be a hell of a walk into town, but I refused to entertain the thought of going back inside, and however hard it would be to walk, it beat hanging out with a corpse. I shuffled forward, unable to see well enough to warrant a quicker pace.

"I forgot something," Darren said.

Startled, I let out a yell and lost my balance and, flailing to right myself, snagged a handful of his jacket. His hand supported my elbow until I was stable.

"Gotcha!" he said, and chuckled.

He'd been standing behind me, yet when I turned, I couldn't find him.

"Where are you?" I asked, convinced that he was going to hurt me in some way.

"Heading over the horizon, dude. Think I'll go buy myself a souvenir. Make myself feel better. Maybe one of those bumper stickers shaped like a sombrero. You seen the ones I mean? The ones got 'Regresa A Mexico' printed on 'em. Come Back to Mexico. Should read, 'Come Back to Mexico. Next Time We Kill Your Ass, Stuff Your Body with Dope, and Mail You to L.A.' Know what I'm saying? I like a cool bumper sticker. Cool bumper sticker always cheers me up."

He sounded like the old Darren, but not being able to see him worried me, and I thought the reason the air was so black might be that he had dissolved in it.

"You'd figure we'd have something like that sombrero decal up in the States," he said. "Guess we don't have like a national hat."

"Cowboy."

"Maybe years back, but not now."

"Camo helmet."

"Yeah, that might get it. 'Come Back to the U.S.A' . . . Shit! I can't think how to make it better."

" 'Or Our Soldiers Will Come to You,' " I suggested.

"That's the one! You got the gift, man. No fucking doubt."

Off along the side of La Vida Es Muerto, somebody revved a motorcycle engine; the ripping sound made me nauseous, violated some organic principle, some fundamental cellular assumption, and when I thought of Brauer's body—and Incarnación's—cooling in the dark, the blood congealing, a thousand minute changes beginning to occur (I imagined their flesh efflorescing, the cells glowing blackly, an obsidian mosaic), the death beetles getting their feet sticky in the spills, my stomach rebelled and I vomited into the weeds. As I stood gasping with hands on knees and strings of saliva trailing from my mouth, Darren said, "It's a bitch, huh?"

I straightened, wiped my mouth. My legs trembled and I was tempted to let myself collapse. The wind was asking questions about me and God was in His voyeur mode, watching from lizard perches and insect eyes. Phosphorescent lights floated everywhere. Wispy vapors rose from the degraded fabric of reality. I could not tell earth from air.

"Damn! I almost forgot again." Darren's voice seemed to issue from beyond a barrier, made faint less by distance than by the phantom ground whereon he stood. "If I was you, I'd check on the girl. I think she might still be ticking."

Chapter 22

Before Therese and I left the States I returned once to Nogales and tried to find La Vida Es Muerto. What I found was a large concrete building (not nearly so large as I had perceived it to be) painted navy blue, with a roof of corrugated iron and no name above the entrance, no façade of plastic trees, no fanciful interior, just an enormous drafty room, a flyspecked bar with a brass rail that ran the length of one wall, thin wooden supports, dozens of rickety tables, echoing acoustics that turned love songs into billows of warped noise, the place patronized by a predictable assortment of unattractive hookers and men in straw hats and work clothes. Only the bartender resembled what I believe I saw on the night Treat and Brauer died. His eyes were normal, but otherwise he was the gray-haired Navajo Serpent Guide of legend. He did not remember me.

What this says about that particular night or about my life, about prayerstyle . . . I've been going over things in my mind for a couple of years now and haven't reached a conclusion as to whether I experienced a season of miraculous coincidence of which La Vida Es Muerto was a part, if one thing after another fell into place so as to contrive what appears in retrospect to have been an almost mystical ambiguity, or if prayerstyle had a bigger influence on my life than I could have ever imagined. I don't guess it makes much difference one way or another. Trinket Jesus or Wardlin Stuart. Ineffectual prophet or ex-con with a parlor trick. Nor do I think it serves any purpose to ponder over whether Darren was a stalker or the Lord of Loneliness made flesh.

The fingerprints on the gun with which he killed Brauer matched those of a small-time thief named Darren House, thirty-six, the possessor of dual American-Mexican citizenship, the child of an American father and a Mexican mother; but since he was never brought to the bar, and since neither his family nor anyone who knew him was located, the sole evidence of Darren's existence is a computer record. Proof enough for the authors of our consensus, perhaps, but not for me.

More important, to my mind, is whether or not anyone deserving derived a benefit from that night or from my pass through the world of celebrity. Incarnación, now the manager of the new improved 'Zona Madness, may qualify . . . and yet I'm not sure how deserving a person she is. She's good with the store, but treats her boyfriend like a dog who crapped on her couch and seems—due to those hardscrabble days in Nogales, I assume—to have the same disposition and general view of humanity as a crocodile. There are those who testify, of course, that prayerstyle changed their lives, but I don't believe them. If their lives were changed, then prayerstyle was simply a lever. Had prayerstyle been unavailable, they might have discovered that staring at a stick or serial self-abuse would effect equivalent change, so long as the remedy was promoted by the right pitchman. If the universe can be influenced by the human mind, I suspect that any concentrative act will do.

Robert W. Kinkade and Degan Mellory were prosecuted for conspiracy by the state of Arizona. Kinkade is currently doing a five-spot in a Club Fed. Degan was acquitted and parlayed her fifteen minutes and centerfold looks into a book contract and her own talk show. She regularly calls my agent and invites me to be a guest. Like Sue Billick once said, I have a golden touch. The scandal that accumulated around the deaths of Monroe Treat and Galen Brauer, the mysterious inaccessability of the mysterious Darren House, and my refreshed image as a noble victim, a spiritual man assailed by contemporary Sanhedrin, that intrigue catapulted sales of *Handbook* into the troposphere and confirmed prayerstyle's status as a bona fide religion, at least so said *People, Newsweek* (*Time* begged to differ), and a host of TV pundits, notably Duval Rowan, who bagged a steady gig on

MSNBC, perhaps the result of successful prayer. Temples were built, Wardlin Stuart events were held. I was revered and, yea, virtually worshiped at a thousand Web site shrines. L. Ron Hubbard was not so loved. Absent gods are always the most alluring. My most egregious mistake had turned into stock portfolios, real estate, numbered bank accounts, and shielded investments, the whole shebang managed by strangers who knew not where I lived or even what I looked like anymore. I knew damn well I didn't deserve any of it. When I was out stumping for prayerstyle, half the time I felt like the world's luckiest sociopath, and the other half I was either befuddled or embarrassed or afraid I'd be caught at some miscreance that I imagined I was committing. But as with the flowers reputed to have sprung from the Buddha's footprints, everywhere I puked, a money tree bloomed.

One morning not long ago, I walked down to the beach with Therese. We had on jeans, sweaters, and rain slickers against the cold, and carried a thermos of coffee. She had taken to wearing her hair down over her shoulders, coloring it brown; I had adopted a beard, earrings, and altered my hairline with a razor. The beach was a tawny, pebbly shingle that bulged with a slight convexity out into the water; tumbles of iron-colored rock—big as houses, some of them—guarded each end. The sea, under a lowering sky, slapped at the shore, explosive slaps blurred by the rush of less concussive surf, leaving creamy curds of foam scattered across the shore. After each series of waves, the water would be sucked down the slope of the shingle, creating a deep trough, and then, seconds later, the sea would surge forward again, lifting its slate-gray hands to deliver another blow. From the beach, the hills built inland—a somber Irish green—and tucked among them, beyond the coastal road, a white town with tile roofs. Higher yet, occupying the side of a hill, a many-leveled house of dark stone, constructed—I've been told—by an eccentric who moved from a jungle place in Argentina to this part of Patagonia (the sole benefit I had derived from my time with Brauer, his description of the place) to escape evil spirits whose metaphysical natures were ill-suited to the region. Even on warm days you can sense the chill rising from the bottom of the world;

perhaps that is what kept him spiritfree. Whatever the case, fleeing our own evil spirits, we suitably inhabit the relic of his pathology.

That morning we sat among the rocks at the north end of the beach, there sheltered from the worst of the wind and the spray, and drank coffee and talked, as we often do, about how we might use all the world-enough-and-time we had acquired. Therese talked about the writing she was doing—stories, poems—and it made me happy to hear her enthuse, but I had no equivalent enthusiasm. The very idea of accomplishment seemed inconsequential. Listening to her, though, I had a revelation. I understood that my days of accomplishment, at least for the moment, were done and this was Therese's time. Through the accident of a prison letter and all that followed—the destruction of the shop whose trivial business had stolen her energies being most instrumental—she had reached a place in which she could thrive and explore and experiment and perhaps come to terms with her dysfunctions, her failures, things I had, in my self-absorption, not treated seriously or simply ignored. It was my time to support her, to assist however I could, and in that devotion, not the specious devotion of prayerstyle, I might find true salvation. And yet I saw the potential lie of this even as I thought it. I knew I could make it false, live it falsely—that was my greatest talent, my most abundant gift. Love might prove insufficient to overwhelm my inherent duplicity. I had come to love as I had come to prayer, through an act of desperation. What gave me cause to hope for any better a result? But the cynical proscriptions against love that I attempted then to reembrace were subsumed into the tenderness she had nourished in me, and I cautiously accepted that I might be able to escape my shallowness, my Trinket Jesus nature, the fundamental human indifference that allows us to ignore the fact that we are surrounded by screams of pain, and do something right for a change. I sat with her hip to hip and I suggested certain narrative strategies and poetic tricks, and, in the space of an hour, found within myself a fresh enthusiasm, a flicker at first, and then a fire.

The thermos almost empty, we prepared to walk back up into the hills, and as I stood, dusting off my jeans, I spotted a figure at the far end of the beach. A man dressed in black and standing close to the tidal margin. During the past months, I had seen similar men on the outskirts of my life, rendered anonymous by distance, in crowds or on a hillside or rounding a street corner. I had never tried to close the distance between us, nor had they. But this man raised a hand in salute.

Therese came up behind me, peered over my shoulder. She put her arms around my waist. "You think it's him, don't you?"

"No," I said.

"Yeah, you do. Otherwise you wouldn't be about to jump out of your skin."

"Okay. Maybe it's him."

The man put something in his mouth. Smoke billowed up and was snatched away by the wind.

"If it is him," I said, "it's no big deal."

"Why not?"

"Because whatever all that was about, it's finished."

"And yet you're worried." She rested her chin on my shoulder, then turned me about to face her. "It's not him. You know why?"

"Say."

"I know you've made this huge case for things being a certain way, and I agree, the whole experience was weird. But you can't live your life expecting some bogeyman who crawled out of your head is waiting around every corner. When you go to obsessing about it, give yourself a smack. It's ridiculous!"

"You weren't there. You never talked to him."

She gave a sigh of mock exasperation. "You obviously don't understand the power of denial."

"Just because *you* can deny it, because you tell me something's not there, that doesn't mean it'll disappear."

She grinned. "Well, this bogeyman's disappeared, anyway."

The beach was empty.

"Where'd he'd go?" I asked.

"I wasn't watching. Into the rocks, I guess. He must have been getting soaked where he was standing."

I scanned the beach, the rocks, the sea.

"He's probably a tourist," Therese said. "Nobody but tourists wave at strangers down here."

"Suppose he's not a bogeyman? Suppose it's plain old Darren House?"

"No one's found us yet. No reporters, no TV jerks. I don't think a crazy fan can do better than them."

Beyond the break, the sea heaved sluggishly, as if some cold monster had grown restless in its deep. A claw of gray water slashed downward, detonating on the shingle.

Therese tapped me on the chest. "Hey! Stay with me!"

I looked at her until I seemed to find myself in her green eyes. "How brain damaged you figure I am?" I asked.

"Let's go home," she said.

It started raining as we crossed the coastal road, but it was a gentle rain and we refused to let it hurry us. The hills were steep, hundreds of feet high, their slopes folded together in waves of grass, earth, and stone, and from the crest of our hill you could see the Andes, white and perilous—every west wind bore an icy touch of their solitude—and in the summer condors soared above the valleys, silent as spy planes, and the feeling you got was not of isolation—Pershing had been isolated, suffocating under its chaotic American quilt—but of an isolate privilege, of cold green quiet and natural splendor. I did not want to lose that place, to have it polluted by my old life, and I wondered how I would handle Darren if he were to reappear. Therese was right, I realized. Denial might be the most appropriate tool. Certain lives seem controlled by simple laws, by regulations that might be distilled from a children's story: magic demands belief in order to exist, evil can be reduced to ashes by means of a spell, and so forth. Mine might be such a life. At any rate, I had no better weapon. Legal remedies had long since proved ineffective and I am done with murder, and, though now and then I feel an urge, a powerful need to revisit and reemploy the process that made me who I am today, the product that contains not a single cancer-causing agent and will someday put my kids through college, yours for a wallet-friendly $19.95, I never pray.